THE
HISTORY
MAKERS

The BookLogix Young Writers Collection

Attack at Cyberwold

Messages from the Breathless

Rapunzel: Retold

Nothing But Your Memories

Thieves of the Flame

The Silver Key

The Girl I Never Met

The Dragons of Kingsland

THE
HISTORY
MAKERS

VAL BODURTHA

LANIER
PRESS

LANIER
PRESS *an Imprint of BookLogix*

Alpharetta, GA

ISBN: 978-1-61005-847-6

Library of Congress Control Number: 2017906644

10 9 8 7 6 5 4 3 2   0 5 0 8 1 7

Printed in the United States of America

♾This paper meets the requirements of ANSI/NISO Z39.48-1992 (Permanence of Paper)

For my high school, my own enlightenment.

We are not makers of history. We are made by history.
—Martin Luther King Jr.

ACKNOWLEDGMENTS

First, thank you for reading.

I'd like to acknowledge the BookLogix team for selecting my book for publication and choosing to tell my story. Thank you to the whole BookLogix team for all their help.

I'd then like to thank my mother, Alison Leigh Cowan, whose unstinting devotion to this book not only got it out there, but also inspired me to keep writing. And thanks to Jennifer English, who patiently supported and believed in me.

A big thank-you to every amazing teacher I've ever had. Thank you to Horace Mann School for teaching me how to think after other places tried and failed to curb my imagination. It's rare that such a distinguished institution cares so much about its students and encourages their passions. Thank you to Dr. Schiller, Dr. Kelly, Dr. Wallach, Dr. Delanty, and the other tireless people who made the school what it is.

To Dr. Groppi, who assigned the small, fun, creative story to my AP World class that inspired seventeen-year-old me to write this book. That whole history department, give yourselves a hand. I had Dr. Oldham, Mr. Bienstock, and Dr. Groppi, and I lucked out every time.

And while I can thank my parents for giving me my main writing influence—namely, books—I must also acknowledge the writing teacher who made me love it. Mrs. Woods, looking at you.

Another noteworthy thing about Horace Mann is how I had standout teachers and mentors in every arena, people who made me who I am: Dr. Ladd, Sr. Dalo, Mr. Ho, Ms. Kolinski, Mr. Nye, Mr. Farmer, and Ms. Bartels, to name a few.

I'd also like to thank Joshua Vera, Omie Hsu, Professor Jonathan Hall, David Smithyman, and Chanda Brodnax for their keen instruction and infectious enthusiasm.

And finally, my family and friends. Thank you to those who have stuck by me, put up with me, and loved me. I love you too.

PROLOGUE

In your average world history class, the Aztec Empire will be covered briefly, focusing mainly on events after 1492. Perhaps it is because so much was wiped out in the following colonization. Even so, in their time, the Aztecs were the greatest nation the world had ever seen.

Such little things influenced the Aztecs' downfall. When the Spanish explorer Hernán Cortés arrived in Mesoamerica, the Aztec tributaries were in a period of revolt. Cortés joined with the Aztec Empire's enemies to conquer them. Soon after, the diseases that the Spanish brought over killed most of the Aztec population. The decline of the Aztecs was a perfect storm.

If only one detail of the conquest had been changed, would the Aztecs have remained in their position of high power? And what would their society look like today? What would have happened had the storm not been so perfect?

CHAPTER 1

PRESENT DAY

The chatter of Azteca's upper class filled Café Quetz, a trendy eatery overlooking Lake Texcoco. Adding to the din were Myla and Quinel, two girls whose elite nature was evident both in what they wore and how they spoke. Myla checked her phone, hopeful.

"He still hasn't called?" Quinel asked.

"No."

"Cut him some slack, My. You know he has work to do."

It was true. The mission had taken Cint from the city for a whole week. Of course, Myla understood why—doing the gods' work, saving the world, and the like. But she missed her boyfriend too.

She gazed out over the lake, chewing on her nails. Ambient music poured from the speakers behind the bar, but it was hard to hear over the talk of the patrons. Myla noticed two girls about her age seated by the café's giant windows, one guffawing at something the other said.

Quinel ran her fingers through her smooth mane. "Did you hear about that priest's wife who got caught fooling around with that Under?" she asked, eyes scanning over the artwork that lined the café walls.

"Yeah, I did."

"They got her as she was leaving the city."

"Really?"

"Yeah. What an idiot. I do all *my* cheating at my own residence."

Myla snorted into her drink, then composed herself.

"Quinel, you can't *say* stuff like that. It'll get you up on the pyramid."

"Oh, lighten up. You're not gonna have any fun if you're all tense."

Myla wished she *could* lighten up and channel more of Quinel's effortless snark, but she felt tied in knots now. Tomorrow was her seventeenth birthday, and soon she could get a proposal from Cint, the man who had claimed her six months before. She didn't know how to feel about it.

Quinel must have sensed something was off from the look on Myla's face. "Are you feeling okay?"

Myla forced a smile. "I'm fine."

"You know what's the answer to everything?"

"I'm not humoring you."

"That's correct! Mild alcoholism!"

Quinel jumped up and grabbed two shots of pulque, their go-to liquor. Myla examined hers. The milky white liquid swirled around inside the crystal shot glass shaped like an infant's skull. She paused, thinking about how everything was going to change. Then she poured the sour, burning liquid down her throat.

The two girls left Café Quetz a half hour later, much more intoxicated. Myla liked this time of day, when the sun had left its peak in the sky, and the stylish skyscrapers of the inner city cast long shadows on the more old-fashioned buildings to the east. Myla liked the boxy, adobe-brick look of the older architecture too, but wasn't about to shed tears over its replacement. The city planners were still in the process of substituting the wood, brick, and stone of the old world with the steel and concrete of the new. Yet the essentials of the old city remained: giant sets of stairs, geometric patterns, and doorways featuring intricately carved designs of various gods.

Myla and Quinel paused here and there to window-shop at the street's many designer stores. Their day had taken them to the nicest part of town, and they strolled down the bustling street, confident that no one would harass them.

Myla giggled. "So what else for tonight?"

"Well, let's stop at my house to get ready, and then I thought . . . Chinampa 9?" Often, Quinel had to do a bit of convincing before Myla would agree to such a raucous party spot.

"Mm . . . fine," Myla conceded.

"Yes! Ah, my powers of persuasion do it again." Quinel batted her eyelashes at Myla. "One of the many things that make me irresistible."

Myla rolled her eyes, and so she didn't see the Under that she stumbled into. He looked straight at the sidewalk and stammered, "My apologies. It was my fault. Please forgive me."

His nose was pierced with a small iron loop and he had a dark, swirling tattoo on his chin—a leaf blower from the northern part of town. All Unders were marked according to their line of work (cheek tattoos for chauffeurs, lip piercings for midwives, and so on), both to make them easy to identify and to keep them in line. If piercings and tattoos had ever been a trend with Azteca's elite, they weren't now. Myla herself could never picture marring her face or skin in such a lasting way, even if her parents would approve.

"Go now, Under. Leave us," Quinel commanded. He bowed and ran away, eager to blend back into the crowd.

"Someone needs to control them," Myla said.

"Yeah. Next time, we'll call his handler. It's okay, he's gone now."

Myla tripped over her own foot, this time jostling Quinel. She groaned, "Why did I let you let me drink so much?"

They arrived at Quinel's apartment building and punched in the code for entry, no need for the Hemopanel's assistance.

The first and only time Maya had touched one, she was four years old and slipped her finger into the small impression in her home's Hemopanel surface. She felt a quick pinch, and tugged her finger away. A minuscule dot of red appeared on her finger as the panel turned green.

"No, no, sweetie!" her mother had exclaimed, pulling her away from the door. "We don't use those. Those are for the lowest class. Don't cry, don't cry."

But Myla hadn't cried, staring in wonder at her finger and the blood pooling there. "What is it for?" she had asked, but her mother was already distracted by something else, she couldn't remember what.

Now she was older and she knew it was to pay tribute to the gods. To gain entry to most buildings, Unders had to sacrifice one drop of blood, one of the ways the gods received what they were owed.

Once inside, the girls chatted as their Unders did their hair and makeup. Red and gold beads were being fastened into Myla's braids when Myla's ringtone went off.

"Cint!" she exclaimed.

"Hey, baby." The use of this familiar endearment relaxed Myla. Cint hadn't forgotten about her yet. He complained, "Ugh, can't wait to get back. You miss me?"

"Of course. Where are you now?"

"Don't tell anybody, but I'm in the northern territories. I'm gonna shut a bunch of stuff down."

"How come?"

"They've been doing solar power stuff and Chief Speaker Matutslan can't let them continue. Or the *gods* will get angry." He sounded biting on that last comment, like he was trying to make a joke.

"What do you mean?"

"Well, I mean . . . You'll understand soon enough, I guess. I'm out here wasting my time. Whatever, at least I'm getting paid."

"What? Cint, what do you mean?"

"Hey, I have to go. I'll be back tomorrow, for your birthday. Something tells me it'll be a special day, babe. See you then!" He hung up, leaving Myla feeling even more confused than before.

"What's Cint up to?" Quinel pressed, blowing on her nails.

"He was being super cryptic. I don't know."

"Hey, it's fine. He'll be back tomorrow, right? Nice! One more night of freedom then!" Quinel glanced at Myla and kept talking. "Not that I don't *want* him to come back of course. He's fine. Like is he the *most* interesting person I've ever met? No. Is he nice to look at? Yes. So no, I don't mind having him around, making my girl happy . . ."

Quinel kept going as Myla let her Under, an older, skinny woman with large eyes, fix her hair. Thoughts buzzed around her head like flies. What did Cint mean by what he'd said about the gods? It didn't matter. Quinel was right. She wasn't going to let this ruin her night.

They left Quinel's building as a taxi was pulling up to the curb. The driver took them to the docks, where they waited for Number 9 to float by.

Chinampa 9 floated on Lake Texcoco, circling Azteca and hosting the hottest partiers in the city. Myla checked her watch. The club arrived on time, music pumping from within that resonated all the way down to Myla's stomach.

The mirrors all along the outside of Chinampa 9's pyramid walls reflected the lights from the city. They were one-way, giving the partygoers inside a beautiful view while concealing their activities.

Myla and Quinel stepped onto the floating island, anxious to get inside and start the evening. Quinel wore a blue bracelet, indication that she was not yet claimed. Myla's green bracelet would show all the men of Chinampa 9 that she was with Cint. Myla was off limits.

As they were about to enter the main room, Myla stumbled.

"Okay, okay. No more for you. I understand," Quinel slurred.

"Thanks, Quinel. I love you, okay?"

Quinel paused for a moment, grinning at her, then dashed inside. Myla too hesitated, and then ran in after her. The club was packed with girls, each wearing a green or blue bracelet. Lights of all colors glowed from three of the walls, pulsing with the beats of the electronic music.

The fourth wall was a dark one-way window, and the men's half of the club lay beyond. Myla always wondered what it looked like. Did the men dance too? Did they drink and laugh with their friends? Or maybe it was silent, each man's eyes trained on the girls' side of the club.

Myla located Quinel on the dance floor, bobbing to the beat as she threw back a shot of liquor. It was so typical. Myla couldn't help laughing.

She went to dance with her friend, their jewelry reflecting the harsh lights of the club. Myla often felt insecure while dancing, certain she looked foolish. Then again, dancing at Chinampa 9 was how she'd met Cint six months prior.

He had been beyond the dark window at the fourth wall. He spotted her while she was dancing with Quinel, the two girls wearing matching blue bracelets. She remembered how her name was announced over the music, how each girl in the club had envied her, except Quinel. She had given Myla a huge thumbs-up and a suggestive wink.

Myla was ushered to a door that led beyond the dark wall. It opened to a dim corridor lined with red curtains. One curtain was pulled aside and she was taken into a little room. It featured a couch, a small table with drinks, and Cint.

He was twenty and handsome, with copper hair streaked with gold. His smile lit up the room. She was the luckiest girl in Azteca. Quinel would be so proud.

He stood up to greet her when she entered, an antiquated formality. Myla had liked it. She was used to men pretending she didn't exist when she entered a room, speaking about her rather than to her. He extended his hand. "I'm Cint," he said.

"I'm Myla."

"I couldn't help but notice you out there, Myla. It would mean a lot to me if we could spend some time together. How old are you?"

"Sixteen."

His smile deepened, and he reached for her wrist. Myla understood and grasped her blue bracelet. She hesitated, but saw nothing threatening in his eyes and slid it off her arm. In turn, he clasped her hand in his own. He locked eyes with her as he fastened a new green bracelet onto her right wrist. She was his for as long as he liked.

She thanked Chalchiu. You never knew who was going to claim you, and some of Myla's friends had been selected by fat and balding men their fathers' age. There wasn't much you could do about it, unless your family was better connected than the man and your parents felt like doing you a favor.

Quinel had been claimed three different times, even though she had only just turned sixteen. It was easy to see how, with her smooth, black hair that fell in ringlets around her heart-shaped face.

Once Myla had asked Quinel why all three men had returned her blue bracelet after a matter of weeks. Quinel shrugged and said, "I'm a lot to handle." Myla liked that such a large personality lay beyond the pretty face and hoped that one day a man would be able to keep up with her friend.

Even now, a circle formed around Quinel, many in the club stopping to watch her let loose. Her energy was infectious and Myla couldn't help joining in.

After a good hour of drinks and dancing, Quinel and Myla left Chinampa 9. Myla's head buzzed and she longed for her apartment's soft bed and quiet. She thudded down on the dock, covering her eyes with her hands.

Quinel heaved her upward. "Come on, My. One more stop and then we can go home." She hailed a cab and half shoved, half carried Myla inside. Once in the cab, Quinel took a deep breath and said, "The Temple Mayor."

Myla considered asking Quinel if they could skip the ceremony that night. They weren't Unders, if they did it wasn't punishable by death or anything. But she visualized one of the priest patrols picking her and Quinel up, returning them to their parents, and decided against such social suicide. And she knew how her parents could get when it came to besmirching the family name.

Myla rested on Quinel's shoulder as the cab sped toward the center of Tenochtitlan. As they got closer, the pyramid loomed, surrounded by a crowd of people thousands thick.

The Temple Mayor had been the center of Azteca for centuries. It never stopped astounding Myla. It had been built 592 times since its original structure, and now stood over sixty stories tall. A gleaming steel pyramid with glass walls to reflect the light and power of the sun.

As the two approached, the crowd at the base parted, noting Myla and Quinel's unblemished faces. The two girls went to the inner circle at the base of the pyramid, an area lined with golden bricks, where they awaited the rest of the upper class. There was an open bar, and Under servers swept the crowd with samples of fine foods.

Quinel grabbed four mini quiches from a woman missing a left earlobe and looked up at the top of the temple. Myla joined her.

On a small balcony at the top of the pyramid stood the chief speaker, Matutslan. A tall, broad man, Matutslan had led ceremonies for over a decade. When he spoke, people wouldn't risk talking over him. Giant screens on the pyramid broadcasted a close-up of his face: that weathered skin, the short, dark hair streaked with white, and those piercing gray eyes gazing out over the city. Tonight, he wore a dark, double-breasted suit and a thin ceremonial necklace of feathers and beads, all red. He carried a long steel scythe at his side.

The pyramid glowed red from the light of the sunset. The priest's wife, that cheater Quinel had scoffed at, was brought forth and set kneeling in front of Matutslan. The screens showed her close up as well, and if she was beautiful, she didn't look it now. Her brown hair was messy and she looked exhausted.

"Idiot girl deserves it," Quinel said.

"Yeah, I guess. Gods gotta eat," Myla responded.

The chief speaker's voice boomed through speakers. "Greetings, people of Azteca. Another day has passed, and the gods have given us one more day of sunlight. For centuries and centuries, we have paid our daily measure warding off the end of the light, the end of the world.

"The other nations do not see the truth. The Spanish demons tried to end the world and all in it five hundred years ago. But we fought back and destroyed all who challenged us!"

Myla rolled her eyes as Quinel whispered, "Okay, okay. Let's keep it moving. The gods are hungry."

The priest continued. "So we will pay our daily penance. We will fight to the last man to ensure the sacrifice is made and the gods can give us one more day. We perform this ritual as our ancestors centuries ago did. It must never change, we must remain to do this good work or forever be lost to the peril of the gods."

Myla's phone rang. A top-ten hit. The people around her shot her glares, but the girls giggled.

Matutslan had approached the table. "For the sun!" he proclaimed. And as the people of Tenochtitlan chanted it back to him, he raised the scythe. It stayed for a moment, casting a red beam of the sun's reflection, and then sliced across the woman's neck. She didn't have time to scream.

The two apprentices raised their swords and set upon the woman, as Matutslan said the ancient words that must accompany every kill. For a second a crushing guilt weighed on Myla's chest, like everything was her fault. She pushed the thought away.

Matutslan stepped back and raised his blood-soaked hands to the sky. "For the sun!" he called. The words sent shivers down Myla's spine. *Suppress it. Be good*, Myla forced herself to think.

The pieces of the sacrifice were thrown down the long staircase. It took a minute, and the woman's head landed at the bottom last. The blood had marked nearly every step.

CHAPTER 2

Myla awoke in her bedroom, the half light of the early morning pressing through the blinds. She sat up, pushing back her covers. Quinel was next to her, still passed out and snoring. Nothing would get that girl up.

Myla staggered to her bathroom and washed out her mouth. *Never again.* She knew this would happen yesterday and still drank that much.

Amid the pounding headache, a thought appeared. It was her birthday. Excitement ran through her, with a hint of apprehension. She was marriageable age now.

Quinel stirred. She opened one eye. "Happy birthday, My," she groaned. "Sorry I'm not in a more festive mood."

Myla smirked. "You're fine, Quin. Get some more sleep." Throwing on a robe, she plodded out of her bedroom, away from Quinel's resumed snores.

When she reached her roof, she pulled her robe closer around her. The morning chill was palpable, cutting into her bones. But still she stood at the railing, gazing out over the Tenochtitlan skyline. The sun was minutes away from peeking up in the east, pushed up one more day by the gods.

Myla enjoyed coming up there the moments before sunrise. She liked finding the last star to blink out in the daylight, lingering for a few minutes more before popping out of existence and into night elsewhere with the others. She never stayed for the rest of the sunrise.

Taking a deep lungful of air with her, Myla climbed downstairs and walked into her kitchen. She reached inside a cupboard and pulled out a box of painkillers. Suddenly, someone jumped out at her. Myla gasped and dropped the box. Then she sighed. It was her little brother, Aktu.

He laughed at how scared she had been, doubling over and then falling on the floor. "Aktu, that was not cool!" she scolded. "You scared me half to death."

"Your face!"

Myla kneeled to clean up the scattered pills. "Yeah, I know. It was hilarious."

Aktu was having trouble breathing. "You . . . had . . . *no idea.*"

"All right. That's enough. Come on, you." She lifted him to his feet, straining to pick him up the slightest bit. He was nine now and looking older every day, even with the brown, frizzy chaos of his hair sticking up in all directions.

He calmed down after a minute. "Happy birthday, Myla," he mustered. "Mom and Dad left you something." He gestured at the counter.

A small, pink, and perfect cake sat on a small, crystal serving platter. It had white flowers and delicate icing spelling her name.

"And mine!" Aktu announced, thrusting a purple disaster in her face. Aktu's cake was a chocolate-and-purple-frosting mess with his handprint adorning the center. Myla loved it.

She took out plates and forks from the cabinet and set three places. She took Aktu's cake and cut it. "Thank you! It looks delicious."

He grinned wide. She placed a slice on his plate, her own, and Quinel's. They ate, and Myla knew this would be her favorite part of her day. "Quinel," she called. "Come and get it!"

Her friend stumbled out of the room, saw the cake, and perked up. "For me?" she sputtered. "Myla, you shouldn't have." When she saw the look on Myla's face, she broke into a grin. "Happy birthday, sweetie . . . Where are your parents?"

"Oh, they've left by now. They have stuff to do. I'm thankful for the silence."

Quinel shrugged and sat with them, digging into her slice of purple mush. "Aktu, you are a chef. This is fabulous," she said.

"Come on," Myla said. "We should all get going."

They all stood, cleaned their plates, and got ready for their tutoring sessions, eager for after: a trip to the beach. Then they'd end up at Myla's big party during the sacrificial ceremony at sunset. Cint would be there. Myla's stomach churned, and it wasn't because of the cake.

Quinel had trudged up the school's stairs, while Myla took them two at a time. It was a classical building, a blocky pyramid made of patterned bricks, featuring Azteca's most prominent pictographs: jaguars, eagles, and many more. Xantic, their tutor, excused their lateness, maybe because it was her birthday.

They took their seats, and Myla noticed Quinel already looking at the clock, eager to get out of there and enjoy the sunshine. Myla was too, but she, unlike Quinel, appreciated that day's class: speech.

Speaking was an important skill to have as a lady of the Tenochtitlan upper class. Someday Myla would sponsor a priest, host events, maybe even bestow awards. She felt excited about all that, but enjoyed learning how to speak and debating ethics among her peers, a group of ten or so girls.

Xantic handed out sheets of paper, the first topic of the day. Myla chewed on her fingernails as two friends of hers wove arguments supporting immigration, opposing immigration. They were good, but they had missed a few key points that had been critical in the debate.

Myla was up next. She was put against Cyotel, a quiet girl who made Myla grateful debate came to her naturally. She demolished her argument about the legalization of the organ trade in a near-record three minutes. Xantic had given Myla an approving nod as she and Quinel left the room.

After a long afternoon of sunning and relaxing at the beach, Myla's usual chestnut color had gone darker and redder around her cheeks. Her frizzy, dark-brown hair was beginning to show signs of golden highlights.

She and Quinel sat in a cab on the way to the Temple Mayor. They had dropped off Aktu with his friends on the way back from the beach. Myla was wearing a short, shimmery green dress that Quinel had picked out for her and Quinel was wearing an all-black outfit that contrasted with her blue bracelet.

"Is something wrong, My? You've been awfully quiet."

"It's my seventeenth birthday, Quin. It's a big day."

Quinel's expression softened. She still had a few months before she had to worry about marriage. "It'll be okay, Myla. Cint is cute and nice to you and it won't change anything you don't want it to."

"He's nice to me, you're right. But sometimes . . . I don't know. I feel sometimes like he doesn't see me as more than a stupid girl who can't handle anything going on his mind. We've never had a real conversation."

"Maybe he's an idiot. *Someone* has to marry the idiots, Myla."

Myla laughed. "I'm doing the nation a service, Quinel."

"Have you *seen* Cint, Myla? Can I join in on your charitable work?"

Myla chuckled and put her arm around Quinel. "I'm glad you're here."

Soon they reached the pyramid, where Myla's party was in full swing. Her parents were there, her dad in his usual dark suit, but featuring a small pin of jewel-tone feathers, a sign of wealth and power. Her mom dressed in a full-length sparkling gown that caught the light with her every move. She approached Myla, brushing her painted lips against her cheek. Up close, her mother's face was a garish wash of color, the beads in her hair clashing with her purple eye makeup.

"Myla! Happy birthday, darling. Enjoy the party!" she gushed as she and Myla's father brushed past her and Quinel.

"Lovely to see you too," Quinel muttered. She turned to Myla. "Forget about them. This night is about you. Let's go mingle."

As usual, Quinel was right. Her parents, Coyol and Tlazo, weren't even worth the effort. Myla described their ambitions, needs, cares, and dreams in three words: the public eye. They bought her cars and threw her lavish parties, but didn't think much of it when they used to leave an eight-year-old Myla alone for hours at home with her new baby brother.

Her father was a stranger. Aside from the annual blunt instructions on how to conduct herself, they didn't talk. He seemed interchangeable with her friends' dads—suits barking into phones and managing factories in Azteca's tributaries. Myla's family owned a wire factory.

Her mother had a few redeemable qualities when Myla thought about it. Curtailed taxi conversations had proved her to be somewhat relatable, and Myla had tried to uncover her mother's true character whenever possible. When they were alone, Myla could talk to her without trying too hard. They shared a passion for horror movies, bad poetry, and dance.

But it was times like these, when her mother was breezy and shallow, when Myla felt she didn't know her at all. Myla felt identical to any seventeen-year-old, upper-class girl to her parents that night. She could be anyone, but her father would nod and her mother would kiss her on the cheek and move on. And of course, she hated them for what had happened seven years ago. And herself.

The two girls danced and drank, laughing with each other and the other kids at the party. There was pulque served at every bar and fried foods from all over the region going around on trays.

"Honey ants from Tlaxcala?" an Under with nose piercings asked Myla. Myla thanked her and took one. Her parents had gone all out on this one. Tlaxcala was one of the states conquered by Azteca centuries ago. The states had always supplied tributes of food and gold, but recently there had been rumors of unrest there.

The party paused and they all stood as Matutslan conducted the ceremony. Myla had known this would happen when she chose the pyramid's inner circle as her party location, but didn't mind. Choosing the Temple Mayor was as good a way as any to ensure a good turnout at a party.

Today the sacrifice was some Under. The priests must have been out of convicts or prisoners of war to make examples of. The Under was sedated to keep him calm, and he didn't even seem to realize it when the chief speaker read out the ancient words and the scythe caught his neck. The sound the metal made biting into the soft flesh echoed around the pyramid, amplified by speakers.

The party resumed as the lower class dispersed from the foot of the pyramid. Myla mingled, finding herself full of empty words: "Thank you for comings" and "Oh, you toos."

Her father was by her side. "Myla, please join your mother and me." She followed him to the edge of the party and into a car where her mother was waiting. Myla got in and slid closer to her.

Her mother spoke. "So, Myla, it's your seventeenth birthday. It's an important day."

"Yeah, I know. Because of Cint." Myla kind of hated that her parents loved Cint so much.

"Well, yes, dear. But also because you are now old enough to be enlightened."

"Enlightened?"

"Yes . . . it's customary to do this today, but . . ." Her mother looked at her father, who gave her a stern stare.

"It should be now, Coyol."

"Right at the party? It's a bit of a shock."

"It has to be now."

"Couldn't we wait until tomorrow morning?"

Her father's nostrils flared. "We're doing this now, and if you have anything more to say about it you can walk home!"

Myla stared at her parents, her mother now quiet and gazing out the window. Where were they going with this? She was used to them talking about her like she wasn't even there, but this was different.

Her mother cleared her throat, looked at Myla, and said, "You can now learn the great truth of how our society stays together and functions."

Myla had not seen anything like that coming. She listened, enrapt.

"Centuries ago, at the start of Azteca, a group of wise men decided that to have a working society, people must be willing to accept their places in the society," her mother began. "But how to ensure this? Finally, a solution arose."

Her father took over. "The group of men started calling themselves the Priesthood. They told everyone about apocalyptic visions, that the world would end unless the people worked as they should and the gods received a daily ration of blood.

"The blood sacrifice subdued the lower class. It made them feel that their toil was serving a greater purpose—to help the sun rise one more day."

They both sat back, her mother regarding her curiously. Myla's mouth hung open, her wide eyes gaping at her parents. She was stunned. Her beliefs, her whole way of life—a lie. "Are you serious?" she stammered.

It was like her mother expected her shock. "Very much so. Only the Priesthood and the upper class know the truth. We wait to tell our children until we believe they are mature enough to understand why we do what we do."

"It's all a lie?"

"Not a lie," her mother replied, pausing as she mulled her next words over. "It's a necessary belief. Without it, we would descend into chaos."

"And the priests . . . are just *acting*?"

"It's for the success of Azteca, Myla," her mother continued. "We all play our part."

"And us, what is our part?"

"We support the Priesthood and through them, Aztecism. Our class exists to reap the rewards of the Unders' labor and dispense them to the thinkers, the priests, as we see fit. They are motivated by our support, and they work hard to ensure that this civilization flows smoothly."

Her father nodded in agreement.

"I guess . . . I understand," Myla conceded.

"Wonderful," her mother said while applying lipstick. "Oh, and don't tell anyone under seventeen about this, or we'll all be next on the top of the pyramid. Now get out there and enjoy the party."

Myla started out of the car, then paused. "If it means nothing, then it wasn't necessary . . . what happened."

Her mother looked away, voice faltering. "I don't know what you're talking about." It was clear their time together was up.

CHAPTER 3

Myla left the car and sat down on the pavement. She didn't know what to think. She didn't know anything about political philosophy and what it took for a nation to prosper, and she couldn't decide how she felt about this new revelation.

She took deep breaths, wondering what would happen if she told anyone who wasn't supposed to know that the sun rose by itself. She took a minute to process that. *The sun rose by itself.* Her mind danced around this new thought until she could stomach it.

Like anyone else, she had harbored some doubts throughout her life, wondering what was out there. But it seemed ludicrous to test the priests' words; there was too much at stake. For centuries, they had been sacrificing each night, and for centuries their society had thrived, existed for one more day.

She stood up and made her way back into the party, stopping for two shots of pulque. That helped.

Anger. So much anger. Myla felt like she was a kid again, powerless to stop what she couldn't understand. She wiped away the hot tears threatening to dribble down her cheeks.

At least this explained what Cint had been talking about. He knew the truth about Azteca and was annoyed that he was assigned to projects with no actual purpose. His whole job was perpetuating a lie—a *belief*, she corrected herself.

Though her faith had never expressed itself through prayer, she wanted to ask the gods for guidance in that moment. Her parents were modern in their beliefs, and they had raised Myla to be the same. As a family, they rarely engaged in the daily rituals to the gods and only attended the daily sacrifices and the annual feast of Huitzilopochtli, which was more of a party and less of a devout religious festival.

But Myla had believed in the gods. She saw them less as divine, all-seeing forces that played an active role in her life, and more as spiritual guides. They were a higher force, pushing the world toward good. Did that mean they didn't exist? Or maybe that no one knew if they existed or not. She took comfort at that thought as she stumbled around the party, seeing no familiar faces.

Men and women intermixed for this party, as the night was about Myla and not focused on claiming.

Myla tended to enjoy these kinds of parties, found them more relaxing than the others. She felt someone take her arm and looked up. Cint had appeared, his smile gleaming at her. "You look ravishing." He kissed her on the cheek.

She managed a "hey." Myla couldn't handle anything else big that night. She paused for a moment and then added, "Glad you could make it."

"Wouldn't miss this day for all the gods in the world," he said with a wink. "Now, why don't we find somewhere more private to celebrate?"

Myla's heartbeat quickened. "Oh, I don't know. It's my party, I should stay and mingle." Her voice was quiet. Her head spun from the pulque and what she had just learned.

"You don't want to do that, and you know it." He took her hand and guided her toward the pyramid. Myla looked around for Quinel, Aktu, anyone, but the crowd was too thick. She looked around for her phone but she had left her bag back at her table.

He hurried her toward the opening of the pyramid, led her through the double doors and past the elegant lounge inside. It was dark and quiet. They stepped into an elevator. Myla wrung her hair with her hands.

"Do you even know where you're going?" Myla asked.

"Of course. I work here, remember? I know where to go."

His finger hovered over the bottom floor's button. He shot a quick grin at Myla and pressed. The elevator lurched downward, startling Myla. The doors slid open to a dark, abandoned hallway with doors and tunnels leading off in all directions.

"No one's used these halls for years," Cint assured. "We'll be alone down here."

Myla peered down the empty corridor. "How far down does it go?"

"Miles. This passageway network goes all through the city. But we won't get lost, I promise." He put one hand at the small of her back and steered her down the hall. They stopped at a door that led into a small office. Cint turned on a lamp and they both leaned on the desk.

"There. Now we can talk." The lamp threw yellow spots of light into his round eyes.

"I think we should go back to the party now, Cint."

"But it's nice and quiet down here."

"Okay. Then how about you tell me what you meant on the phone. I know what's going—" He leaned in and cut her off with a kiss.

Myla drew back. He had kissed her before—about as far as they had gone together—but something felt off. She didn't like the strange urgency in his eyes.

"What's wrong now?" He sounded annoyed.

"Nothing, I promise. I just . . . would like it if you talked to me. Especially right now."

"What are you talking about? I talk to you all the time!"

"I know, I know. I need someone to talk to right now. I feel insane and I don't know what's happening."

"But we're finally alone."

"I can't do this. Too much is going on."

"Fine. What's happening?"

"My parents enlightened me."

He sighed with relief. "So you're a bit surprised. It's okay."

"What? How can you be so nonchalant about this? It's *insane*. Unders die one a day like clockwork and it doesn't even do anything!"

"Why are you freaking out, Myla? It doesn't have anything to do with us."

Myla turned away from him and put her head in her hands. It was too much. The past seventeen years had had at least *some* underlying logic to them. And then, her enlightenment. She needed air.

Cint put his hands on her shoulders and bent to rest his cheek against hers. "It's all about societal harmony, babe. Without it, we'd be working class like them." His fingers traced a line down her back.

Myla stiffened and stood. "I get that, Cint. I do. But I still feel upside down." She wiped her sweaty palms on her dress.

Cint produced a flask and offered it to her. "You'll get used to it. But don't worry too much about what the Priesthood does. You'll move in with me and we'll live our new life together."

Myla turned down the drink. "Our life together?"

He shrugged. "Yeah. Marry me."

Myla had known it was coming that night, but still felt it crash on her like a ton of bricks. "What?"

"You heard me. You're seventeen now and we should get married. I think you're great."

"You think . . . I'm great." Myla's eyes narrowed.

"Yes."

"And that's your number-one reason for wanting to marry me."

He nodded, smiling. Myla got up and brushed out of the door. She didn't even look where she was going, she had to get out of there. Cint called her name. She took a right and then a left.

The hall darkened as she proceeded. She must have been heading deeper and deeper underground. She no longer heard Cint calling to her through the labyrinth, the air around her getting cold and stale.

Voices echoed around the next corner. The glow of a flashlight reflected off the opposite wall. She crept closer to listen. There were the sounds of footsteps, not more than a few people.

". . . and how can we know that you're telling the truth?" It was a girl's voice, about Myla's age. Her tone was as sharp as a dagger.

A second voice, this one male, spoke. "Oh, yeah, that makes sense. I *knew* they were going to kill me,

Amihan. Why would I tell them anything?" His voice was bright and mocking.

"You could be working for them. It was easy to break you out. Too easy, in my opinion."

"You got me, I fell in love with the high priest and have decided to betray you all."

"Both of you *calm down*," a third voice boomed through the corridor. This boy's low, firm tone sent chills down Myla's spine. The other two silenced under his stern command.

The second boy said, "Tezca is right. We have much more to do. We can argue about who is or isn't a spy later. What's next?"

Myla's blood pounded all throughout her body. These people were criminals. She clutched her hands to her chest to stop them shaking as she crept a little bit closer to the outlaws.

"Small mission," the girl said. "Planting cameras in zones three and five, bottom floors. Zone two is covered."

"This has to be done quickly and quietly. They'll notice your absence in about an hour, Tona. We need to be in the tunnels by then," the deep-voiced boy asserted.

"Okay then," responded the other boy, Tona.

There was a pause as they all seemed to take one breath together. At the sound of footfalls, Myla realized with a jolt that they were coming toward her hiding place. She tried to run but was frozen in place.

A flashlight blinded her and she put up one arm and averted her eyes.

"What the hell?" the girl gasped.

As the flashlight moved down from her face, Myla couldn't see at all. But soon her eyes adjusted. She made out three figures in the darkness, all holding guns pointed right at her.

Myla had heard stories about the deserters. They were ruthless rebels who sought anarchy. The priests had even preached that they were demons. Myla had never visualized them before. The rebels were supposed to be a vague, textbook-bad-guy force, not three real people standing in front of her with guns. She held her breath.

"Don't move," the tallest figure said. His was the deep voice from before. Tezca. "What are you doing down here?" he asked.

"I . . . I was at a party and I left. I'm lost down here."

The girl, Amihan, spoke sharply. "She's heard too much. We can't leave her here. She's upper class. She'll talk."

"We could tie her up somewhere," Tona cut in. "They won't find her until we're long gone."

Amihan said, "Perhaps. But she knows that we have cameras down here." She cocked her gun. "We need to take care of this here."

Myla's heart beat faster and faster in her ears. They were going to kill her. What about Aktu? What would he do without her? She forced herself to calm down, taking deep breaths and clearing her mind. She could get out of this. She *would* get out of this.

"Don't shoot. Look, I know you think you can't trust me, but please keep in mind that I have no idea how big your operation is. I don't know who around me works with you. Why would I risk my safety telling anyone anything?" Myla had watched her parents work as Priesthood benefactors her whole life. She had persuasive abilities, but would they work there?

Tona considered it. "She has a point." He looked at Tezca. "What should we do?"

The tall boy, Tezca, was the leader of the operation. If Myla got him on her side, he'd overrule the trigger-happy girl, Amihan. Myla trembled.

Tezca was thinking it over when they heard footsteps coming from far away. Myla's breath caught as she heard Cint calling out to her.

Amihan stepped forward, pointing the gun at her forehead. "Friend of yours?"

"He's . . . my boyfriend, I guess. He's looking for me. If you let me go to him, I'll get him to leave. He knows nothing."

Amihan sneered. "How stupid do you think we are?" Cint was getting closer. Through the darkness,

Myla sensed Amihan preparing to kill her, seeing the quick shot in her mind's eye. Should she run?

Then, Tezca spoke. "Ami, tie her up." She obeyed, lashing Myla's wrists together with a black cord from her backpack. Myla's heartbeat tore through her chest as Tezca explained, "We're taking her with us."

CHAPTER 4

Soon Myla was being shoved deeper and deeper underground by her captors. They were arguing. Cint's voice had long disappeared.

"We can still place the cameras," Amihan insisted.

"It's too risky. We need to get her out of here and back to base," Tezca said, his deep voice echoing down the corridor.

Myla struggled with the ropes that bound her. They were small but thick, but maybe she could chew them off. If only the cold-blooded Amihan would put her gun down, Myla could think straight. But still, even stumbling through the darkness, the girl kept the gun pointed at Myla's forehead.

After Amihan seemed to accept the lost mission, Tona broke the silence. "Thank you to the two of you, by the way. A most impressive rescue mission." He turned to Myla with a slight grin. "My two knights in shining armor. Now they must fight for my love."

"Oh, shut up, Tona," Amihan snapped.

"Stop antagonizing the prisoner," Tezca said in a measured voice with a hint of affection in it.

So that was what Myla was. A prisoner. If this were a movie, she'd be tied to a chair and tortured and made to talk. But what would they want from her? What were these rebels even trying to accomplish?

Myla played with the idea of turning the two boys against Amihan. If she provoked an argument, she could escape. She couldn't leave Aktu on his own. Everyone would think she was a deserter, a girl who'd learned the truth about Azteca and left, unable to handle it. Her parents would hate her. Quinel would never understand why her best friend had left without saying goodbye. With a heavy feeling, she realized that Cint wouldn't miss her too much.

The walls of the tunnel got older as they went along. They had started out as halls you'd see in a hospital, with fluorescent lighting and floor tiles. But the tiles had fed into a dirt floor, with torch holders instead of electric lights. Myla sensed she was far below the surface, too aware of the heavy tons of rock and dirt waiting above her head.

Amihan and Tona fell behind bickering and Tezca fell into step with Myla. "Are you okay?" he asked, his deep voice struggling to remain indifferent despite the newfound concern. Myla hadn't even realized she'd been shaking, her breathing quick and shallow.

"Physically, yes," she managed. "I'm a little bit claustrophobic. Or it could be the, you know, kidnapping." Tezca looked straight ahead. She tried again. "What do you even *want*?"

"What do you mean?"

"What are you hoping to get out of planting cameras, infiltrating the Temple Mayor, kidnapping me?"

"This was supposed to be a rescue mission. Tona was picked up by the patrols while on surveillance, and Ami and I came here to break him out of holding. I hope you'll understand if I don't tell you our other plans."

"But why? Surely you can tell me that."

Tezca paused, then said, "How old are you?"

Myla sighed. "Today was my seventeenth birthday." Of course. Everything centered on her enlightenment.

He looked at her, and there might have been a harsh glint in his eyes. "So you know then?"

"I was enlightened a couple hours ago."

"And how do you feel about the news? The fact that eighty percent of Azteca is enslaved for nothing? How the Priesthood kills one Under, *one human being*, a day to perpetuate a false religion?" He must have thought these words through, over and over, until he was sure they packed a punch.

"I don't know, to be honest. I felt sick at the mindless sacrifice at first, but then I realized . . . maybe it isn't mindless." Tezca's stare burned, but she continued. "I don't know anything about politics or the foundations of society. Maybe letting one group of people believe one thing to ensure societal harmony isn't such a bad thing."

"Take it from someone who does know something about politics, there are other ways. Are you someone who can look at a daily slaughter and turn off your humanity in the name of societal harmony?"

"Well, is it possible that the daily slaughter prevents a civil war that would kill many more people? Maybe the Priesthood is saving lives in the long run."

"That's a great hypothetical you've got there. Societal harmony never exists. You're not saving anyone, you're exploiting them."

Myla didn't know what to say to that. Her thoughts drifted to what had happened seven years ago. She had sided with the Priesthood then; she could do it now.

They walked in silence for a while. Tezca had holstered his gun. If Myla got her fingers around the handle . . . But then she'd be a girl with tied wrists clutching a gun she didn't know how to operate versus two other people with guns. Running seemed like her best option.

Tezca tried again. "That girl who had an affair with an Under, the priest's wife, did she deserve to die?"

Myla knew the answer to this one. She had learned from tutors and had heard Cint rail against her type a dozen times. "She is an example. How will other women learn to be faithful to their husbands?"

Tezca sighed. "What if women didn't have to worry about falling in love with someone else because they could choose whom to be with? It's not *that* crazy of an idea." Myla was sure he saw her gaping, because he went on. "Were those words yours just now?"

Damn. This boy had every angle figured out. Even Myla couldn't talk her way out of this one. Who *was* he?

"So that's your mission? Take down the whole civilization?"

"You and I have different ideas of what is civilized."

"What would your alternate plans be?"

He flashed her a small grin. "You'll see." He stopped walking, and Myla stopped with him. His flashlight met the floor, showing a small hatch. "Here," he said. Tona and Amihan caught up with them and pointed their flashlights at the door as well.

Their attention was on the hole. Myla edged backward. The three rebels kneeled, trying out different crowbars on the edge of the door. "Ow!" Tona yelped. He held up his hand, a shallow gash running across his palm. That was Myla's chance.

She turned and bolted down the hallway. Flashlights glanced up her way and the rebels called, "She's running!" and "Stop her!" As she ran, she bit at the cord on her wrists, hoping to loosen it. Thank the gods Quinel had given her a short dress.

Myla was halfway through the first cord when she tripped. A small groove in the floor was her downfall. She heard the crack before she felt it. She'd read in a book once that pain travels as fast as lightning but it was taking forever. When her ankle twisted, the pain was unbelievable. She had broken her finger when she was seven. This was nothing like that. Every time her pulse traveled through her ankle, it throbbed with pain.

She caught herself from the dark earth with both forearms and then turned over, panting. She felt a flashlight on her face and looked up to see Tezca standing over her. He seemed relieved that she didn't get away, but his respite turned to concern as he realized why she hadn't stopped gasping.

"Ami! Get over here! She's hurt." He kneeled at her side and inspected her with the flashlight. Myla felt like she was going to pass out.

Tona and Amihan trotted up. The latter seemed triumphant. "Good going, Tezca. You got her!"

Tezca scowled at her. "Patch her up please, Ami." She squatted and inspected the ankle as Tona and Tezca held up the flashlights. Finally, Myla saw what the girl looked like. She was Asian—from the Philippines, Myla guessed—with small, delicate features. Half her head was shaved; the rest of her hair hung down low, swooping over one eye.

What caught Myla's attention was how *pretty* she was. From her demeanor and voice, Myla was expecting someone more physically intimidating and fierce. Amihan looked downright fragile.

As if she had read Myla's mind, Amihan looked up and glared at her. "Your ankle is sprained pretty badly. I'm going to have to set it for a splint." Myla barely had time to process this before Amihan grabbed her foot and snapped it hard into place, shooting new pain up Myla's body.

Amihan used materials from her bag to make a splint, removing Myla's left shoe. Tezca seemed to want to distract Myla from the pain. In the darkness beside her, he kneeled, cut the rest of her restraints, and took her hand.

"What is your name?" he asked.

"Myla," she gasped in the effort. Amihan was taking every opportunity to wrench the ankle around.

"I'm Tezca, that's Tona, and that's Amihan," he continued. "Do you have any family, Myla?"

"I have a brother . . . he's nine."

"What's his name?"

"Aktu. I'm . . . I'm worried about him," she said, a final plea for letting her go.

Tezca paused, thinking. He withdrew his hand and stood. "Well, that's something I understand." Amihan put the finishing touches on the splint and Tona helped prop Myla up.

"We're never going to get out carrying her like this," he said.

"We're close. We'll take turns supporting her," Tezca responded. And so, they trudged back to the hatch, helping Myla hop along on her good foot.

Tona pried open the hatch, revealing a ladder leading deep down into blackness. A musty, dank smell wafted out of the hole.

Tezca looked up at Myla. "Time to get okay with being underground." Out of her apprehension, Myla had the strange urge to laugh.

"I can't climb like this." She nodded to her foot.

"You won't have to." Tezca handed his flashlight to Amihan and hoisted Myla over one shoulder. As she processed how tall he was, her stomach lurched.

"Whoa, whoa! Stop!" she protested, struggling in his iron grip. Tona laughed and she was conscious of how ridiculous she looked.

"No sense fighting it. You can't get down by yourself," Tona said, a small laugh in his voice. Myla realized Tezca was *enjoying* this! Ass. The tips of her ears burned.

Tezca handed his backpack to Tona and started down the ladder, taking care to not bump Myla's ankle. Myla pushed down on his shoulder with her own hands to make the load easier. Soon the circle of light cast by the flashlights above shrank until with a lurch, Tezca hit the ground.

He lifted Myla off his shoulder and laid her out on the ground. "Sit here for a moment." The ground was cold stone, and Myla heard running water nearby, a dank smell hitting her like a wave. "Are we in the sewers?" she asked.

Amihan had made it down the ladder. "What, can't handle a little bit of grime?"

"Oh, lay off, Amihan," Tona called from above. "The first time we brought *you* here, you weren't happy either."

Tezca helped Myla to her feet. "We're almost there, I promise." He paused, then added, "I'm sorry about your ankle. We'll fix it when we get back."

"It's fine." Myla laughed dryly and added, "I can't blame you for the worst escape attempt ever."

The small group moved through the sewer, their footsteps echoing through the darkness that extended for miles. It gave Myla time to think. Tezca, this crazy, rebel deserter, had given her much to consider. Why had she accepted the Priesthood's rule without question? Was she going to grow up into her parents? Hadn't she shown herself to be a little bit rebellious in abandoning Cint? And why was everything Tezca was saying earlier making so much sense?

Soon she felt fresh air on her skin. The sewer's stream emptied out through a circular exit ahead. They had emerged on the edge of Tenochtitlan. Over the great lake, the neighboring suburbs of Tlacopan and Texcoco loomed. Tenochtitlan towered over them, blocking the few stars that shone through the smog.

"Where are we going?" Myla ventured. She had accepted that these people didn't want to hurt her—well, two of them, anyway. But what were they going to do with her once they got back to wherever they were hiding out? They wouldn't ransom her back to her parents, not with what she knew.

"You'll see soon enough," Tezca said, his flashlight scanning the dark water before them. The beam passed over then hovered on a dark shape in the water about the size of a truck. Myla shivered. The priests had told her stories about sun-swallowing demons that lived in the huge lake, anxious to wreak havoc on the people of Azteca. It took her a moment to realize that it was all part of their great lie. She didn't know if that made her feel better or not.

But then the thing under the water moved. It was coming closer and closer to them. Myla felt the urge to run back into the dank sewer but was aware of Tezca's hand on her waist, supportive and light now, but capable of restraint if need be.

In the light of the moon, Myla was at last able to make out what Tona and Tezca looked like. Tona was short and broad shouldered, with shaggy, dark hair patterned with thin rows of red streaks. He had kind, round eyes and a large mouth, a mouth that could break into a dazzling smile.

But what caught Myla's attention were his mutilations. Tona was missing his left earlobe and had a small loop going through his eyebrow. He was—had been a carpenter, an Under.

Tezca was tall and somewhat lanky, with a small waist and wide shoulders. He had close-cropped hair that grew straight up, adding to his height, and he looked about nineteen. Myla saw no mutilations, but a furrowed brow and pursed lips gave him an intense, serious look. He matched his voice perfectly.

At last, the object surfaced. With a low creak, a hatch opened to reveal a pale face, a plain girl with long, blond hair in many braids pressed to her scalp. Soon a boy about Myla's color peeked his shaved head through the hatch as well. The boy had large gauges an inch in diameter in both ears, a former Under as well, and he carried a gun. The girl had a flashlight.

The object was a submarine covered in mirrors, save for the dark iron top. It was nearly invisible, reflecting the water on all sides. Myla had never been inside a submarine before and felt a new anxiety creeping in on her.

"Lisbeth, good to see you," Tona said, a coy smile traveling across his face.

"Get in, Tona. We should go. The bridge is closing," the girl, Lisbeth, responded, unsmiling. Her Nahuatl, Azteca's language, was good but accented. This girl was from some Scandinavian country.

"Well, I'm happy to see you alive and not sacrificed too," Tona muttered as he lurched onto the submarine's surface.

"Wait," the boy with the shaved head said. "Who's she?" Lisbeth's flashlight beam found her and the boy cocked his gun.

"Tez found himself a little souvenir," Amihan mumbled, low enough to deny what she said later. She would have to because Tezca turned and glared at her.

"She overheard our plans. She's just a kid. We decided to bring her underground," Tezca stated, like it was the simplest, most everyday thing in the world. Little tears grew in Myla's eyes, like hearing it out loud made it more real.

There was an awkward pause as the weight of what Tezca said sank in. The boy with the shaved head did not alter the trajectory of his gun and Lisbeth seemed angry and puzzled.

"They're not going to like this back at base," the boy ventured.

"Okay. So shoot her. Tie up this loose end," Tezca deadpanned. His hands clamped down on Myla's arms. What was going on? Amihan gave a satisfied grunt, egging the boy on.

The boy pointed his gun at Myla, but he locked his gaze on Tezca. Myla stared down the barrel of the gun, thinking of her brother and her friends and, hell, even her parents. She forced herself to think. They wouldn't have taken her this far only to kill her there. Tezca had *carried* her down the damn ladder.

The boy sighed and slung the gun's strap over his shoulder. "Come on, let's get going." Tezca picked up Myla once again to carry her into the submarine.

Myla was starting to feel used to being treated as a backpack and didn't struggle this time. Once down the ladder and in the belly of the submarine, she caught a quick glance around before being set down. The submarine's interior looked old, from at least fifty years ago or so, with aged yellow light filling the cabin and rusted metal pipes working their way through the ship. The air was as musty as the air in the sewer had been. A few portholes let in ghostly, water-filtered moonlight.

"Is this thing safe?" she asked no one in particular. No answer.

Amihan said something above on the ladder, then Tona's signature laugh drifted down as he responded, "Well, he never could learn to share."

Myla turned bright red. They were talking about her.

Tona said, "I've got it from here," and she felt two hands on her shoulders steering her forward. Tona sat her down on one of the bunks and instructed her to not move. "You can't escape from this thing, so stay put." Myla nodded.

Amihan approached as Tona said, "Aw, come on. Where is she going to go?"

"Are you going to get out of my way?" Amihan asked.

Tona sighed and left as Amihan untied Myla's hands to handcuff Myla's left wrist to a pipe. "Try anything, rich girl, and I *will* kill you."

CHAPTER 5

Gears clanked and machines pinged as the ship submerged. Myla's five captors ran around making sure everything went according to plan. From the conversations being had close by, she learned that the white, blond girl, Lisbeth, was the captain.

"Check that everything's sealed," she instructed one crew member. "This is our course," she told another. "Should be about an hour."

Despite their efforts to hide their plans, Myla realized they were crossing Lake Texcoco. It made sense. Security on Tenochtitlan's side of the lake was much tighter than on the overgrown, wild side across.

How long had it been since she left Cint? An hour maybe? No one would know that she had disappeared yet. They might have thought she took some time for herself, not that she had been kidnapped or killed.

She would not cry in front of Amihan. That girl was quick to spot weakness, and Myla would not give her the satisfaction. Myla bit her nails, a bad habit she'd had since she was a kid. She hated being restrained too. Something about the cold metal on her skin brought back her childhood nightmares.

Myla sat in silence, listening to the waves churning above her and the whispered conversations about her for what seemed like an eternity. Tezca sat down next to her.

His familiar low voice said, "Can I look at your ankle? The light's much better in here."

"Yeah, I guess," Myla said as she lifted her leg onto the bed beside her. It landed lightly in Tezca's lap, but Myla still winced.

Tezca checked the pulse in the middle of her foot. "It doesn't look too bad."

"How do you know?"

"Well, I'm not a medic, but all mission leaders and participants are trained in first aid. My father also ran the hospital in Tlacopan. From what I've seen, it should heal quickly."

"You may be right. It doesn't hurt that badly anymore." Myla thought she saw a flicker of relief on Tezca's stone face. Maybe she could get some answers. "When your friend pointed his gun at me . . . you could have killed me," she said.

"I'm not the Priesthood," he said. "I don't kill without reason." He aimed that at Myla, like she was to be held responsible for the actions of a secret society centuries old. But still it struck a chord with her. Tezca studied her face.

Myla wasn't going to grovel. "If you're looking for thanks, you won't find them here. My little brother is alone with my parents, and the Priesthood and everyone will think I deserted."

"Well, maybe they'll record you as a deserter. And the people hundreds of years from now will look into history books and see you as one of the first heroes," he countered.

"Well, you've still got some nerve. You don't get a gold star for not murdering me." Myla looked away, though she swore he sported a half smile. She searched for things she could say to convince him of his wrongdoing. "I'm engaged," she said. "My future husband will be heartbroken."

Tezca's poker face returned as he glanced at her green bracelet. Now he looked pissed. Myla could tell he was thinking of mean things to say about how expendable she was to Cint. Plenty of empty-headed upper-class girls with blue bracelets lived in Tenochtitlan. But he kept silent.

Finally, he said, "And . . . you?"

Myla pictured Cint's bright eyes and smile that never seemed to reach them. She thought of the way he laughed by breathing out of his nose and smirking. How they had met in public places and how Cint had nodded every time he met her father, like he was engaging in a business transaction. Hell, Myla had known Tezca, *her captor and a wanted criminal,* for two hours or so and he had made her think more than she ever had with Cint.

Myla changed the subject. "My friend, Quinel, will miss me. She needs me. She's a mess."

Again, that flicker of relief, but a hint of annoyance after. "My parents mistreat my brother," Myla continued. "I take care of him. He needs me."

Now Tezca looked irritated. "It must be hard for you."

"What's that supposed to mean?" Myla asked, her eyes narrowing.

"Stop complaining. Your friends and family are rich and happy enough living off the bloodthirsty system. They'll get on without you. You have no idea what other people are going through."

"Who? You?" Myla asked. "Sorry if I haven't suffered to the standards of a professional sufferer like you. Get over yourself."

Tezca got up and went through a door on the left. Myla put her head in her right hand and closed her eyes. She felt bad about what she'd said. Myla preferred to avoid conflict, but something about this boy made her want to go head to head. Maybe that was because deep down, he was right about her. But he didn't get it. She *had* to be good. That had been her first lesson. Defy the Priesthood and pay with your life. With those familiar thoughts came an old friend: guilt. She wouldn't go there.

When she looked up, Tona stood over her. He cracked a grin. "Hey, it's not like I meant to eavesdrop on your entire conversation . . ." His grin faded and he studied her. "But you should know. If you're looking for a pro sufferer, you were just talking to one. And I don't say that lightly." With that, he left as well. What on earth had he meant?

Before the submarine emerged, Myla sat for an hour and pulled at the cuff chafing her wrist. It was as tight as the bracelet on her right wrist. The five ran around, pulling levers and operating the old machinery. Soon the boy with the shaved head advanced toward her. "Time to go," he said. He unlocked her left cuff.

The rebels assembled near the ladder, anxious to depart. Lisbeth pointed to Myla and said, "She goes first." Tezca approached to take her up the ladder but Tona intercepted.

"Please, buddy. I'll take her this time. Take a break, you must be tired from carrying her all the way here," he teased. One not-amused look from Tezca was enough to evoke a new wave of Tona's laughter.

But Tezca stepped back and Tona hauled Myla over his shoulder, grunting with the effort. It was Tezca's turn to laugh as the tips of Myla's ears burned.

"I could try the ladder . . ." Myla ventured.

"Please!" Tony interrupted. "No, I've got this. I am a big, strong man and you are light as a feather."

"Of course, Tona," Lisbeth sarcastically agreed. "Please affirm your manliness for us."

Myla attempted to lighten his load by holding her own weight with her hands on his shoulders. It must have worked because Tona started up the ladder, careful not to throw Myla.

Once they reached the top, Tona hauled himself out onto the submarine's surface and laid Myla on the nearby shore. Then he collapsed on his back in the sand, panting.

He looked up at Myla and wheezed, "Don't . . . tell. Big . . . strong man . . . remember?"

Myla cracked a smile. Soon Lisbeth popped up from the hatch. Upon seeing Tona, she rolled her eyes and uttered, "Drama queen," under her breath.

Tona sat up and smiled. "You love it." The three waited on the beach, listening to the waves, until everyone had surfaced.

The boy with the shaved head came up last and sealed the submarine behind him. They all worked together to cover it below the surface with seaweed and branches. It occurred to Myla that it wasn't the first time they had executed this.

Finally, Lisbeth seemed satisfied. The boy with the shaved head helped her to her feet and helped her walk into the jungle. As she limped along, he said, "I'm Mectel, by the way."

She responded, "Myla."

They walked for under an hour before reached paved ground. Myla, one foot in a fancy flat, one foot in a splint, stumbled plenty of times, sure that she was irritating Mectel with how often he had to catch her. Though, to be fair, they *were* bringing a crippled girl through unpaved jungle. He would get over it.

Once on the road, she could hear a car coming, saw its headlights. But instead of running and hiding like she expected the rebels to do, they walked toward it. It stopped in front of them, a woman over thirty in the driver's seat.

She rolled down the window. "What did you do?" Her voice was husky, and even in the dim light Myla saw she was plain looking, with wide-set brown eyes.

"I'll explain on the way," Tezca said as he opened the car door.

"I'm glad everyone's so overjoyed to see me alive," Tona muttered as he got in as well.

Soon Myla was sitting in what turned out to be a van, squished in between Lisbeth and Amihan. No one seemed happy about it.

They drove for maybe thirty minutes before the driver slowed. The woman driving whispered, "We've got a patrol coming."

"What? I thought you said this road was clear now!" Amihan accused.

"What do we do?" Tona asked as the van rolled to a stop.

The Priesthood patrol approached the car, as everyone held their breath. Myla felt Amihan's gun pressed into her side. "Say anything and you're dead," Amihan hissed.

The priest was next to the car. The woman in the front rolled down her window.

"Please roll down all the windows," the priest commanded.

She complied as the priest shone a flashlight, illuminating the rebels and Myla one by one.

"Where are you headed?" the priest demanded of the woman.

"We're on the way to the beach coming from Texcoco. We're meeting family there."

The priest's light rested on Tona's face. The priest drew his gun and held it up with the light. "What are those *Unders* doing here?" he growled. The woman was at a loss for words. Amihan cocked her gun. The priest looked at the passengers, then back at the driver. "Get out of the car, all of you."

"Is there a *problem*?" Myla drawled in her best impression of her mother deciding that she needed to "speak with a manager."

Everyone, including the priest, turned and stared at Myla. Amihan dug her gun deeper into Myla's ribs. Myla didn't let her fear show.

"We are so *late* as is. I don't need—and *you* don't need—my father angry," she huffed. The priest looked surprised. So did the passengers of the car. Myla struggled to keep her voice even.

Myla gestured to Mectel and Tona. "This Under is my translator. The carpenter is building a new deck for my family once we get to my beach house. I have all the necessary paperwork for them, if you *need* to see it." She had no idea what the paperwork for taking an Under out of town would even begin to look like.

Her bluff seemed to work, though. The priest lowered his gun and said, "I'm just doing my job, ma'am."

"Yes, well next time, stop the right people. Can we *go* now? It's my *birthday*," she whined. That last part did the trick. The priest paused, then nodded and waved them along.

"Have a good night. Drive safe," he said in parting. The woman in the front of the car rolled up the windows and drove. Everyone else was still staring at Myla.

CHAPTER 6

"That was insane!" Tona broke the silence. A gigantic smile lit up his face. Lisbeth and Mectel agreed, nodding in awe. Amihan looked like she had smelled something bad.

Tezca, if Myla had to place it, looked downright disillusioned and contemptuous. He added, "It was a role she was born to play."

Myla opened her mouth, but couldn't think of anything to say, a rarity. Instead she shrugged and turned forward. "You're welcome," she said.

She wasn't going to let him get to her. He was wrong about her; she would show him. He had *no idea* about her past. She would let him go ahead and call himself a "pro sufferer" all he liked. Her big performance was just that, a performance. At least, she hoped it was.

And she had given up her last chance at freedom to save them. Why had she done it? Pure instinct had kicked in, in the moment. Maybe it was because she knew they would be sacrificed if they were caught. And maybe something Tezca had said earlier about how certain people didn't deserve to die had gotten to her.

Or maybe it was something else. Myla was not an adrenaline junkie, and she wasn't crazy about the thrills of that night. But something felt real about this little group and their purpose. No one had lied to her or put on a fake smile for her for the past few hours. It felt strange to Myla.

Then again, there was the possibility of this new rage against the Priesthood affecting her judgment. Since her parents enlightened her several hours ago, the old voice had surfaced—the voice she hadn't heard screaming at her since she buried it after *it* happened. She had controlled it for so long . . . why was she slipping now?

After a half hour of silence, Mectel turned to Tona. "Hey, you okay?"

Tona smiled. "If you're wondering whether I told them anything, I didn't. They tried to get it out of me, though. Tried."

Mectel looked concerned. "I didn't mean that, man. I know you'd never do that."

"It's fine. They got it all done the first week they had me. I'm close to healed. And they cauterized anything that could have gotten infected."

"You're the strongest of us, Tona," Tezca murmured.

Tona touched Lisbeth on the shoulder. "I am, you know," he told her. "And the most sensitive. It's like a 'strong and stoic but with a gooey center' type thing."

Lisbeth rolled her eyes. "I'm glad you're back, Tona," she said sarcastically enough, but Myla swore she wiped something from her eye.

"I'm sorry about Ixa," Tona told the lady in the front. The woman shrugged and said, "She knew the risk."

The woman addressed Myla. "I'm Huelta, by the way. Ixa was that priest's wife that was executed recently. She was one of ours." She paused and added, "She was my little sister."

Myla was shocked. "I'm so sorry." She remembered how that night she had watched the sacrifice, sipping alcohol and laughing with Quinel. For a split second, she hated herself.

Huelta said, "She got us information for a year. That's a long life-span for an infiltrator. She'd want us to move on. What did they charge her with?" she asked Myla.

"Cheating on her husband. With an Under." Myla heard the disgust in her voice, programmed into it, and caught herself, trying to sound empathetic.

"That's good. Sends a message to the loving wives of Tenochtitlan," Lisbeth hissed.

"Yeah, it's airtight. No way they can prove it," Huelta agreed. "We'll add her to the memorial when we get back. And who was tonight?"

Amihan said, "A food-service Under called Tlazo. He was thirty-seven and had three children."

"Not for nothing," Tezca stated, his expression murky. The other passengers murmured the same back to him after, staring out the window into the endless, moonlit jungle.

After three hours of driving, Myla felt exhausted and cramped. The dress she was wearing wasn't comfortable and her ankle ached. But wary of Tezca's snide comments, she kept silent.

They went off the main road onto a small dirt path obscured by jungle growth. The path ended soon after and Huelta parked the van on the side, careful to conceal the vehicle with large leaves as Lisbeth helped Myla out of the van and onto the soft, wet earth.

As they walked through the jungle, Tezca, Amihan, and Tona explained to the rest of the crew how they'd come upon Myla and decided to take her with them.

"I was against it," Amihan insisted.

"Yeah, well, without her we'd all be up on the pyramid by now," Huelta responded.

They all approached a cave. "This is going to get tricky," Huelta said. She looked at Myla. "It's too rocky for you to navigate with that leg." Tezca started toward her to pick her up. Myla's teeth clenched as she was hoisted up off the ground.

"I'm not happy about this either," Tezca hissed in her ear.

Tona looked at him quizzically, his eyes dancing with laughter, and said, *"Aren't* you?" Tezca sighed and entered the cave.

The cave was a rocky mess, but a short one. They emerged from the other side of the cave as dawn was breaking. It served as a tunnel, a doorway to the compound. Myla's vision adjusted to this new light and she saw their base.

It was impressive, for a ragtag group of rebels. They had long log cabins, scattered wells, and fire pits here and there. Gardens and trees on the tops of all the buildings protected them from an aerial spotting. Long rows of corn and other vegetables stretched behind the cabins. Construction projects and half-finished cabins stood around too, but it was too early for anyone to be out working on them.

"Good thing we're in time for breakfast," Mectel said. Myla agreed. She hadn't realized how hungry and tired she was. She had been awake for almost twenty-four hours and hadn't eaten in at least eight.

"It'll have to wait," Huelta said. "We have to take Myla to the rest of the council, consult them on what should be done." They marched her to the longest, widest building. Vines hung from the rooftop garden to meet the flowing grass below. The morning mosquitos' tiny needles pricked Myla's exposed skin.

There were no doors, only hanging drapes and mesh guarding the indoors from outside. Lisbeth pulled away the curtain to reveal a well-lit room, wooden walls and floor, with several old couches. Plastic tables and chairs were stacked up against one wall.

Huelta and Tona broke off and helped Myla through a curtain on the right. They took her down a wooden flight of stairs that smelled of lemon polish fighting a losing battle to mold and into a dark room at the bottom. There was a door leading to this room, a heavy steel one with a thick glass window. Inside there was a small cot, a lamp on a table, a bookcase, and a door that led to a bathroom.

"You have to stay here for now. But we'll get you out soon, I promise," Tona assured her. "We're going to send you a medic to check out that ankle. Wait here."

Myla nodded and entered the room with Huelta's help, settling on the bed. She glanced up with a quick thank-you, and then they were gone. She was left alone in the room.

The titles on the bookshelf in front of her were all in English and German, and Myla had heard of none of them. The nightstand's drawers held paper, a pen, and paper towels. The lamp was one solid piece of plastic, and was bolted into the wall. Myla felt stunted in the exploration of the new space.

Her head was heavy as a rock, and the pillow welcomed it, spouting up a celebration of dust. Before Myla could stop herself, she planned her next day. She would go on that boat trip she'd always wanted to go on with Quinel.

Myla burst into tears, feeling sorry for herself. She liked her life back home, but wasn't sure if she could continue to live under the Priesthood, given the new information. Then again, roughing it out here with a group of rebels, half of whom wanted to kill her, didn't seem ideal either. It was hopeless.

While she cried, an older man, midforties and bespectacled, entered the room carrying a large duffel bag.

"Hello, Myla," he said, "I'm Izel. I'm here to look at your leg."

She sat up, moving her leg forward. He kneeled at the side of the bed and removed the crude splint Amihan had implemented.

"Please tell me what's going on out there. I'm going crazy in here by myself," Myla begged.

"Lie still. I need to assess the damage," he responded. Myla was not going to get anything out of him. He reminded her of a tutor in a movie whom you wouldn't feel bad about getting pranked.

Izel changed her bandages and splint with dazzling efficiency and delicacy. He even gave her something for the pain. When he was done, he stood. "Don't put too much weight on it. It should be better in a couple weeks." And with that he was out the door before Myla could say thank you.

Myla stood and hobbled to the bathroom on the crutch he gave her. The tiny room looked like it was from a hundred years ago. She bent at the small porcelain sink and splashed water on her face, pausing before letting herself study the spotted mirror above it.

She looked terrible. When Myla cried, her face got puffy and her eyes looked red for hours after. She dreamed about a cosmetic Under with a full kit showing up out of thin air and correcting the mess on her face. It would be one tiny, normal detail that would make her feel safe in her own skin. After years of constant touch-ups, the streaky, frizzy, and swollen girl in the mirror was a stranger.

They had left a starchy T-shirt and a flowing pair of unisex shorts hanging on the bathroom door. Myla ditched the tight, filthy party dress for the comfortable relief of the clean clothes. Able to breathe, she flopped down on the bed and fell asleep.

CHAPTER 7

Myla awoke to a grinning Tona. "Hey there, my favorite hostage!" Why was he in her room? Wait . . . no. Her bleary eyes focused and she remembered. She had been kidnapped. The Priesthood were liars, and she was still figuring out whether to continue to support them. Oh, and she'd twisted her ankle.

"Am I supposed to say you're my favorite captor?" Myla said, rubbing her eyes.

"Wait 'til I tell the guys!" he said mock excitedly. "Now come on. The council wants to see you."

Myla swung herself to a sitting position. "What time is it?"

Tona shrugged. "You've been asleep for three hours or so. Here let me help." He helped her support herself on the crutch and hobble her way to the stairs.

Climbing up the stairs was no easy feat. She wished Tezca were there to expedite the process.

Tona then led her back into the main room and through a door that went outside.

Behind the cabin there was a large amphitheater carved into the earth. Despite being modeled after ancient architecture, the gleaming white stone looked brand new. Sitting surrounding the stage were at least five hundred people, all buzzing with excitement. Below Myla, six people sat at a table awaiting her. Tezca sat in the middle. Amihan sat on the far right. It took Myla a second to realize that she was unaccustomed to seeing a girl sitting at equal rank with a boy. Other women served on the panel as well.

She stumbled down the steps, pretending not to hear the whispers about her. Most seemed curious, but one rebel looked her straight in the eyes and said, "Priesthood scum." Myla kept walking. When she reached the stage, a chair was produced for her facing the table.

"Hello, Myla," Tezca said, his deep voice reverberating throughout the space. "We were just discussing your role here, whether you should be treated as one of us or kept separate." He sounded different. The deep voice was still there, but it was no longer as stern and serious. Commanding, yes, but now his words also brimmed with possibility. You *wanted* to listen to him. The furrow in his brow was also gone.

"We've never had a . . . visitor before," he continued. "And of course, you are a special case. We were hoping you would want to give us some input as to why you spoke up in the van last night."

Hmm. What did Myla want out of this? She still wasn't sure whether she wanted to try to escape. She needed to get them to allow her some freedom, and she would take advantage of it if needed. She didn't want to be locked up.

She knew what to do, found the words, but before she spoke, Amihan interrupted. "This girl is Priesthood, through and through. If we are not careful with her, then she will escape, and we'll all be done for. She's jeopardizing everything we've worked for."

The crowd held their breath, with some clear nods and angry faces.

Myla spoke up. "If I may shed some light on my actions, I was enlightened last night. I knew nothing of the Priesthood's secrets, and it took me by surprise. However, I was trained well and I let myself believe that it was all for the greater good . . . at first. After speaking at length with Tezca here, I realized that maybe my instinctual sickness at what the Priesthood is doing was correct. By the time we were pulled over, I was sure that whatever happened with your people, I couldn't go back to Tenochtitlan."

She paused, reading the crowd. No one looked murderous yet. She stood up, hopefully inciting sympathy over her ankle. She continued. "Why did I speak up in the van? For multiple reasons, the first of which being that I appeared to be traveling with you. I was already associated with rebels, and I would have been sacrificed, executed with the rest of you. The second was that I don't believe any of you deserve to die. I was thinking for myself for the first time in my life. I realized I don't want to save you for the next fight. I want to be there with you."

"Liar!" Amihan yelled, and all eyes strayed from Myla. "You expect us to believe you flipped like that? Once upper class, always upper class." Amihan turned from Myla to the crowd. "Her people, her family and friends, they killed your loved ones! It was her!"

Myla's stomach dropped as the parts of the crowd murmured their assent. Someone screamed, "She's lying!" Another yelled, "Priesthood spy!" And a select few cheered them on.

Tezca interceded, holding his hands up. "So what would you do with her, Ami?"

Her answer was quick. "Make her an example, a warning. Send her back to her mommy and daddy in three different shipments."

That divided the crowd even further. Some looked more incited than before, others glanced around, uncomfortable with such a blatant request for violence.

Myla took advantage of that, hobbling toward Amihan. "You are right to not trust me, Amihan. You are even right in hating me and what my family stands for. But I *cannot* be the first person here who was persuaded by Tezca. I can't be the only one who sat by and did nothing . . . and now regrets it more than anything.

"The Priesthood has hurt too many. I want to join the cause." She waited a moment before adding, "Not for nothing."

That did it. Scattered applause, then more joined in. Everyone but a small section of the audience was smiling and clapping. Up on the panel, the council nodded, except Amihan, who was pouting, and Tezca. His expression looked impressed . . . but knowing, like he was going to allow the crowd their moment but he knew what Myla was doing.

Myla could have told them what had happened when she was ten; perhaps that would have convinced Tezca. But she had so many conflicting feelings about it that she wasn't sure it would have come off as well. The Myla who subdued the feelings of rage and betrayal and decided to live as a good little Aztec girl might have come out. She still was the one whispering in Myla's ear, telling her to run back home and tell everyone everything. That Myla was scared. She had learned her lesson.

And Myla had warped the event so much in her own mind that she couldn't be sure she knew what had happened anymore. Angry Myla who reared up right afterward remembered it one way and Scared Myla remembered it another.

But she was right to avoid the subject. An older council member, a man in his late twenties with long hair tied back, stood and said, "I think I speak for everyone when I say it doesn't matter how you got here. Anyone who wants to join the cause can."

That last part hung in the air for a moment before it was disrupted by Amihan standing and protesting once more: "She's everything we've ever fought against. You're signing our death sentence."

The man pondered that for a minute, then said, "Motion to vote . . . All in favor."

Myla could barely bring herself to look at the panel, but when she did she saw four hands in the air, signaling their support to her. She swore she heard Amihan grinding her teeth from afar.

The council adjourned and Tona came up to Myla. "Hooray for Stockholm syndrome!" he cheered. Myla had no idea what he was talking about, so she smiled and nodded. Then Tezca came up to her.

"Nice speech," he said. He was looking at her with the same cautious disdain from earlier, but now there was something else . . . respect?

"You too," Myla said.

"I thought I'd mention that there's miles and miles of jungle surrounding the camp, and we block the roads when we're not using them. If you were curious, of course."

Okay, so he didn't buy her whole "reformed rebel" speech, saw she still had doubts.

She tried to look indifferent. "Thanks, Tezca," she said sarcastically.

They stared each other down for a few more moments before he broke. "Breakfast is in the pavilion. Would you like me to show you?" The cold, stern Tezca was back. But Myla could do it too.

"That would be lovely, thank you."

He took her past the amphitheater to a standing tent under which people were serving corn tortillas, rice, and beans out of dozens of large bowls. People were taking their plates out to picnic on the field. It was simpler fare than she was used to—she and her parents used to order in all the time from restaurants featuring more worldly cuisine. But still it all looked rather pleasant to Myla and she dug in with vigor, sitting with Lisbeth, Huelta, Tezca, and Tona. The older council member with long hair sat with them as well.

Myla sat in silence, eating and listening to the long-haired man discuss council matters with Tezca. They appeared to be in the highest seats on the panel. Myla was not surprised given Tezca's incredible transformation into a likable leader earlier.

Tezca turned to Myla and said, "Well, it seems that you will be staying with us for a while."

"What will I be doing here?"

"Well, my hope is to keep you in minimum security, let you see how things are done here. Might have to put you to work though." He chuckled when he saw her horrified expression. "Relax. We're not going to send you into any silver mines or anything."

"What will I have to do?" she ventured.

"Well . . . what are you good at?" he asked. Myla hadn't thought about it before. She was fine in math and history. Her English was passable and she knew a little Chinese. She was glib in speech and could think in tough situations. But what set her apart? What could she offer a rudimentary society?

Enough time had passed for Tezca to save her with "It's okay. We'll find you something to do. But there won't be many parties to throw or priests to sponsor." With that, he got up and left.

He had her pegged. He had given her the chance to surprise him with a hidden talent like hunting or chopping wood. But now he got to be correct about how she had always expected to go into sponsoring priests as a businessman's wife, like the good little upper-class girl she was. She felt foolish, useless, and then angry. Was it her fault that no one had taught her how to catch a damn fish? She was a fast learner. She would prove him wrong.

After everyone had eaten and placed their plates in the basins under the pavilion, they all set off to work. Myla was left standing alone, unsure where to go.

Soon Huelta, who was holding one of the full basins, found her. "Come on, Myla. You're with me in the kitchen."

Myla breathed a sigh of relief. A kitchen. She knew how those worked. She started off in Huelta's direction but stopped when she cleared her throat and gestured with her head to the remaining basins. Myla smiled and lifted one tub full of glasses. It was heavier than she'd expected, and Huelta had made it look easy. Myla heaved it off the table under one arm and trudged after Huelta on her crutch, careful to walk around the small shrubberies here and there in her path.

Though plenty of people used the grounds, no clear paths connected the buildings. Everyone cut across the grass, which was thick and soft, elevating Myla at least an inch off the ground.

The kitchen was its own building, another cabin with several chimneys and a water pump outside. Like the main cabin, ivy ran down its sides from the rooftop garden and made it look like it had grown from the grass around it. Myla was reminded for a moment of the sharp and standoffish glass and steel of the city. She didn't like one more than the other yet, but she did concede that she would appreciate an Under and a cab for her ankle. After a moment, she itched to bite her nails.

"This is it," Huelta said, a hint of excitement in her voice. She swung open the door to reveal a modern kitchen, out of place with the old-fashioned outdoors. They had a gigantic, gleaming oven, a stove with a dozen places for pots, and several sinks, all glossy chrome.

"The pump outside is for emergencies," she continued as she set down her basin on a counter. Myla did the same as half a dozen rebels she hadn't seen before entered with the remaining bins. There was no one younger than Myla, and it was full of women. Myla noticed one black woman and one white woman speaking in English as they placed their bins.

"I know what you're thinking," Huelta said. "You're wondering how we got all of this equipment. It's interesting. We had a bureaucrat on the inside for a while. He forged the papers for an expansion of one of Tarasca's factories and made a request for factory-size kitchen supplies. Once it was out of Tenochtitlan, we intercepted it and here we are."

She smiled and clapped her hands together. "These are the kitchen workers, and I'm the closest thing we have to a chef. We can do introductions later. Dishes first!"

Everyone stood near a sink with a basin and Myla got the hint to do the same. For a half hour, they washed, dried, and stored the flatware, and soon Myla's hands were red with scrubbing. It was a simple enough task, though, and Myla was glad that there were few ways she could screw it up.

At some point, Huelta brought out an old-looking boom box, the kind Myla had had as a kid, pink with puppies all over it. The sounds of Mezin, a type of fusion music featuring Spanish guitar and Aztecan drums that had been popular fifty years ago, filled the air.

Once the dishes were sorted into new bins, Huelta clapped her hands again. "Okay, quick break, everyone. Then we start on lunch." Myla filed behind the line of people going outside and flopped down on the grass. Her ankle was throbbing. Soon a man and a woman sat down beside her. The man was late twenties and the woman was well into her forties, her skin delicately worn like one of Myla's mom's handbags. The man had a thick beard that seemed to cover most of his face.

"Hello, I'm Zimi. And this is Monty. We liked what you had to say this morning," the woman started.

"Oh, thank you so much. I'm Myla."

"We know," Monty interceded. "Welcome to the kitchen. It's light work, but we have the longest days. We hope you'll like it here."

"Is everyone assigned their jobs?" Myla asked.

Zimi responded, "Newcomers are if they have no specific skills. Then they're given an opportunity after a while to switch if they'd like. But we appreciated a more relaxed environment."

Huelta was calling them back in to prepare lunch. It was mixed grilled vegetables and lean cuts of chicken on green wraps. Myla helped to slice the vegetables, surprised they trusted her with a knife, though she did catch a few wary glances from some of the other workers. They arranged them on large platters and took them out to the pavilion.

Myla sat with Monty and Zimi for that meal and chatted with them about food production on the compound. She was interested to learn that they stole what they could from neighboring factories and even infiltrated Tenochtitlan's parties to carry off cases of gourmet meat. However, most of what they ate came from the gardens and the small supply of livestock they had. After lunch's dishes, Huelta took her around the compound and showed her the barn. Myla wrinkled her nose in disgust at the smell at first, but forced a calm, attentive expression on her face. She needed to make a good impression.

Huelta also showed her the vast wheat fields, the living cabins, and the mission-base building. The people who had captured her were inside, planning the next mission to steal food or hurt the Priesthood. Tezca was probably inside, his brow furrowed over a map, calculating chances of survival.

She prepared dinner, listening to the benign conversation and Mezin, allowing herself to indulge in one calm moment. However, her ankle protested more with every passing hour despite the light painkillers Huelta had given her, and she had only gotten three hours of sleep. Myla felt ready to drop by the time she was sitting eating dinner.

Over the whole camp eating on the field, a megaphone crackled. Everyone fell silent. The megaphone belonged to Tezca. His deep voice rumbled over the field. "Tonight, it was an Under named Minual. He was a bricklayer. No children. Not for nothing."

The whole camp rumbled as it responded, "Not for nothing," then resumed conversation.

Huelta took her to the long-haired council member from before for her rooming assignment. He introduced himself as Quent, the copresident of the council. Myla could tell he wanted her to feel flattered at his presence, so she smiled wide and thanked him for every little thing. If only everyone were this easy to manipulate.

He gave her Cabin Four, and Huelta was nice enough to steer her in the right direction. Myla was the first one there and found a cot not yet taken among the two dozen or so there. After sitting for a few minutes, she got up and walked among the beds. All of them were made, and on the shelves above were small keepsakes the owners had taken with them when they fled wherever they had come from.

Myla spotted a tube of lipstick on one, a pair of dancing shoes on another. A mandolin, a fancy headband, a tiny, silver bell. There were pictures of all kinds of people, young and old, Unders and whole. Finally, she found a small photo of an Asian family with a smiling mother, father, young son, and someone who looked a lot like—

"What the hell are you doing with my stuff?" Amihan was next to her, staring her down.

Myla put her hands up in a gesture of peace. "I wasn't touching anything."

"Get out of here. Before I make you leave," Amihan huffed.

"This is the cabin I was assigned to," Myla stated.

Amihan turned her back on her, strolling among the cots. As she paced, she pulled out a knife and played with it, twirling it around her fingers. Myla watched, mesmerized, wishing she had pocketed the one she was using earlier, just in case.

"If I see you anywhere near my bed again, little Miss Upper Class . . ." The knife was at Myla's throat, the cold blade moving with her pulse. Amihan smiled so sweetly, Myla had to remind herself to breathe. Amihan continued. "I'll cut you up into little tiny pieces and feed you to the pigs. Everyone will think you tried to escape." She giggled, an unnatural sound.

"What are you trying to get out of this? I'm not scared of you."

Amihan's smile reached her eyes. "I'll start with your throat. Rip out your lovely vocal cords. Let's see you talk your way out of everything like that."

The door opened, women spilling into the room, and the knife was gone. Somehow Amihan made it disappear. Myla was impressed, and giving Amihan one more forced "you're adorable" look, she went back to her bed.

In the women who came in, she recognized Lisbeth and Zimi. Luckily, Zimi came and sat on a bed across from Myla's. Her bed was the one with the lipstick above it. Myla's shelf looked empty, and she wished she had a photo of Aktu or Quinel to fill up the space. Zimi wished her goodnight and the lights went out.

Myla climbed into bed, ready to drop from exhaustion. It was a moonless night and dark as it had ever been inside the room. Myla closed her eyes and tried to shut out all that had happened, but tossed and turned for nearly an hour.

Suddenly, Myla bolted upright, certain she had heard breathing right next to her bed. Out of the darkness came a quiet giggle, the flash of a blade, and a whisper of "Good night, Your Holiness."

CHAPTER 8

Myla awoke the next morning easily. Amihan's warning had provided her with a restless sleep, her trying to keep that one eye open. After Myla showered in one of the cabin's bathrooms and dressed in the clothes they had given her, she walked over to the kitchen to help prepare breakfast.

As she cooked beans and rice, Huelta approached her to talk. "Myla, we're glad you're adjusting to the kitchen work, but we hoped you could attend a class after breakfast instead of doing dishes. It's customary for newcomers here to meet with our historians who run our school for the few kids here on the compound. It will help clear up any myths you still think true of the Priesthood."

Myla had only just learned that most of what her tutors had been feeding her was propaganda. Would this "class" teach her anything truthful? The survivalist Myla stepped aside for a moment, letting the curious Myla through to wonder . . . what *had* the Priesthood been hiding? Were any of her history lessons fact?

"I'd love to go," Myla mustered after a while, if only for Huelta's approving smile.

Myla started out alone for breakfast that day, as no friendly faces appeared in the crowd before her. But right before she sat down, she heard an overexuberant "MYLA! Over here!" coming from behind her. She turned to see Tona sitting with Lisbeth and Tezca on the far side of the field. The other two looked annoyed at Tona's invitation. That was what set Myla striding across to them.

"Good morning, everyone," she said. Lisbeth gave her a smile that was genuine, if somewhat uncomfortable. She would take it. Tona grinned in his usual way that made Myla feel right at home. Tezca's face was a blank wall.

"How are the kitchens?" Tona ventured.

"I like it, though my hands might disagree," Myla joked, holding up her raw fingers. Tezca smirked at her previously unworked hands.

Myla ignored him. "What are you guys up to?"

Tona blathered on about their newest mission to plant the rest of the cameras in the Temple Mayor. Tezca looked outraged.

"Oh, Tona. You don't want to bore our new friend with technicalities," he said, struggling to remain indifferent.

"Yeah, you're right," Tona shrugged. "Let's talk about something fun . . ." A wicked glint entered his eye. "There's a party tonight in the amphitheater. There'll be a bonfire and music." He looked expectantly at the group. "You all can come, right?"

Tezca looked away. "I have some work I have to do. I'll see if I can stop by."

Lisbeth said, "Okay, Tona. I'll check it out," and Myla smiled. "That sounds great, Tona. I'm flattered you invited me."

Tezca made a sound in the back of his throat and stood up. He cleared his dishes and stalked off. Myla looked at her food.

"Sorry about that. He's sensitive and quick to judge," Tona offered.

"No, it's fine. I can't believe that cold person is the same speaker I saw yesterday."

Tona laughed. "Yeah, he's a politician through and through. But he does care about the cause and the people here."

"I'm sure once he gets to know you and he knows he can trust you, everything will be fine," Lisbeth added.

"But he was warm, even caring at first," Myla responded. "What did I do wrong?"

Tona and Lisbeth shrugged, but Myla thought she knew the answer to her own question already. Tezca had been attentive and friendly when they engaged on a real level, debating matters of the world. When Myla had turned it into her own issues, he had seen them as menial, and concluded that she was yet another empty-headed, upper-class girl. The fact that he'd seen through her speech the other day made her a treacherous one as well. It didn't look good. She bit into her tortilla.

"I wouldn't worry about it," Tona answered. "At least he's not an extremist."

"An extremist?"

"One of Amihan's crew. They were the ones giving you those dirty looks yesterday. Most of us believe that the caste system should be changed and the sacrifices abolished. They think that we should invert the system, enslaving the upper classes and killing one a day for no reason other than revenge. Most of them are former Unders."

He caught her eyeing his piercings and mutilations. Myla asked, "Why aren't you with them, then?"

He shrugged. "I like believing we're all the same deep down."

"Yet you still wear your piercings."

"Doesn't mean I can't serve as a reminder to those around me of the atrocities committed against my people. And to myself."

He said all of this calmly. A small part of Myla still felt weird about sitting and eating with an Under. But Tona was so open to knowing her that it made it feel normal.

"And then why is Amihan an extremist? She isn't an Under," Myla probed.

"No, but practically. She was shipped from the Philippines to the factories in Tlaxcala. Most of the workers there aren't even natives anymore. They're teenagers imported from all over the world who need to send money back to their families. But they aren't coming to jobs. The 'housing' they're promised is cells, and they can't leave. Amihan escaped during one of the riots last year."

"Wow. I had no idea. And you, Lisbeth. How did you get here?"

Tona interrupted, "She caught one glimpse of me and decided to follow me wherever I may go."

"Ha-ha. I'm from Europe, Sweden to be exact. My family was wealthy and I decided to go to Azteca as part of a student-exchange program. Once I got here and witnessed all Azteca was doing firsthand, I knew I had to join the resistance," Lisbeth said.

"Not everyone uses the caste system?"

"Well . . . there are forms of cruelty and subjugation all over the world—the factories in rural China, similar to yours here, the slave trade in Africa and Asia, and the conflict in the Middle East. In most of these cases, knowledge and education is the key to resolving the conflict, but in no case is it as direct as it is here."

Myla felt confused. "How will education do anything here?"

Lisbeth continued. "Eighty percent of your population believes a lie. If we could tell them the truth . . ."

"Enlighten them," Myla said.

"Yes . . . enlighten them, we could topple the system and with the right people and a bit of work, it would give way to a more humane, democratic society. Democracy, the way of the ancient Greeks. You can read about them in our library."

Myla had never heard anyone, let alone another girl, speak this way. She swallowed and asked, "What makes you think your system is superior?"

Lisbeth held out her hands, gesturing to the compound. "The success of this compound has convinced me. We have compassionate representatives who do their part to meet our needs. They also work just like the rest of us. A rudimentary society like this one needs a lot of hand-holding in the beginning stages, but as we've progressed and grown, we've added some more sophisticated aspects."

Tona jumped in. "The council was the first thing we established—well, Tezca established. He was our first leader. Then we organized groups for farming and other jobs. Now we're working on expanding past the simple barter system and councilors-as-judges-and-jury legal system."

Tona noticed Myla's worried face and chuckled. "Don't worry. We don't often have to throw someone in the cell you were in. We share everything, so there's not a lot of theft, and there's not much violence."

Myla remembered Amihan's knife and shivered. "What happens when someone wants to leave?"

Tona gave her a cautious look. "Well, we'd have to stop you. We don't trust you yet, sorry. But someone who came of their own accord, we wouldn't want to stop them. It is a dangerous life. And as a precaution, the council decided that whenever someone leaves, we have to uproot and find a new place in the jungle to settle. We've moved twice."

Myla looked around at the people clearing their plates. "Well, breakfast is over. Thank you both for the introduction. It was . . ." she smiled, "enlightening."

CHAPTER 9

After breakfast, Myla was directed by Lisbeth to follow Izel, the man who had resplinted her ankle, to the schoolhouse. He was plowing across the field and Myla had to jog to catch up. She limped alongside him as best she could to keep up with his huge strides. He looked her once at her, nodded, and looked back ahead.

She could make out a small cabin, the schoolhouse. Izel saw what was happening there before Myla did, and increased the length of his stride, crossing the distance in seconds. Myla stood panting next to him a minute later.

A girl was sitting crying outside the cabin, holding her knee. A boy was explaining to Izel about how the girl had fallen. Izel kneeled and removed her hand, revealing a shallow scrape two inches long.

Izel sighed and turned to Myla. "Would you mind taking this girl to the infirmary? I need to begin the lesson."

"I thought you were a medic."

He cleaned his glasses. "I am. But that's part time. I am the head tutor here. I'm teaching literature first. You won't miss anything."

Myla didn't know if she liked Izel or not, but she wanted him to like her. "Of course, I'd be glad to take her." Myla held the girl's hand as she picked herself up. The girl led Myla toward what she assumed was the right building and away from the schoolhouse. Myla looked over her shoulder to see Izel herding the rest of the children into the cabin.

The girl was still crying. Myla asked, "What's your name?"

"Arel."

"I'm Myla."

They had reached another cabin like the schoolhouse. Myla paused outside, then knocked. A short, somewhat-stout woman in her thirties opened the door, her hair pulled back into a little bun on top of her head. She looked up at Myla and then Arel with mild interest and a big smile.

"What's going on?" Her voice was low, yet somehow bursting with joy. Myla liked her immediately.

Arel spoke up. "I hurt my knee." She started crying again.

"Okay, well, come inside. I'll patch you up."

Myla and Arel were bustled into the room. It was immaculate yet cozy for an infirmary. A dozen cots lined the walls, with curtains ready to pull around each one, and medical stations at both ends of the room. Three or four people lay in cots at the other end. Arel was sat upright in the cot closest to them.

"I'm Zuma, by the way," the woman said. "I'm head medic around here." Myla leaned on a counter and Zuma's eyes widened. "Are you going to faint?" There was a new light in her eyes now, an amused warning, an are-you-kidding-me pre-reaction to the idea of Myla fainting like some delicate waif.

Myla stood upright. "No! I mean . . . no, I'm fine. Blood doesn't bother me."

Zuma gave her a relieved "Good," and bandaged the knee. When she was done, she looked at Arel, who was red, puffy, and sniffing. "You're okay now." Arel shed more tears. Zuma asked, "How old are you?"

"Eight."

Zuma nodded, looked her straight in the eyes, and said, "You're fine now. Go back to class." The warmth was still there, but Myla sensed an old toughness in Zuma's voice. It worked too. Arel stopped crying and stood, reaching for Myla's hand.

Zuma stopped them, looking at Myla. "You're that upper-class girl, right?"

"I suppose."

Zuma nodded again, looking in her eyes, and said, "Let's see what you've got in you." It wasn't a warning. It was pure interest. It was motivational and accepting, rather than derisive. Myla would show her. She would prove Tezca wrong and show Zuma what she was made of. With a brief smile, she hurried Arel out the door and back to the schoolhouse.

The cabin was filled with long tables and a whiteboard. Several small children played in the back of the room. A few younger teenagers, around twelve or thirteen, sat in the front. As Arel rejoined her friends, Izel turned to Myla.

"Welcome, Myla. We just finished literature for the younger group. The older group is now here for what you'd like to learn. Most likely you are used to your sessions with Priesthood-approved tutors. I am here to tell you that everything you think you know is wrong. Sit there."

He pointed at a chair in the front of the class. Myla sat down there, next to a thirteen-year-old boy. Izel stood at the front of the room, marker in hand.

"Now we will be discussing similar societal mass delusions to Aztecism and the Priesthood's government."

Myla felt like she should be taking notes, Izel moved so fast. In less than an hour he covered the ancient Indian Brahmans and how they'd perpetuated Hinduism from the top of the social hierarchy, much as Aztecism was spread. Hinduism taught its followers that if they followed the structure and avoided social mobility, they would be rewarded with a step up in the next life. The people at the bottom, "untouchables" if they believed what the priests said, would remain "untouchable" until the day they died. Myla felt uncomfortable, having bought into a similar system days before.

The idea of other religions in other regions had never occurred to her either. She had never thought about it. She knew that the Europeans who tried to conquer her people five hundred years ago did what they had in the name of one supposed "God." But it was always implied that they were primitive and wrong, worshipping people, turning certain ones into "saints," and erecting idols of their god and his "son."

Of course other regions had religion! Myla felt stupid now. The two landmasses made contact through those first "conquistadors," and they both had existed long before that.

Through the lesson, she also had her doubts about whether Izel was telling the truth as well, since she had been brainwashed all these years and wasn't ready for it to happen again. But he showed them pictures in books of archeological digs and relics, and though some were in English, they looked like history books. Izel spoke the truth.

Then they moved on to governmental analysis. Myla already knew that the upper class supported the priests, sponsoring whomever they agreed with. Money acted as votes for different candidates. The priests formed a senate of about two hundred, of which Matutslan was the chief speaker. He had the ultimate power over what was done in the government but was supposed to listen to the advice of the senate.

Izel passed out a picture of an old priest. "This is Priest Honel. He was a popular senate member last year. Now, we all know that Matutslan is in favor of mass governmental regulation of the surrounding factories. It helped him gain total control over the senate because he could arrange it so the sponsors of his political enemies would fail financially. It was a vicious power cycle. Honel wanted to privatize more industry, putting some power back into the hands of the people, even if they were upper class."

The class collectively smirked at the mention of the frivolous, idiotic upper class. Myla got angry, then realized that it was true that this was the first time she had bothered to learn about any of this.

Suddenly, she remembered one night she had stayed up reading until the early hours of the morning. She had overheard her father speaking into the phone, and she crept down to the kitchen to listen.

She had known that her mother and father had made a move to support an up-and-coming new priest, pledging to give him hundreds of thousands of goldit, Azteca's currency. This was after there had been talk of increased governmental regulation of business. Myla hadn't paid attention, but she dug details from her brain to make sense of what her father was saying.

"But he hasn't done it yet? . . . Good, good . . . But this is unfair! No, I *know* he's the chief speaker."

Myla's ears pricked up. What did her father have to do with Matutslan?

Her father was yelling now. "It's my right as a citizen to support whomever I want! . . . Well, if he does decide to wreck me, *everyone* will know it was because of the new guy! They won't stand for it. I have friends in high places."

Not as high as the chief speaker, apparently. He listened to the voice on the phone and quieted. "Fine. Fine, I'll pull support. Just . . . I need assurance he won't wreck my business just to make a point. Uh-huh. Uh-huh. How much? . . . Fine."

What Myla was focused on back then hadn't been the corruption in plain sight, but rather on her father's anger. She sat on the stairs for a long time, remembering what happened when she was ten. Where had been this anger then? Defiant, Angry Myla had risen up that night, itching to confront her parents about why they had laid down and taken all of it. Scared Myla soon replaced her, remembering what happened and wanting to lie there with her parents.

But even so, she had heard it herself. Matutslan had threatened her father with shutting down his factory, all to drain support from the speaker's opponents. She didn't remember the name of the priest her family had wanted to sponsor, but saw now that Matutslan must have disagreed with him on some matter.

Izel continued. "Now regardless of Honel's stance on economy, he also had some ideas regarding military spending that would have saved Azteca millions. But because Matutslan disagreed with him on one matter, Honel couldn't be correct about any matter. Matutslan had him ostracized, as the ancient Greeks called that type of sanction—we covered that last week—and thrown into exile. Here we see a main flaw of Azteca's government: that ideas and innovations are not judged independently of the ideologies of the people who present them. That along with the corruption and sponsorship system."

Myla looked around at the nodding teenagers. How were they getting all of this? Myla thought she understood, so she nodded too. Izel passed out another photo, this one of a young priest whom Myla recognized.

"This is Priest Polumex. He was a radical," Izel breathed. "He advocated for legalization of homosexuality. Well, for as long as he could before he was executed." It clicked for Myla. She remembered this guy. She remembered the night he was killed.

"Again, regardless of his bearing on that matter, he was a senatorial genius. He proposed ideas to Matutslan quicker than anyone else, before he came forward about his beliefs. He knew the government's inner workings and got things done. But then Matutslan refused to employ any idea that he was behind, only because of their disagreement on one matter. Matutslan even agreed with him on some proposed ideas, but struck the ideas down.

"If we had an impartial ruler, someone willing to look beyond conflicting ideology and accept good ideas as good ideas, no matter the source, society could progress at a much faster rate."

The boy next to Myla raised his hand and piped up, "Is that why Tezca invented the anonymous system?"

"Precisely," Izel said, smiling. This was the most emotion Myla had seen yet from the guy. It was weird. "When submitting ideas to your representative, you do it anonymously. It's the same for when council members submit ideas to each other. So far, it's worked rather well. That's how we engaged the rooftop camouflage idea and the idea to move every time one person wants to leave, rather than making them stay."

He paused, looking around his classroom. "Very well, if there are no questions, please take out your math books and work quietly. Myla, you may return to the kitchens."

Myla stood, uttered a quick thank-you, and hurried out as fast as she could. Her brain couldn't take in any more information; she had learned more in that morning than she had in her whole life. The good student in her was cataloguing it for memorization. The Priesthood girl who had hoped these rebels were wrong both in cause and ethics was turning the facts over and shrinking back at what she saw. Myla didn't know it yet, but she would cry for a long time that night.

On a scale from one to ten for my-parents-are-idiots-buying-into-a-terrible-system regarding her support of the Priesthood, Myla was still somewhere in the middle. But she was changing. She and her ankle received blows that night, but both were healing and becoming stronger.

CHAPTER 10

That night at dinner, Tezca's megaphone sang out, "Tonight was a midwife Under by the name of Ibelia. Two children. Not for nothing." Myla found herself chanting it back to him with the other people there, shielding her eyes from the light of the sunset.

After the dinner dishes were done, Myla walked alone to the amphitheater. She could see candles set up around the perimeter, and Huelta's pink boom box hooked up to a speaker system below in the belly of the theater. There were at least three dozen people there, all on the younger side, already.

Lisbeth found Myla, holding a platter of cups. She had warmed up to Myla after their chat that morning. Maybe sharing her story had connected them in some way, but that cautious discomfort was gone, to Myla's relief.

"Hey, you made it!" Lisbeth said happily. It was subdued, as Lisbeth was, but it was there.

"Wouldn't miss it. How's it going?"

"Okay. We haven't gotten the music working yet, and we were hoping for a larger crowd, but it should heat up soon." She handed Myla one of the cups and Myla drank, hoping for pulque. What she got instead was a fruity mixture, overly sweet. It clung to her tongue.

"Wait." Lisbeth stopped her. "Are you seventeen?"

Myla nodded and Lisbeth switched the glass for a differently colored one. It was the same drink but with the sharp tang of alcohol. It was strange how the taste comforted Myla. If she closed her eyes, she could be outside Chinampa 9 with Quinel, laughing and trying to keep it together. She put it out of her mind.

"How old are you?" Myla asked.

"I'm twenty."

Myla was surprised. She looked much younger. Lisbeth gave her a small, knowing smile and admitted, "I know, I look like I'm twelve."

Myla laughed and lifted her glass. "To looking and feeling young, then!" Lisbeth seemed to like it, and they toasted.

"Ladies, please!" Tona was between them. "Stop fighting over me. Form a line."

Lisbeth rolled her eyes. "It's like you have one joke, Tona." Myla took a good look at him. Through the blur of the alcohol, he didn't even look like an Under.

"So what is there to do at rebel parties?" Myla asked.

"Well . . . drinking, thanks to Huelta's homemade distillery out back, games when the party dies down a bit, and dancing," Tona replied.

"Speaking of," Lisbeth spoke up, "let's see if the head of the tech department, yours truly, can get the music up and running."

They set off down the stairs of the amphitheater and toward the speakers mounted on a small table. Lisbeth disappeared behind the speakers for a moment, handing her platter to Tona. Myla watched as she switched wires, opened the back of the speaker, and flipped a switch and music burst from the table. It was unlike anything Myla had ever heard before—the sounds of a fiddle intermixed with a pop beat and rapping. Lisbeth knew all the words.

"When you fix the music, you choose the music!" she yelled over the Scandinavian din.

Tona gave her a look and yelled, "You get *fifteen* minutes of this, woman!" But Lisbeth was already pulling Myla onto the dance floor.

About a dozen people were there, bobbing up and down to the beat. Tona was already there. He nodded at them and started a strange, jerky dance, like twitching your neck while moving your arms in circles. Myla laughed and joined in as much as she could with her ankle. She craved a normal moment in this place more than anything. After a morning of overeducation, it was nice not to think.

People poured out of nowhere, thickening the crowd and upping the energy. Then someone switched the music to a techno riff with a building beat. Everyone went crazy. Lisbeth shrugged and yelled in Myla's ear, "What do you want? We have maybe four albums. We like them."

Myla joined the jumping mass and somehow, she, Lisbeth, Mectel, and Tona ended up in a circle. Out of nowhere, Tezca, wearing his politician smile, crossed the dance floor. He had spotted Tona and Lisbeth, but not Myla. He even danced a little bit on the way over. He danced like her grandfather, shaking his shoulders and tapping his feet. She had to struggle to keep a straight face.

Myla pretended not to see him until he joined the circle. He looked happy to see everyone until his gaze rested on Myla. He stopped short, standing and staring. He looked confused. He hadn't expected to see her there.

Maybe it was the drink, but Myla walked up right next to him across the circle, stood on her tiptoes to reach his ear, and told him outright, "I'm here! Deal with it!" She crossed the circle again, not caring about his reaction, but when she did look over, to her surprise, he was smiling, bemused.

Then he danced again. Myla did too. The four and a half rebels, Lisbeth, Tona, Mectel, Tezca, and Myla, twirled and jumped and shouted in their circle, their little pocket of freedom.

The party was peeling off in small chunks, people leaving to fall into their beds. Even the music stopped. Myla thanked Tona for inviting her and headed back to her bunk. It was getting easier. Even after two days, she found she could rest more and more weight on her ankle.

Her head was spinning from the drinks, and Myla liked it a lot. She breathed in the fresh air, didn't care for a moment, and sighed. When she opened her eyes, the spell broke. Tezca towered over her.

"Oh. Hey," Myla offered. She was in a good mood. She could be civil.

He seemed to agree. There was little hostility in his deep voice when he said, "What are you doing?" He cocked his head.

"Walking back to my bunk. You?"

"No, I don't mean that. Why are you trying? If you're going to try to escape, why are you . . . investing in the life and people here?"

Oh. He still thought she was Priesthood Myla, the girl who had faked an inspiring speech yesterday morning. Of course he was confused when he saw Interested and Serious Myla and Friendly Myla at the party.

"Maybe I'm not as fake as you think I am."

He gave her a skeptical look. She tried again. "I'll admit, the speech yesterday was exaggerated near the end. I didn't want to be locked up. You can't blame me for that."

"You're smarter than I gave you credit for, but you're every bit as fake as I thought you were. Please don't try to convince me that you are anything but a spoiled little Priesthood girl."

She looked him straight in the eye and said, "Tezca, you are mean and judgmental."

He looked shocked at her straightforwardness. It felt good. She continued. "I don't deserve your hate. Yeah, maybe I'm privileged. Yeah, maybe I don't have many practical skills. Yeah, maybe I'm dying a little inside that there isn't a proper shower anywhere on this stupid compound.

"But I'm working hard in the kitchens. I'm impressed by all of you and I see I've been wrong on many topics. I learned so much today. I'm *trying*, Tezca, and that's more than I can say for you."

He opened his mouth, but Myla was in the zone. She held up one finger. "You were nice enough on the way here when we debated Aztecism and gender roles and everything. You decided you hated me when I said I had to go back anyway. But you don't understand. I don't want to go back to keep my brother company. I'm worried about his safety. You have *no idea* what I've been through." She could hear her anger rising with new tears in her eyes.

"If you knew, you'd understand why I am terrified to leave him with my parents. I do not trust them. And I love him so much. So, tell me again what a good little spoiled brat I am."

Tezca's mouth hung open. After a moment, he blinked and looked, Myla hoped, a little mortified.

He stuttered, "Myla . . . I'm—"

This time, she saved him. "Your friends here have done enough to convince me to stay until I learn a bit more about the cause, at least. It's a step in the right direction, I admit. You can help share this place and what it stands for, or you can continue to hate me. But you have my attention."

"That . . . would be good," he said, stunned.

Myla nodded. "Good." She breathed a sigh of relief, the cords of stress untangling in her chest. "And that *felt* good . . . See you tomorrow, then." She turned to go. As she walked, she heard him one more time.

"Myla?"

"Yes?"

"Was that one real?"

She smiled.

CHAPTER 11

Over the next week, Myla ditched the brace on her ankle. She worked in the kitchens, sat with the people she had met, and learned all she could. She felt alive, learning the inner workings of Aztecism and history with Izel and discussing it at meals with her new friends. The long hours scrubbing and chopping and boiling allowed her to muse over what she heard, processing all of it. Izel, to catch her up on items not in his curriculum right then, even met with her at lunch sometimes to tutor her.

Myla learned about the Spanish, the people who had come to conquer all those years ago but were driven back. She learned about the issues with cultural assimilation in Europe now. After its defeat, Spain had all but become a province of Azteca, with Nahuatl people and business moving there.

A current issue under debate in Spain was whether to still teach Spanish in schools there.

Nahuatl had become the main language. The Spanish people worked for Aztecan companies, practiced the religion, and cut their hair like Aztecan celebrities. They had a president, a prop set up by the chief speaker. Spanish culture had all but disappeared.

One by one, European countries—France and Portugal especially—assimilated and accepted the Aztecan way of life. Nearer countries like America had long been conquered by Azteca, prop governments set up as well. But America had its own industry, and fewer Mesoamericans had moved there, so it had been more resistant to the cultural takeover. So far.

She learned about gender roles around the world. She saw a documentary on the oppression of women in Africa and Asia. She read Sei Shonagon's *The Pillow Book*. She tore through a translation of an American book, *The Feminine Mystique*. The fact that women had written books was new to her. She listened as Izel spoke to her about the subjugation of women in different religions, and how Azteca was no different.

Myla never thought about what made men and women different. It seemed ingrained in her. She had always focused more on what made her different from female Unders. As far as the upper class went, women could rarely turn down marriage proposals, spent their days planning galas and events for their husbands and staying in shape, and were never allowed to live alone.

She learned that Under women were given arranged marriages by their upper-class overseers, yet another way to control every aspect of the Unders' lives. In a strange way, Myla felt like she could relate—or at least she could have, back home.

At the compound, the women worked alongside the men, and were as free to love as the ancient Japanese women in *The Pillow Book*. At the compound, Myla felt like her voice was heard when she spoke by men and women alike. Perhaps it was because a struggling, tiny group of rebels couldn't afford to shut out 50 percent of the population. They needed doctors, plumbers, anyone who could help build a cabin. And some of them had been Unders, women who had known work. It boggled Myla's brain in the best way.

One woman in particular vexed her. Amihan made snide comments as she passed, spread rumors about her being a spy, and threatened her whenever they were alone. One night it had gone too far.

Myla was walking back to her cabin after the dinner dishes. She had stayed late, and there was no one around, except one person walking behind her. She felt a creeping fear as the grass muffled his footsteps as much as hers.

From far away, Myla could see another dark figure walking toward her through the cabins. He was coming from the direction of *her* cabin. She stopped and went right, weaving in between two other cabins. Amihan was waiting there for her.

The knife was back at its home on Myla's throat as she was shoved against a wall, Amihan's pretty face inches from hers. The two men from earlier stepped through the gap and barred escape that way.

"What do you want, Amihan?" Myla tried to sound brave.

"I want you out. I want you to leave. You are not welcome here."

Myla knew she could feel the knife moving up and down faster as her heartbeat increased.

"How do I leave?"

"I don't know. I don't care. Walk into the jungle and die like the Priesthood scum you are."

"I can't go anywhere, and you know that. So you can quit it with your threats, okay?"

"Threats, huh?" Amihan reared back and punched Myla in the gut. She was a small girl, but it hurt. Myla doubled over, coughing, wondering why she hadn't screamed. She felt like ten-year-old Myla was watching from above.

The next morning, she didn't tell anyone what had happened. Scared Myla bit her tongue, knowing what happened to people who blew the whistle.

Myla found herself surprised at how most of the people at the camp took to her. She was eager to be helpful, and people appreciated it.

Tezca had been cordial and polite to her, sometimes bordering on friendly. Sometimes she thought she could see him watching her in the corner of her eye, but whenever she looked, she'd find him brow furrowed and staring at his hands. Myla was glad they were rarely left alone.

But one day, it was unavoidable. Tona was sitting between them at dinner, making a nice buffer that helped the conversation unfold without any awkward pauses.

But then he stood. "I've got to go. Mectel needed to talk to me about the next mission. I should find him before dinner ends." And he left, leaving Myla and Tezca sitting in mutual embarrassment. He knew at that point he'd been condemnatory and juvenile. Myla wished she hadn't had her outburst the night of the party.

"So . . ." she ventured. "How's everything?" It was less a question, more an admittance that she had no idea what to say. The sun dipped below the tree line.

"It's good. It's good," he responded, the politician and the speechwriter both with nothing to say.

He tried a question. "Do you like the kitchens?"

"It's nice. I like the people there. I have an idea of something else I'd like to try though."

"Oh. What?"

"That woman at the infirmary, Zuma. She seemed nice."

That brightened his face. "Oh, Zuma? She's the best. A bit crazy, but the nicest person you'll ever meet."

"Oh, good. Maybe I'll put in a request for a transfer . . . How's the mission planning going?"

He looked down at his food. Myla sighed. "You're still not going to tell me anything?"

He glanced up at her through his wrinkled brow. His eyes—they were hazel, Myla hadn't noticed— showed actual concern. "I'm sorry," he said. Then he perked up with new resolve in his face. He grabbed her hand. "Come with me," he murmured.

They deposited their dishes in the basin and Tezca grabbed his megaphone. He took out a small pad of paper with hundreds of names and details written inside. He read the newest one aloud and Myla whispered, "Not for nothing," to the bloodred sunset when he was done.

After, he took her to a room she'd never been to inside the main cabin. It was a small room lit by candlelight. Inside was a black marble wall with nearly ten thousand tiny names carved into it. There was also a book on a small pedestal with the same names.

"This is where all the sacrifices go—at least, the ones we could get records of. It goes back twenty years or so," Tezca said. He let go of her hand as she stepped forward to read all the names. She tried her hardest to not look for a name that would have been about seven years up the list. The memorial did what it was supposed to do, and Myla felt like she would drown in all the blood spilled. Though she pushed it out of her mind, the familiar guilt from what had happened when she was ten surfaced and pricked her eyes to tears.

But when she looked back, Tezca's face was not one of hate. He did not bring her here to accuse her, but instead to do as she had asked: share the camp with her. She held a hand to the cold stone.

"How do you feel?" Tezca asked.

Myla gave herself a minute to answer. She felt upset that it had been happening for centuries. She felt stupid for not seeing what it was, guilty for what she had done when she was ten. She felt like screaming because her little brother was back there with them.

Instead, she turned to Tezca, wiped away a small barrage of tears, and said, "Like I want to *do* something."

He nodded and said, "Welcome."

Myla woke the next day to alarms. Zimi shoved her awake.

"Get up! We need to get ready."

"What? What's going on?" Myla bolted upright, expecting an air raid. She wasn't half wrong.

"Aerial patrol spotted on its way. We need to camo. Now!"

Myla jumped out of bed and charged after Zimi outside. It seemed everyone in the camp was running around. Tezca's megaphone blared, "Three minutes!"

Myla saw Izel leading the children into the main cabin. Zimi brought her to a storage area near the main cabin. Inside were gigantic, thick tarps made of fake grass. They hauled them out on onto the amphitheater, disguising the white stone. The same was done to the wheat fields and farms. The pavilion was dismantled and everyone ran inside. From inside her cabin, Myla could see Tezca and Quent running across the fields, checking one last time that everything was covered. Hopefully, everything from above would look like one big clearing.

Myla panting turned to Zimi. "How often does this happen?"

"Oh, once every six months," she sighed. "Most of the crops are ruined."

They waited inside, keeping away from windows to feel safe, until the sound of jets had long passed and Tezca had given the all clear. She and Zimi stumbled outdoors, helping roll up the tarps. It was true—most of the fruit and vegetables had been crushed under the weight of the tarps. Tezca called a council meeting.

Myla filed in with the rest of the rebels and sat with Huelta. Tezca's low voice boomed, "We are in slight trouble, everyone." Somehow when he said it in his politician affect, it didn't seem so bad.

"Most of the wheat was salvaged, as well as the beans. But it's not enough until the next harvest. We have to eat all of the livestock, leaving none for breeding. Any ideas you all had were submitted to your representative, I trust. I have the ideas that got through before me.

"Number one: Hunt in the surrounding jungle. Number two: Recover saplings and other plants from Tenochtitlan. Number three: Steal food from the next gala and freeze what meat we can get. Number four . . . Eat the Priesthood girl."

There was slight laughter from where the extremists sat. Amihan smirked. Myla could feel everyone looking at her. Tezca's teeth clenched for a moment, then he crumpled up the paper.

"Because this is supposed to be anonymous, none can be held accountable for this cruel mockery of a serious situation. But to those who submitted it, and the council member who allowed it to pass, grow up. Take this seriously. Or leave, and take your prejudices with you."

There was a moment of silence as the people took in the level of controlled but fierce power in Tezca's voice. The extremists looked everywhere but at him and Myla.

"Now the councilors will vote on which option to take." He handed out slips of paper and sat to write his vote. It was a special voting system. Tezca had explained it to Myla. Each council member got three votes in this case and could choose which one, two, or three options to support.

After he read the votes aloud and counted which course of action had the most support, it went to number two. The mission crew left to plan the operation. Word was they were going to break into the Tenochtitlan arboretum.

The day before the mission, Tona came to Myla at breakfast. "Hey, Myla. How are you?"

She smiled. "I'm good, Tona. And you?"

"I'm all right. Bit nervous about the upcoming mission, you know?"

Myla nodded and he went on. "Well, it's somewhat of a tradition before a mission . . . to go on a little outing and celebrate in case something bad happens. And well, I've talked to the gang, and we'd like you to come."

"I'd have to ask Huelta, but I'd love to come. What would we be doing?"

Tona broke into the biggest smile, like he thought she'd never ask. "We are going to the beach!"

CHAPTER 12

An hour later, Huelta had agreed and handed Myla a case filled with fruit and sandwiches to take with them. They departed in Huelta's van, Myla, Tezca, Mectel, Lisbeth, Tona, and Amihan. Izel had been invited, as he was the mission's medic, but declined the offer to teach his class. Mectel wasn't going on the operation, but was still included as the group's guest, like Myla had been.

Lisbeth drove the van and Myla sat squashed in between Tona and Mectel. Amihan and Tezca shared the backseat. Myla could hear them talking in low voices, Tezca chuckling, even. Only they called each other "Tez" and "Ami." People had explained their close relationship by the fact that they were the original two rebels and had founded the compound together. But Tezca lacked that ingrained connection with the people who joined soon after, like Izel,

Lisbeth, and Quent. Had his relationship with Amihan ever progressed past friendship?

Lisbeth played her weird music and Tona chattered away to her and Myla. He explained the tradition of a day-trip before the mission. All of the teenagers knew the risk of going to Tenochtitlan and what would happen if they were caught. A year ago, the council had decided to allot the mission leaders and medics who were going one day of freedom and fun. The mission leaders were the crew in the van, but sometimes people were swapped out if they were busy.

It was all explained to Myla, with Tezca's blessing, everyone's usual roles. Tezca was a planner. He charted their course, with the navigator's, Tona's, help. Tona, through his years as a carpenter in Tenochtitlan, knew the ins and outs of many government and high-profile buildings. He also was Lisbeth's apprentice in technology.

Amihan was there as a marksman. She had manufactured guns during her time in the Tlaxcalan factories and was a better shot than anyone on the compound. Mectel assisted Amihan in security and was trained a bit more than the mission leader in emergency medicine.

Izel was preferred as a medic, as he had more training and experience than Mectel. But he hadn't been used during Tona's rescue mission because it was risky and he couldn't run well or use a gun.

The arboretum would be less guarded, and they decided to bring Izel along instead. Lisbeth was a mechanic and technical expert. When she came to Azteca as part of the student-exchange program, she had been studying to take over her family business in electronics.

Sitting cramped for the two-hour ride, Myla also learned Mectel's and Tona's stories. Mectel had been a worker in the sewers before he ran into the rebels there one day. They convinced him to join them by enlightening him, and he left behind everything he knew. He had had a father who worked alongside him in the sewers, but his father had been chosen for sacrifice once he became unable to work. That was a month before Mectel left. He admitted he didn't know if he would have had the courage to leave if the priests hadn't taken his father. But he had seen an opportunity with the rebel groups, and they welcomed him and his knowledge of the sewers.

Tona told his story as if it were some great tale from hundreds of years ago that no one knew whether it was fact or legend.

"I was a simple boy, toiling as an Under for years. My parents had been carpenters and so was I. I was also religious. I wanted to make the gods happy, so I kept my head down and said nothing as my people were offered up one by one. I wasn't as talkative then.

"You have to understand, Myla, that there were rumors of the Priesthood being liars and a rebel force growing all around the Under communities, no doubt spread by my friends here."

Tezca interjected, "We tried to enlighten the population that way, but rumors weren't enough to topple lifetimes of brainwashing."

"Yeah, I didn't believe any of the planted rumors," Tona agreed. "It was interesting to think about, but what was the cost if we Unders were wrong and stopped the sacrifices? The end of the world. The sun wouldn't rise. I needed confirmation from someone who had been on the inside."

"Which is when he met me," Tezca added.

"Yeah. One night soon after the initiation of the rebel compound, Tezca infiltrated the Unders' ghettos. He went door to door, handing out letters detailing the priest's fabrications and whispering, pleading for help.

"I answered the door that night, not my older brother or parents. I opened it to see this upper-class boy standing in the rain, staring at me with wild eyes. Ixa, Huelta's sister, was with him that night, too. That caught my attention.

"Tezca informed me in his rehearsed speech that he had been a Priesthood apprentice sent from Tlacopan. He had discovered a horrible secret, one that would change my life."

He took a dramatic pause, eliciting a bored sigh from Tezca. "At first, I was cautious. I thought it might be some Priesthood trick to test my loyalty. But then he began to talk about how the sacrifices weren't necessary, and the priests had never even spoken to the gods.

"I knew then that it was the real deal. The Priesthood would never go so far as to cast doubt on Aztecism. Tezca told me that night that I could risk my life with him and work to free my people. I told him I'd need to think about it. He said he'd be back the next night.

"I told my family what had happened, but they seemed to think it was a dream. They warned me about going against the Priesthood. But I had been submissive and quiet my whole life. That night when Tezca came again, I whispered goodbye to my parents and brother as they slept and slipped out the door. That was two years ago, when I was fourteen."

Myla asked, "What happened to your family?"

His face darkened and he said, "I don't know. I went back soon after to look for them. They seemed to have disappeared. Either the Priesthood figured out where I had gone and punished them or they decided to sneak out too, and they're living out there somewhere, looking for me."

Tezca put a hand on Tona's shoulder. "If they had been sacrificed, we would have seen it on the cameras. They would be on the wall."

"Yeah. Yeah. Of course." Tona looked out the window.

The mood brightened when they arrived on the beach. They did not go to Lake Texcoco, but to the coast, on the east of Azteca. It was sparsely populated, and Tona insisted he knew a small cove they could enjoy without fear of being seen. Myla was sure she could talk their way out of it again if they did get seen, but it was nice to not have to worry about it.

They arrived around midday, pulling the car over on the tiny dirt path they had been riding. Tona turned to Myla, holding out his pack and towel.

"Mind holding this for a sec?"

Myla nodded and held out her hands. Upon thrusting the gear at her, he dove headfirst out of the car and ran full stop to the edge of a cliff. He flashed a devious smile back at the car and Myla felt her breath catch as he took a few more steps and threw himself over the side.

Myla jumped out of the van. "Tona!" Myla's voice rose with hysterics until Tezca touched her on the arm and shook his head, smiling with his eyes.

She approached the sandy edge, looking over and expecting to see Tona's broken body on the rocks below. She saw him doing the backstroke. Myla felt something cut the air beside her as Lisbeth followed Tona over the cliff. It must have been forty feet down.

Lisbeth rose from under the waves, spewing water and laughing. Myla felt her brain reoxygenate as she saw the two swimming and splashing each other.

Myla's eyes could not get enough of the cove. Wet, dark rocks dressed in algae towered from the clear water. The blues and greens of the water looked synthetic. Myla marveled at how the water could be clear when washing over the small, gray pebbles of the tiny beach yet contain such a deep palette farther out.

Tezca was by her side. "Jump in. Leave the stuff up here, we can get it later." When his brow wasn't crunched up, his face looked nice. He looked capable of happiness. Happiness was attainable in this place, Myla sensed.

But that wasn't enough. "I'm not great with heights," Myla uttered, backing away from the edge.

Tezca gave her a coy, annoyed look. "Not great with heights, not good with being underground. What *are* we going to do with you?"

"Oh, just *throw her over!*" Tona called from below.

Amihan appeared. She hadn't looked at Myla the whole trip, except now, shooting Myla a petty, sinister look before letting herself fall backward into the water. Her eyes were closed in a moment of bliss in midair. Before she met the water, she straightened out into an elegant dive. Once she surfaced, she swam out from shore.

"I'll climb down, thanks. Still don't trust this ankle," Myla protested. Tezca shrugged and clambered off the cliff, hollering once before crashing into the water.

Myla inched her way down the rocky slope nearby, carrying the gear. Mectel had decided to stay behind and help her down, though she insisted she could do it alone, the tips of her ears burning.

They settled on the small beach and set down the gear that had been abandoned on the cliff. Mectel turned to her. "Do you want to go in at all?"

"Not right this minute, but don't let me stop you."

He smiled and nodded, pausing not one moment more to fling his pack down and sprint into the water. Myla stretched out in the sand, feeling the pebbles massage her back. If she closed her eyes, Quinel would be sunning herself in a tiny bikini next to her, and Aktu would be playing in the shallow waters of Lake Texcoco a few feet away. She let the little cove take her, drifting off in the sun.

By the time she woke, Lisbeth was sunning herself near her. With Lisbeth's sleeves and shorts rolled up as far as they could go, Myla could see how pale the girl was. And muscled. In fact, all the people around her were in shape. It made her feel a tiny bit self-conscious.

Myla stood and made her way into the water, leaving behind her green bracelet so she wouldn't lose it. She took her time, not hesitating until it was waist high. Then she ducked and opened her eyes. She saw bright, silver fish the size of her hand. She took deep breaths above so she could better follow and observe the fish in their home. It was endless, and she hated that she needed to breathe.

She gave up and floated on her back, letting the cold of the water and the heat of the sun battle through her body. She closed her eyes, letting the current take her in, and bumped into someone. She stood.

"Hey," Tezca said. He stood, water chest high, with pink showing on his tan skin, dusting his cheekbones.

"Hi," Myla said. "Sorry I ran into you."

"No, no. Don't worry about it. Sorry I interrupted your float. But since I did, want to join us?"

They were playing a game in the mouth of the cove where two people went up on the shoulders of two other people. The top people tried to throw each other off balance until there was one pair standing.

"Come on, you'll replace Lisbeth on my shoulders," Tezca offered.

"You want to team up with me? I'm not vicious."

He smiled that little smile that barely touched his cheeks but dived into his eyes, and his low voice growled, "Oh, I disagree. Come on, Myla. Let's see that devious side."

With that, he hoisted her up so she was sitting on his strong shoulders.

"Well, I can't say this isn't familiar." Myla laughed and bobbed up and down as Tezca allotted soft laughter. She felt great until Tezca turned around and they faced their opponents.

Amihan, petite and deadly, sat on top of Mectel. Myla's blood froze, and she reassured herself— Amihan wouldn't try anything here, would she?

"Tezca, I'm not sure this is a great idea."

"Oh, give it a try."

"Yeah, Priesthood girl," Amihan sneered. "Try me."

Tezca and Mectel lumbered toward each other. Myla searched Amihan's form. She couldn't hide a knife on her anywhere, but then again, she had produced it from nowhere before.

The two girls clashed, the boys on the bottom clueless to the amount of hate exchanged between the two. It was a game to all but Amihan and Myla. Amihan grabbed her shoulders, and Myla did the same. Amihan might have been stronger, but Myla outweighed her. She could feel that power surging up inside her, strength she didn't know she had, to push Amihan back farther and farther.

Myla was aware of Tona and Lisbeth cheering her on from the beach. But all she could see was

Amihan's sweet face contorted in rage. Myla tasted victory until she felt Amihan's hands move to her neck.

Panic. Her lungs wondered where the air had gone and her hands slapped out to Amihan's face, striking her again and again, but the tiny fingers tightened.

Suddenly, she was flung into the water. She surfaced, gasping, to see Mectel and Amihan in jubilation over their conquest. Amihan flashed a beautiful smile. Myla stared and forced more air into her throat. Had no one seen what had happened?

Tezca stood nearby, smiling sheepishly, and he helped Myla up. "It's okay. We'll get them next time. You had her for a second." She turned and waded back to the beach. Tezca splashed after her.

"Hey, it's okay. It's just a game." He wore his politician smile, the conflict resolver, the people pleaser, as he said it.

"Yeah," Amihan agreed from the water, "just a game."

Myla wasn't going to let her have this one. She smiled as sweetly as Amihan. "Sure, yeah. I was just cold." She sat down on the beach and Tezca joined her.

"How about I teach you some self-defense moves? As an inductee of the cause you should learn it."

Myla nodded. That didn't sound like a bad idea. Maybe she'd be prepared the next time Amihan's knife appeared.

"Come on, let's climb the cliff. There's not a lot of room down here," Tezca said, pulling her up. She followed him up the narrow path onto the plateau overlooking the cove. She took a moment, lingering.

"You coming?"

"Yeah. It's nice here. I didn't believe anywhere like this existed."

He stood beside her, feeling the sun as she did. After another second, he walked backward and challenged her. "What first, Myla?"

Myla rubbed her throat. "Teach me how to get out of chokeholds."

"Fun."

They sparred until late afternoon. Myla learned the three chokeholds—front, back, and bar arm— and how to get out of them. Her favorite was the back chokehold. Tezca grabbed her neck from behind and she raised her left arm, rotated left, and trapped his left arm under her elbow. He taught her that it freed up her right hand to attack, either a push upward with the heel of the palm or a good, old-fashioned punch.

He taught her how, when she was knocked down on her back, to swivel around, propped up on her elbows, kicking at any advances. Myla soon felt sweaty and hot, but also powerful. She had little to no upper-body strength, but it didn't mean her thick legs weren't useful. She could feel her body weight and strength contributing to every move. She felt as fluid as the water below, as solid as the cliff.

By the time they were called from below to eat, Tezca looked sweaty and worn out as well. Myla stopped him midattack.

"Maybe we should stop. You have a mission tomorrow."

He smiled that eye-smile. "What, think I can't handle it?"

"Hey, I don't want you too sore to run right when the patrols are cornering you."

"Oh? You don't want your vicious captors getting what they had coming?"

Myla raised her eyebrows. This light conversation was disguising something else. She joked, "Well, I never said *that*."

The smile was replaced. "But . . . you would like for me, for us, to come back . . . right?" The slightest furrow had creased his eyebrows.

Myla decided to play it off. She rolled her eyes. "Yes, Tezca. I don't want you all to die. Happy?"

He looked out into the dipping sun. "Sure."

Myla led him down the cliff. They reached the bottom and joined in on the mini feast of tortillas and fruit with their friends. The six unspooled there, capable of enjoying the colors of the cove without a single thought as to who would or wouldn't be returning the next day.

CHAPTER 13

Myla held her breath for twenty-four hours. And then all five of them returned. But something was wrong. Tezca was being supported by Tona and Amihan, yet somehow he retained his composure as he addressed the camp.

"The mission was successful. We have enough seeds and saplings now. Planting will begin tomorrow. Quent will be reading the sacrifice tonight, as I may be . . . detained." His voice shook with effort.

"Oh, screw this. I'm taking you to the infirmary," Tona said.

"It's a flesh wound. I'm fine."

Tona looked at Amihan and they agreed. Fighting Tezca's feeble struggle, they took him to the infirmary. Myla raced ahead to find Zuma.

Once there, she flung open the infirmary door, to Zuma's surprise.

"Tezca was hurt during the mission. Let's prepare a bed for him."

Zuma processed the news. "Okay. Move bed four up close to the door."

Myla set to the task. No sooner than the bed was in place, Tona, Amihan, and Tezca appeared in the door.

Zuma was ready for them. "Lay him there." She looked up at Myla. "You said you were okay with blood? Cut the clothing around the wound and clean it." She handed her gloves, scissors, gauze, and saline. Myla stood helpless for a moment, but the blood spreading from Tezca's abdomen prompted her to action.

After pulling on the gloves, she cut away the lower part of his shirt, noting two bullet holes two inches left of his belly button. Tezca was losing the poise he had earlier. He groaned and sweated. Myla brushed his arm while cleaning around the wounds. His skin was cold.

By the time Myla was done, Zuma had the materials for surgery out. With Myla's help, she rolled Tezca onto his left side. She said, "The first bullet went through, just bandage that one. I need to find the other one. Get the anesthetic out of the left cupboard."

Myla dashed away and searched for anything that looked like it could be anesthetic. She found a tank with a mask attached and brought it to Zuma.

Amihan and Tona were hovering by the door, averting their eyes. Myla hadn't even noticed them.

Once Tezca was under, Myla assisted Zuma in surgery, handing her different tools and wiping the occasional accumulation of blood. Soon, Zuma extracted a small, metal bullet from inside Tezca's abdomen. Tezca, unconscious, let out one long sigh of relief, like he could tell the trouble was over.

"Apply bulky dressings to both sides and hook him up to the wall oxygen. Use the nasal cannula on the desk," Zuma said, washing her hands.

Myla first tried to remember all that was bid of her, then grabbed the gauze on the desk. She laid it in thick layers across his abdomen and back and used medical tape she found in a drawer. Zuma came back to apply pressure and stop the bleeding while Myla hooked up the oxygen.

First, she picked up a large plastic mask, but a "No, the other one" from Zuma sent her to a tube that went in Tezca's nose and around his ears. She attached it to a nozzle on the wall and cranked it so the tube made a small hissing noise in his nose. Then and only then, Myla took a breath.

She heard Amihan's harsh voice behind her, demanding from Zuma, "Well? Is he okay? Is he going to be okay?" her voice rising into hysterics.

Tona looked lost. "We never should have let him address the camp, the idiot," he murmured to no one in particular.

Zuma was still applying pressure with the tips of her fingers to Tezca's wound. She grunted at Myla, "Get her out of here."

Myla took Amihan's arm and led her outside. Amihan did not struggle. When she was outside, she paced in circles and muttered, "I'll kill them. I'll kill all of them. I'll kill their families," over and over. Myla decided to not take it personally. She went back inside.

Tona was leading against the inside wall, bringing his head against it over and over again. "You okay?" Myla offered. His face was blank, in shock, but for his panicked eyes.

"Fine, fine. Fine." He looked everywhere but at Myla. "He's such a stupid, noble ass. Reckless even. Idiot."

"Does Tezca have parents? Is there anyone we should get?" Tona stared at her, unseeing.

"Myla! Take over," Zuma called. Myla took her place at Tezca's side, stopping the blood flow with her hands. Zuma went over to Tona. "It didn't puncture any organs," she said. "He lost a lot of blood. He's in shock. But he should be okay."

Myla heard Tona utter, "Idiot," one last time before leaving. She focused on the warm mass below her fingers that once was flesh. The bullet holes had been tiny, though. Why did they feel so much bigger to Myla now?

She stood there for ten minutes, her legs locking up, staring at her gloved hands. She didn't think. Her heart beat slower and slower. She prompted her breaths each time.

Zuma came over with a chair. Myla hadn't been aware of her this whole time. "Do you mind staying with me tonight? To watch him?" Myla shook her head no.

Myla removed her hands from Tezca and sat after changing her gloves. She tried to process what had occurred and found that she wasn't having much trouble doing so. She had been there the whole time, hadn't she? She was like a canal of rushing, cold water, the thoughts flowing through her. Tezca had been shot twice, he underwent surgery, and she had his blood on her hands for a while. She felt in control, ready for anything.

She chalked it up to her improvisational abilities. She never had issues thinking midcrisis. So what if the stakes were higher now? She kept waiting for the moment when the world would come crashing down on her and she'd break down crying like in the movies. But it never came.

Tezca awoke eight hours later to Quent, Tona, Amihan, Mectel, Lisbeth, Zuma, Izel, and a tired Myla. She didn't feel it, though. He surfaced for about six seconds, did his strange smile from his eyes, and conked out again. Tona brought Myla some food and she dug in. She had been afraid the blood and gore would diminish her appetite, but found it full and waiting.

She sat by Tezca's bed, watching his chest rise and fall, the whole time, getting up twice for the bathroom and to help Zuma with another patient.

Soon the sun rose. Zuma came up to Myla, smiling. "You're good at this. I appreciate the unflinching type."

Myla smiled and shrugged. "I watch a lot of horror movies. In the moment, I wasn't even thinking about it."

Zuma giggled. "Oh, I used to *love* horror movies. Anyway, I do need some extra help in here, if you'd like to switch."

"I'd love to. I was meaning to put in for a transfer. I mean, the people in the kitchen are nice and everything, but I think I might be cut out for this."

Zuma never stopped smiling, a teeth-showing grin that brightened every word she spoke. "Oh, *good*. I'm glad to have you on board."

Myla brimmed with affection for this welcoming woman. She wanted to make her proud. She had been cool and collected when digging around inside Tezca. It inspired Myla. She *was* tough enough. She *could* do this.

What's more, Myla couldn't help comparing Zuma to the people in her life, even her old self. Zuma, bright and engaged, was everything that

Myla's mother was not, everything Myla hoped she could someday be.

She stayed until Izel tapped her on the shoulder that afternoon and told her that she could take a break. She got back to her bunk and flopped down on her bed with her shoes still on. She woke up right before dawn—no one had wanted to rouse her.

Myla was surprised at how tired she was. Being in that focused state of mind had its consequences. But she realigned her mind back into it and strode back to the infirmary. When she got there, Tezca was awake and chatting with Quent. He stopped when he saw her.

"I heard you were pining," he joked.

"I was not. I was monitoring your breathing. I don't pine."

"Not even a little bit? You weren't here for twenty hours?"

"And then I left," she said, feigning indifference.

Quent stood. "I'll postpone any council stuff until you're better. Thank you for getting what we needed. I'll talk to you later."

"Okay. I'll see you." Tezca reached out and clasped hands with him once, a formal yet affectionate gesture, before Quent left.

Tezca looked at her a moment before speaking. "It's because you said you might be the slightest bit sad if I died. I didn't want to upset you."

"That's gracious of you, Tezca. I and the people of the world thank you."

"Hmm, no tears of joy? No gasping that you'll never let me go again?"

"Mmm . . . nope."

He stared at the ceiling. "Well, that's no fun."

"What were you expecting?"

He sighed. "You weren't the *slightest* bit scared?"

"I don't know what you want, but you're not going to get it here." He was starting to tick her off a little bit. Then Tona flung open the curtain.

"You're alive!" he crowed, throwing his body over Tezca's. "I was *terrified* you were going to die! You looked dead!" He held Tezca's face in his hands. "Don't *do* that again!"

Tezca was laughing. "I'll try my best to not get shot, Tona. Look, I'm fine." He turned to Myla. "Do you see how it's done?"

"Well, excuse me if I didn't faint clutching my pearls," she said, smirking.

"No, no, you're right. I was . . . being stupid. I have Tona here to fawn over me."

"That's-right-I'm-never-leaving-you-again-you-idiot," Tona rushed in one breath.

Myla smiled and turned to Tezca. "Is there anything I can get you? I've seen where Zuma keeps the extra pillows."

"Nah, thanks, though. Wouldn't want you to get in trouble."

"Don't worry about me."

"It's okay. Thanks though."

"No problem."

Tona glanced at Tezca, then at Myla, then back again. "Oh, guys, sorry. I have this thing. I gotta go."

Tezca's brow crumpled. "I thought you were never-leaving-me-alone-again-you-idiot?"

"Yeah, yeah. I'll be back. I'll . . . give you two some space." He was giggling as he left, stopping to flash seductive eyes and pull the curtain around the bed.

Myla was laughing even as she turned back to Tezca with his hands covering his face. She eased them off.

"You shouldn't worry so much."

"Oh jeez, I'm so sorry. He's the worst sometimes." His embarrassment was endearing to Myla.

"He's looking out for you. I get it."

Now he was interested. "*Do* you?" His eyebrows skyrocketed.

She chuckled. "No, no. I didn't mean it that way. I'm still indifferent to your outcome, I promise."

"Oh, good."

She sat in the chair by his bedside. "I feel bad. We shouldn't have sparred two days ago. I kept on thinking, what if that was what slowed you? Made you open to the fire?"

"Don't, Myla. It wasn't your fault at all. The patrol was chasing us and I dropped some seeds. They told me to leave them, but I was too rash. I ran back, got hit, and Amihan and Tona had to carry me out of there. I jeopardized the whole mission."

"Don't say that. You're the reason it could happen. You're the reason these people are here. You made one mistake. You paid the price for it. And you won't do it again. *Nobody* is going to blame you for this."

"Thanks, Myla."

"It's my pleasure. Hey, and some good came out of it. I'm Zuma's new assistant."

"That's great. She did tell me earlier that you were a natural, undaunted in the face of duty."

Myla flushed with pleasure. "She said that?"

Tezca nodded.

"Well, it wasn't *easy*, I promise. It happened quickly, and I guess I could keep up."

Tezca gave her a courteous smile.

Myla couldn't resist asking, "Who have you spoken to since you woke up?"

"Well, I woke up to all of you that first time. Since then, Izel, Quent, Tona, and you."

"Nobody else?"

"No . . ."

"No parents?" In the two or so weeks she had known him, he had never brought up any family. She knew he was former upper class, and his father used to run the hospital in Tlacopan, but that was it.

He sighed and looked at the ceiling. "Do you want to know?"

Myla nodded.

"I used to be upper class. My father ran a hospital, my older brother was about to take over the business, and my mother didn't do much all day. I still loved them. We'd go to play festivals and family trips. We even ate dinner together. They were a fun-loving family, more open to the needs of the Unders. The Unders that my father employed were paid fairly and not abused. I think that's why I was so affected by my enlightenment.

"A second son, I was sent to Tenochtitlan to work as an apprentice for the priests. I thought I was doing holy work. I was enlightened there, and I didn't take it well. On the one hand, my family was prepping me to go far as a priest, maybe one day even make chief speaker. On the other, I had even made friends with some of my father's employees over the years. I couldn't stand the thought of their being sacrificed to fake gods."

He paused, and Myla asked, "So you left?"

"Not then. On one vacation from the city, I confronted my parents and brother on what they thought of the system. They seemed distraught about it, but had never known any other way. They were too afraid of the Priesthood to act.

"I proposed we run. We'd infiltrate the Under ghettos, starting with our own workers, and convince them one by one to join us. We'd set up somewhere in the jungle, building until we had enough people to take on the Priesthood.

"On the way out, we were stopped. One of the Unders at my dad's hospital had informed the Priesthood on what we planned to do. I was the only one who made it out, and I wandered the jungle until I met Ami. We found Quent and Lisbeth soon after. Most of the Unders helped, spreading information to interested participants. We got it up and running, and my family's names are the first three on the memorial wall."

His face looked serene enough. It was his deep voice that carried the old hurt. He looked at Myla and continued. "It's why I can't fail, Myla. They're all dead. After that, there's only me."

She took his hand, warmth permeating into his cold skin. "Us, you idiot."

CHAPTER 14

For the week and a half that Tezca was in the infirmary, Quent took over reading the names at sunset, no council meetings took place, and most of the people on the compound took shifts in planting the new seeds and saplings from Tenochtitlan.

Myla served her time squatting in the dirt with a trowel. She didn't complain, but it didn't mean she liked it. She had gotten more used to the dirtiness of the compound, switching between two outfits day to day, and her hair's natural rat's nest state. Still, the hours in the dirt made her long even more than usual for her apartment's roomy shower instead of the cramped compartments with hoses attached in the cabins. She never thought the thing she'd miss most would be water pressure.

She ate her meals with Tezca in the infirmary, joined often by Tona, Quent, Lisbeth, Mectel, and Amihan. The last was civil to Myla, not even meeting her eyes, still worried about Tezca. But it didn't mean that when Myla walked back to her cabin each night, she wasn't checking over her shoulder every second.

Tona had agreed to help her continue her self-defense training. He wasn't as good of an instructor as Tezca, but he was willing enough to meet during the hours Zuma gave Myla off. Mectel had also offered to take her to the shooting range. She hadn't taken him up on the offer yet, but she planned to.

What she had been doing was learning from Zuma, and there was much of it to do. She absorbed everything Zuma threw at her, following her around the infirmary.

Myla was surprised at how much cleaning was involved. She learned how to wipe down the beds and chairs and equipment in a sterile solution. She learned how to make the beds after. It was another job that it was hard to be bad at, and Myla was glad. She also learned minor tasks: taking out IVs, cleaning and dressing wounds, taking vitals, and splinting. Four days in, Zuma took thirty minutes to teach Myla cardiac resuscitation, how to push the chest and blow air into the lungs to restart a failed heart.

There weren't that many patients, however. Lisbeth came in twice to fill up her inhaler and once due to a minor asthma attack. The compound had a few old people with some needs and kids who never seemed to run out of ways to get hurt, but Zuma and

Myla never had more than four or five patients at a time. The one who was there the whole time was Tezca.

He would watch entranced as Myla changed his dressings. Myla could sense him watching her as she sashayed around the infirmary, recording vitals and cleaning sheets. She got annoyed when he did this and told him so.

"What else am I supposed to do?" he countered. The next day she brought him a book from the main cabin.

There was one serious patient other than Tezca that week. A farmer named Umer put on his shoe to find a scorpion waiting for him. He was rushed to Zuma, who at first said it wasn't that serious. She tasked Myla with putting cool compresses on the foot affected while she searched for the antivenom.

The man had been out cold before he reached the infirmary, but as Myla was monitoring him, his breathing stopped. She tapped him, listened for signs for breathing, and felt for a pulse. She tried three different spots and got nothing.

"Is he okay?" she could hear Tezca two beds over asking. She turned, made quick eye contact with him, and instructed him to yell for Zuma until she came. He began as Myla supported the man's head and shoulders and tugged him off the bed. Once on a hard surface, she began the resuscitation, doing it as Zuma taught her.

She was aware of Zuma running about behind her, preparing the antivenom in a syringe. But Myla didn't look up. She stared at her bitten nails, pumping blood into this man's heart.

After four rounds, he coughed, but he didn't open his eyes. Myla watched with satisfaction as his chest rose with new air. She and Zuma lifted him onto the bed together and Zuma injected him with the antivenom.

"It was the shock of it that triggered a heart attack," Zuma explained. "Quick thinking, Myla. You saved his life."

"It's a good thing you taught it to me, Zuma. He and I should be thanking *you*."

"No, this one's all yours."

"Well, at least let me thank you for letting me join up."

Zuma chuckled. "Okay, okay, you win. But I like having you here. Why don't you take a breather for now, though, and monitor Umer?"

Myla nodded and sat, watching his chest move. She counted breaths per minute out of habit. She could do it without even focusing on it now. Tezca was sitting upright in his bed, watching her again.

"I told you I hate that," she said, not looking at him.

"Well, I finished my book."

She looked over her shoulder at him, keeping one eye on Umer. "Please lie down for your own health.

I don't want something rearranging in there that Zuma and I have to go in and fix. I want you to get better."

"You don't want me here, keeping you company at all hours?"

She smiled. "Stop twisting my words."

She could see him flopping down on the bed, exasperated. She had tried to keep hating him, she really had. Was this a good time? She decided yes.

"Hey, Tezca?"

"Yeah?"

"I've been here three weeks. I've joined the cause. I'd like to stay."

"But . . .?"

"I know you don't like hearing this, but I'm still worried about my brother. If there were any way to contact him . . . just so he knows I'm okay . . ." She let herself trail off, turning back to watch the man in front of her.

She could tell Tezca's brow was furrowed when he answered in a brusque tone, "I'm sorry. There's no way."

"Over the phone? Or maybe I could send him a note?"

He tried a different approach. The politician crept into his voice. "I'm sorry, Myla. I'd do all I could to help you. But it's not possible now." He might as well have added, "Thank you, and have a nice day." For some reason, it reminded her of Cint.

She gave him the same look he had given her on her first day when she gave her speech at the council meeting. "Are you just saying that?"

His silence answered her question for him.

One morning about a week after Tezca got out of the hospital, Myla decided to take Mectel up on his offer of the shooting range. He took her below the main cabin to a long, narrow hall.

"It's soundproof down here. Most likely the shots wouldn't be heard by anyone dangerous at this distance, but we like to play it safe."

He handed Myla a small handgun and a pair of headphones. She was surprised at how heavy the former felt.

"Where do you get all the guns and ammunition from?" Myla asked.

"There was one difficult mission a year and a half ago to recover guns. We got some ammo then as well, but we intercept guard trucks and patrols to steal extras. At this point, we've stockpiled a pretty big amount."

Mectel taught her how to load the gun, sliding the small, golden tubes into the canister and inserting it into the butt of the gun. He posted up a target about thirty feet away on the range, then came behind Myla and showed her how to plant her feet and square her shoulders. After warning her about the gun's recoil, he stepped back and put on his headphones. Myla did the same. She was nervous. Unlike scrubbing pots and making beds, this was one job that she could screw up.

She turned to the target, turned off the safety, cocked the gun, and fired once. The gun bucked upward. The shock of it nearly blew her back a step, but when she looked up, the right upper-hand corner of the target bore a small, clean hole.

"Hey, look at that. You got it." Mectel sounded impressed.

Myla shrugged. "Beginner's luck."

It turned out to be. She practiced for a half hour, but couldn't make it more than a few inches into the target. Mectel was being nice about it. He cheered her on when she got that little bit closer and said nothing when she missed. He had been silent for the past fifteen minutes.

On the way out of the main cabin, Myla saw the door to the memorial was ajar. She peeked inside. Tezca stood in front of the black stone. He was nearly as tall as it, and therefore could reach the top. His hand was poised above his head on the first few names written. Myla backed away and left, sensing she would have been disturbing a private moment.

She went through the rest of the day jubilant, having enjoyed the lesson and new knowledge that came with it. These days Myla felt bottomless, absorbing skills in medicine, self-defense, and now this. She never knew what she was capable of and enjoyed the awe she had of herself.

Myla liked being in the infirmary. For some reason, it reminded her of her storage room at home—or more realistically, her father's storage room. It used to be a home office, but her father was a meticulous record keeper, and it was soon filled with old documents and letters. Now it sat, rustic and cobwebbed. It was impossible to navigate through with the stacks and stacks of cardboard boxes. Any furniture that had been there once was moved out. It was now lit by a single, dangling lightbulb.

One night, Myla had stumbled home drunk and ended up in the storage room somehow. She stood under the circle of illumination cast by the lightbulb and scanned the desert of boxes in front of her. She had wondered about the afterlife. If her dad died one day and woke up in this room, unable to leave, looking through the records of his old business triumphs, would he be content? Poring over and reliving each transaction on paper, maybe finding the odd crayon-drawn note from his children here and there . . . would he smile to himself as he did? Did the summation of his entire life stuffed in boxes in a room help or hinder his happiness?

Myla, on the other hand, knew she liked where she was, full of records of a different kind. All around her in the infirmary were memories, like the time she and Zuma had run out of sheets and had to conspire to steal some from the laundry center, or the time Zuma had shown Myla her hidden cookie stash, or the first time Myla had hooked up the heart monitor as Zuma stood by watching with pride. She felt like she could be trapped in the infirmary forever, watching these old films, and she would be content.

One day, Myla was restocking the cabinets in the medical stations when she heard a knock on the door. It was a quiet day, with one snoozing patient at the far end of the room. She opened the door to see Tezca.

"Hey."

"Hey, what's up? Is everything okay?"

"Yeah. My stomach hurts. Can I come in?"

Myla looked around the barren infirmary. "I guess. Take bed five." Tezca lumbered over to the cot and sat while Myla washed her hands and changed her gloves, smiling to herself.

"Did you bring a book?" she asked.

"I don't feel like reading."

She took his temperature and vital signs. It all came out normal, but he still insisted that the pain in his abdomen was severe. Myla checked the bullet wounds to be safe. They didn't look infected at all.

"Well, your bullet wounds have healed well. They won't even leave a scar."

"Good to know," she heard from above while palpating his stomach for any rigidity or swelling.

"Does the pain worsen when I press somewhere?" she asked.

"No. Not at all."

Myla glanced up to see those hazel eyes staring at her. She resumed her inspection.

"What have you eaten today?"

"The usual."

"Okay, well, from what I can tell, there's nothing wrong with you. Zuma's shift starts in six hours if you want to come back then and see the expert."

"Oh. Okay. But would you mind if I stayed here?" He gazed up at her, eyes round and hopeful. He looked away and added, "Just in case."

"I guess." The answer had the effect of a fizzy soda on her stomach, which increased when looking at him lying on the bed. Myla washed her hands and resumed her cabinet stocking. "Lie down and see if you feel better. Do you want me to close the curtain?"

"No, please. It's fine. I don't mind it open. Do your work and forget I'm here."

Myla nodded once and went back to work, checking on her patient on the last bed. He was snoring, so she began a routine cleaning of the room.

Maybe now was the time. She went to Tezca's bedside. He looked up at her. She asked, "Have you thought about my request to contact my brother somehow? And please . . . honest answer."

He opened his mouth and closed it. Finally, he stared at the ceiling and said, "Not yet." Myla would take it. She resumed washing the counters and machines.

She became aware of Tezca's eyes on her. She pretended not to notice until she couldn't take it anymore. Myla broke the silence with "How have the council meetings been going?"

"Pretty well. We're working on implementing the new legal system. I'd like it to be a compound-wide silent vote after a trial. But if it's unanimous among all council members to disagree with the popular vote's decision, we can call a retrial."

"I thought support was supposed to be anonymous. You shouldn't be telling me."

He propped himself up on his elbows, cocking his head. "Can I trust you, Myla?"

"You can, if you like."

"Not still the Priesthood's number-one fan?"

She stopped scrubbing the counter and looked up at him. "That's not funny, Tezca."

"Oh. Yeah. Okay, I'm sorry."

Myla continued rubbing down the counter, pressing a little too hard with the antiseptic cloth.

Tezca tried again. "How do you feel about the years you spent there now?"

Myla sighed, left the cleaning, and moved to sit on the edge of his bed. "How was it for you, Tezca?"

"Traumatizing. I wouldn't leave my room for a few days. We didn't just dip our toes in the blood. We and our families and our ancestors before them bathed in it, patting ourselves on the back for coming up with such an ingenious way of obtaining it.

"I was named for Tezcatlipoca, the god of night and fate. My namesake invented war as a means of providing prisoners of war, and therefore sacrificial food and drink for the gods, so the priests say. And that . . . makes my compliance with the system much worse."

Myla said, "What's incredible is how harmless, funny, it seems in the moment. And then for the rest of your life you turn it over and over in your hands, saying ifs and thens. I'm always thinking about it. I never stop imagining fantasies where I knew better, where I stopped everything and was a hero. I feel so stupid. You made a mistake and though you push it down as far as it will go in your mind, the guilt always finds ways to surface."

"Are we still talking about the sacrifices?" Tezca asked. Myla hadn't rambled like that since the night of the party. He continued. "You can tell me what happened."

She looked up at him and smiled. "Can I trust you, Tezca?"

He shrugged. As she stood and grabbed the cleaning supplies, she looked over her shoulder and offered one promise: "Not yet."

CHAPTER 15

Tona circled her, a devious gleam in his eyes. Every half turn or so, he'd sprint toward her, and back away when she showed her "ready" fighting position. He reversed his direction. Myla adjusted.

"Good. Good," Tona granted her. "You've improved." Myla caught his words somewhere in the back of her brain, but she was still focused on his sternum, as he had taught her.

She tried to anticipate what he'd do next: a standing kick? A flip? A tackle? Her brain sparked with listing the counterattacks to these and for a second she was distracted. And then, he was behind her, his hands clamped down on her neck. "Don't think, Myla."

She tried to lift her arm and turn sideways as Tezca had shown her, but Tona knew that move. His hold cut off escape. The chokehold wasn't hurting, but it wasn't comfortable either. Myla went rigid, searching her brain for a way to escape. Then, Tona released her.

"You're too used to being calculating in the face of adversity. Fighting isn't like persuasion."

"How can I fix it?"

"It's not a conscious thing you can fix. You need to feel natural in combat. You need to relax."

"I'm trying to—"

He interrupted her. "On a rare serious note, Myla, when you're out there in the Temple Mayor tunnels or wherever and you've got fifty patrols heading your way, you don't have time to overthink. When you're there, to think is to die."

He retreated to his original circling, looked Myla in the eyes, and said, "Now . . . again!"

A week later, a storm hit the compound. The rebels ran around, scrambling to prepare for the monsoon. Myla was told to stay at the infirmary alone, in case any storm-related injuries should be rushed in. The drawers and cabinets were stocked, the room spotless, and there were no patients. So Myla sat, reading a new book from the compound's tiny library. It was about a civilization that existed thousands of years ago and whom they worshipped.

The "mythology" was gripping to Myla. She was surprised at how she could picture future historians discussing Aztecism, how silly it could sound in the right context. Suddenly, a knock on the door.

Myla was unsurprised to see Tezca outside. He had been in the infirmary every day for the past week, sometimes complaining of ailments that couldn't be proved, sometimes just hanging around. Myla wasn't sure whether she liked it yet or not.

"What is it this time?"

"Headache. Can I come in?"

She stared at him, eyes narrowed, for a moment, to keep him in suspense. Then she sighed for effect and stood aside. He entered, shaking off the rain from outside.

"What's going on out there?" Myla asked.

"For me, mission planning. Everyone else is doing what they can to save the plants and stuff like that. How's it been in here?"

"Quiet."

"But you still like it?"

"I love it. I mean, I know there's not much I can do to take care of the patients with serious medical issues, that's Zuma's job. But I like taking care of her, making her job easier so she can focus on the stuff only she can do."

He looked at her straight in the eyes while she talked. She loved it. She felt like Cint had only listened to her as a courtesy. While she spoke, she had been alternating looking at him and then his hands clasped together. His fingers were long and perfect looking. His forearms had this hard and lean quality, with light veins tracing the surface.

"You wouldn't want to leave this job? Even for another part-time job?"

"What do you mean?"

"Well, I know this is a big turnaround from wanting you to know nothing about the missions, but you are the third most medically qualified person on the compound, maybe even better than Izel. I was thinking of proposing it to the mission group . . . How would you like to come with us on our next operation?"

"Would that be wise? I don't know my way around a gun . . ."

"Mectel says you're fine. You think quickly in a crisis and can run faster than Izel."

"I don't know. I feel like I haven't had enough training."

"That's normal. My first mission was getting out of Tenochtitlan and I didn't have any training then. I was scared too, but you'll be with us, and it should go smoothly."

"I'm not sure. I've only been taking self-defense from Tona for a few weeks now."

He smiled from his eyes. "I'll give you a crash course." He stood up.

"What? Right now?"

He gestured around the empty infirmary. "Do you have anything else to do?"

"What about your headache?"

He looked puzzled for a moment, then it rang a bell. "Oh! Yeah, my headache. I feel much better."

She gave him the most skeptical look she could muster. He shrugged and said, "You're a miracle worker, Myla."

She laughed and stood up. He circled her and she stood in the main defense stance, left foot forward and hands in fists guarding her face.

"What have you been doing with Tona?"

"Oh, standing kicks, palm heels, rolling, stuff like that."

He circled around behind her. "What about bear hugs?"

"What about *what*?" But suddenly, he was upon her, lifting her up, his arms pinning hers at her sides. Their faces were close.

"What? You never learned these?" He looked too happy about the given situation. She writhed, trying to escape. Finally, she sighed and went limp.

"Okay, okay. How do I get out of these?"

"Well it's hard when you're so tiny and you have such a tall, strong opponent. But try struggling 'til you can get your feet to touch the floor." She did as she was told, and got the tips of her toes down.

"Now wrap your arms around me. Use your legs to get a boost and lift me just enough for me to lose my balance. Then tilt over, landing on top of me."

"Are you sure you want me to try this?"

He nodded.

He must have been going easy on her, because it was over in a minute, with Myla pinning him flat on the infirmary floor. She did as Tona taught her and sat on top of him, pinning his arms under her knees. They were both laughing hard as Tezca struggled.

Suddenly she heard a familiar voice. "Tez, what the hell are you doing?"

Myla looked up to see Amihan silhouetted against the storm behind her. As soon as Tezca heard her, he lifted Myla off him and put her aside. She landed on the cold floor with an unceremonious bump. He stood.

"Myla and I were practicing her self-defense."

"I don't care." Amihan didn't look her normal, frosty self; she looked alarmed. "You are needed at the mission center. You've been needed for the past week. I guess this is where you have been, with the Priesthood girl."

"Yes, yes. I'm sorry, Ami. I'll be right there."

He hadn't looked at Myla once since Amihan had arrived.

"Sorry, I have to go," he said, eyeing the floor. And with that he walked out the door, leaving Myla sitting on the ground, bewildered.

He had been ditching mission work to come hang out with her? Well, whatever he had done, Myla was unhappy that he obeyed Amihan. It bothered her that the girl that hated her so much had such control over Tezca. And the way he shoved her off him . . . was he ashamed of her in front of Amihan?

Myla straightened up as she lingered in the doorway. Myla eyed the area around her for a weapon, but Amihan wouldn't attack with Tezca so close by, would she?

She stepped in closer toward Myla, and Myla thought she could detect a hint of fear in her eyes. "Stay away from him," she said.

"No. And besides, he's the one who keeps coming to me."

"I don't know what he sees in you. You're the same spoiled brat we picked up that night."

"I don't think so. I think I've changed, but you've got a lot of issues and don't want to see it. You should try channeling all of that anger toward something useful." Myla allowed her tone to be sharp. She was sick and tired of all the crap Amihan put her through.

But for once, Amihan didn't look like she wanted to hurt Myla in any way. Her eyes were wide, like Myla had struck a nerve. She looked beautiful.

She said, "That's idiotic."

"Is it?"

"No one can change, really."

Myla shrugged. "I feel different. And I don't think I'd go back if I had the chance."

Amihan stood there in silence, staring at Myla.

Myla continued. "I feel alive out here."

She snorted. "What does that even mean?"

"I don't know . . . I think it's like, we feel alive when we feel like we're affecting the world around us, when we experience strong, *real* reactions to our actions. Everyone interprets that differently, but with you guys I feel like I'm engaging much more than I was before. It's like I can't even remember *thinking*, having actual thoughts, before I came out here. So yeah, I feel alive."

Whoa. Myla felt a slight head rush from spilling so much. She had no idea where it came from, why she was opening up to someone who wished her bodily harm. Maybe it was to humanize her in Amihan's eyes. Maybe she needed to vent. Or maybe there wasn't an angle to that speech.

Amihan stared at her, mouth agape. Then her eyes cleared, like she remembered where she was.

"You're not one of us. I worked for too long for evil people like you. *You don't get to be the hero*." And with that, she stalked out into the storm.

Tezca had planted the seed of an idea in Myla's head, and she couldn't stop thinking about joining the mission group, at least part time. She pictured running around, garbed in all black, saving the day over and over again. She imagined returning to the camp with supplies, hailed a hero as Amihan sulked. She had come this far. Why not?

Two days later at breakfast, she brought it up to Lisbeth and Mectel. "Tezca said some of you were thinking of including me on the next mission . . . is it true?"

Lisbeth swallowed what she was chewing. "Yes, though some of us disagreed with the idea."

Myla rolled her eyes. "I wonder who you could be talking about."

Mectel jumped in. "Yeah, well, for this next mission your presence would be helpful."

"I'd slow you down."

Lisbeth and Mectel looked at each other. Lisbeth started, "I don't know about that, Myla. You see, for this next mission, we're going to your family's factory."

"How do you know what my family does?" Myla asked with trepidation.

Lisbeth admitted, clearing her throat, "Well, after we took you with us that night, we sent our moles in Tenochtitlan to find out everything they could about you. Some were still afraid you were a Priesthood plant who was hoping to be captured.

"So we got our upper-class people to investigate the party that was going on that night—happy birthday, by the way—and found you."

Mectel intercepted. "We did surveillance on your family for about a week after you came here. We were able to find out what you all did."

Myla felt her breath catch in her throat. "How did they take my disappearance?"

Lisbeth looked away. "From what we could tell, as of that time, they pretended like nothing was wrong. Nothing was reported to the Priesthood patrol and if anyone asked, they said you were vacationing in America."

"Did you see my little brother, Aktu? Was he okay?"

"It wasn't us there, Myla. And the moles didn't tell us anything about a little brother."

Myla was upset about this dead end regarding her brother's well-being. "Oh, okay then." She paused. "What would you have me do?"

Mectel looked happy with her willingness to go with them. "Stop by the mission center when you can. We'll fill you in on everything then."

Myla nodded and resumed her breakfast. Lisbeth grinned. "Oh, and there's another get-together tonight, if you're interested." It was Myla's turn to smile.

Myla headed over to the mission center after Zuma took over for the afternoon. It had been a slow day—one food poisoning and one migraine. The mission center was a cabin like every other building on the compound, but Myla had learned to not judge things by how they looked on the outside. Anything could be inside the cozy cabin: a chrome, electronic haven featuring footage shot on the infiltrating cameras in Tenochtitlan, a dark basement littered with maps and photos, anything.

The result was, as she expected, unexpected. Lots of natural light filtered throughout the room onto a large, wooden office table. Whiteboards were on each wall with a few maps tacked up here and there. It looked like it could have been an architect's office. The table had a few guns on it here, some camera equipment there, and plenty of paper and pencils. Tezca, Amihan, Tona, and Mectel were there.

"Hey, guys," Myla ventured. "I was told to stop by."

Tezca looked surprised and a little bit relieved to see her. "Hey, Myla. We were outlining the best getaway options for the operation."

"What is the operation?"

"Well, we have cameras giving us visuals in Tenochtitlan all throughout the Temple Mayor. And we were hoping to expand into sound as well, for the offices of the higher-ups in the senate. Obtaining sound is vital for us. If we can hear what they are planning, we'll be ahead of them at every move. But we don't have the equipment. Your family's factory wouldn't have the best selection of microphones and electronics, but it should be adequate."

"The plan is to steal some microphones? What do you need me for?"

"For now, information. Have you ever been to the factory?" He offered her a chair, and she took it.

"A couple times, the most recent being three years ago."

"Well, we have a good idea of the outside security: some patrols, a barbed-wire fence, and decent security camera footage. But as for what they have inside, we have no idea. We were hoping you could fill us in."

Myla searched her mind, trying to recall the one tour her father took her on three years prior. "There was a security desk at the main entrance. I remember they had more coverage the closer you got to the worker housing." She could see Amihan's eyes narrowing, her hands gripping the back of a chair too tight. She continued. "In the management areas, I don't remember seeing any cameras, and there weren't any guards."

"Okay, that's helpful, Myla, thank you." He was using his politician voice. He was about to ask her for something big.

"There's one more thing that would help . . . we want you to be the first one to infiltrate the factory."

"How would I do that?"

He paused. "The front door."

CHAPTER 16

After he filled her in on the official plan, she agreed. As far as plans went, it didn't seem too dangerous. She was still scared, though. She had been worried about her sudden presence at the factory.

She had asked Tezca and the rebels, "What if my parents have reported my disappearance by now? Won't it be weird if the deserter daughter showed up at the factory?"

She saw the mission group exchanging looks and asked, "What is it?"

Tezca reassured her, "We know for a fact your parents haven't reported your disappearance."

She was confused. "How would you know that?"

"I asked them yesterday."

It turned out Tezca had snuck into Tenochtitlan, posed as one of Myla's friends, and came to her apartment pretending to look for her. Her parents had greeted him and insisted that Myla was on vacation abroad, but should be back soon. They must have been afraid she had deserted, but didn't want to tell anyone for the judgment it would bring down on them. If Quinel or Cint had inquired about her, they had been fed the same lie.

"What the *hell*? You didn't think to *tell me*, Tezca?"

"I'm telling you now."

"Well, it's nice to know they're so worried about me." She paused. "Did you see my brother?"

Tezca smiled. "I did. He believes what your parents are saying and misses you a lot. He's fine and happy, though."

"Oh, thank goodness."

"But anyway, you see how you'd still be welcome at the facility."

"I suppose so."

Tezca could be so *frustrating* sometimes. He knew she was worrying about her brother—why wouldn't he be more up front with her? He had stepped to the side with Amihan, the two whispering. Myla didn't like seeing them together. She didn't like how Tezca could be one person with her and another with Amihan. What if he still saw her as a Priesthood supporter? What if all this newfound trust was a lie?

They were going to leave in three days, Tezca informed her, after the meeting. He and Myla stayed behind, Amihan jostling her as she brushed past. He pretended to arrange the papers on the table before him.

"Thank you for agreeing to this, Myla."

"Anything I can do to help."

"Will I see you at the party tonight?"

"Yeah, maybe. I was thinking of going."

"Oh, good. I'll see you there."

Myla decided to play it cool. She called on the way out, "Yeah, maybe."

Myla brought a book to the party. She decided she was going to try to appear aloof and indifferent, even though her mother always told her it was bad manners to not mingle and entertain at parties. Myla was surprised at how much she had been trained about social interactions, how many little chores she knew to do, and how quickly they were being shoved out of her brain to be replaced by something better.

But hard as she may have tried, she couldn't say no when Tona pushed her toward the dance floor. He was a crazy dancer, flailing his arms and jumping. Myla let herself go as well, laughing to imagine what her mother would think of her dancing with this Under.

She looked back and saw Tona take Lisbeth's hands in his. He danced differently now, more subdued, but the insane happiness was still there. Lisbeth hesitated and joined in. They weaved in and out between each other, leaning out only to have their connected hands reverse their direction so they could circle each other once more.

Lisbeth seemed to take a labored breath at one point and shook her head, leaving to sit on the sidelines. Tona wilted, then noticed Myla watching. He perked up to dance over and shout in her ear that he had just tired Lisbeth out and how it was difficult to play so hard to get when she wanted him that badly. Myla laughed for his sake, but then gave him a hug for the same reason.

It was enough. He was ready to dance again, and Myla joined him. But then, as it had been for the past week, Tezca was there, looming as best he could. He ranged from the friendly, on-top-of-everything politician to the brooding, stern mission leader to the boy at the party that wanted to have fun but didn't know how. Myla thought she liked this one best.

She took his hand and led him in the dance that Tona and Lisbeth were doing earlier. It felt comfortable. When they danced, sparred, and even when he had to carry her out of the sewers, it felt like their bodies knew how to act around each other. He wasn't such a bad dancer. Their minds had synced with the beat and their bodies knew where to step next to complete the other's movement.

They danced until the songs changed to a slow, acoustic guitar song. Myla left the dance floor to catch her breath, but Tezca didn't seem to want to go. He gave in and followed her to the drinks table, where she handed him a large glass of the fruity, alcoholic drink.

They sat on the steps of the amphitheater and slurped the cold drinks. Soon, Myla decided it was time.

"Tezca."

"Mm?" He was smiling that smile with his eyes, but teeth were shown this time. He looked like he was having a good time.

"So, I'm going to be infiltrating a factory for the cause. My family's factory."

"Yeah?"

"Well, it would be so easy to leave my brother a note, give it to an employee to deliver to him."

The smile melted off his face, and he gave her the same stubborn look as before, but now there was something else . . . pity?

"Myla, I'm sorry."

"Yeah, yeah. I know. What if it fell into the wrong hands, blah, blah, blah."

"Look, there's something I should tell you . . ."

A petite figure appeared before them, swaying in time with the music. Tezca straightened up, leaning away from Myla.

"Hey, guys!" Amihan wore a smile, a real one. She beamed at Myla and Tezca, looking like she was at a photo shoot for some skin product. She sat down in between them. "How are you enjoying the party?"

Tezca looked nonplussed by the performance as well. He stuttered, "Um . . . it's okay. Fun."

She sighed. "Yeah. I'm having the *best* time. Aren't you, Myla?"

Myla regarded her warily and nodded.

Amihan next turned to Tezca and looked at him straight in the eyes. "You know you're important to me, right?" she said. "I care about you a lot." Tezca's eyes went wide, and then he smiled.

What was this girl trying to pull?

Myla would have to wait to find out, as the sky broke open and rained down on them. Tezca hustled for cover with Amihan, her tiny arm thrown over his hulking frame, as the party dispersed.

She was left sitting there, getting more and more soaked, when Tona came up from behind her and sat next to her. He handed her a drink that was half rain in content. She could tell he had seen what had happened.

"I wouldn't worry about it, Myla. They're close old friends. It's never been that way between them."

"I can talk, Tona. You know me . . . I can talk my way out of any situation. But when it comes to expressing real feelings out loud . . . I get flustered. It's easier when it's fake." She couldn't lay it all out for Tezca like Amihan had. It made Myla conscious of how Tezca must see her versus Amihan.

"I won't tell you he's not judgmental, because he can be. But from the way he acts around you, I wouldn't worry about embarrassing yourself. Just don't turn everything into a joke to make yourself less uncomfortable, like I do."

Myla stared at him, this sudden show of emotion, as he continued. "Don't look at me that way. I know I do it." He took a long swig from his drink. "And when you make everything a joke, everything *is* a joke."

She put an arm around him and he laid his head on her shoulder. "Lisbeth is missing out," she offered.

"Nah, it's not even about her. I mean, she's great and everything. Smart, kind, beautiful, clever . . . I'd love to be with her, but I'm not mooning over her in particular."

"So . . . what is it?"

"Everyone wants the prince, never the court jester. It just . . . sucks to feel like a side character in your own life. I know that's melodramatic . . ."

Maybe it was the drinking or the way the rain pounded, making it so someone a foot away couldn't hear what they were saying, but Myla could feel her brain churning, working through the emotional barricades set up.

"Tona, it's all about finding the girl who makes you feel like you are the leading man. Turning everything into a joke is your way of communicating, coping. You'll find someone who sees the world your way someday."

"I'm not so sure."

"It's funny. This is reminding me of the conversations I'd have with an old friend from home. She was like you, a bit more cynical and skeptical, but the same 'free spirit' quality was there."

He sat up and wiggled her eyebrows at her. "Well, when this is all over, if the Priesthood hasn't killed all of us, maybe I can snag her number."

Myla laughed. Tona had gotten all he had needed to out. They sat sipping their drinks in the rain, trying to understand what to do next. The two weren't glad the other was in the same boat, but both were glad for the company.

CHAPTER 17

Two days later they left for the little beach they had visited before, this time with Myla as part of the mission group. They sat as they had before, with Tezca and Amihan in the back, but this time Amihan would giggle every couple of minutes. Everyone pretended to not notice and Myla forced herself to not look back at them. Tezca hadn't spoken to her that day.

Amihan also made sure to use "Tez" as much as possible and loudly, like Myla hadn't already known they had those nicknames for each other. Lisbeth, Tona, and Mectel all seemed thrown off by Amihan's change in behavior, and the conversation to the beach was strained and forced. Myla was happy when they arrived.

Everyone hopped out of the car, ditching the stuff and jumping off the cliff. Myla approached the drop-off, still deciding whether to climb down. She ran back to put her stuff back in the car and tried to undo her bracelet. She didn't want to lose it; it was all she had from home, even if it had been Cint who gave it to her. She was fiddling with the clasp when she heard someone behind her. Tezca, soaking wet, had climbed up the cliff to the car.

"I need my towel." Myla stepped aside to let him get it and he noticed the bracelet.

"Here, let me get it," he said as he unfastened the bracelet's tiny clasp. She waited for him to let go of her wrist but he did no such thing. He gave her other hand the bracelet as his left hand's fingers slid down to hers.

"You know, I once gave someone a bracelet like this."

Myla wasn't in the mood for one of his talks. She was worried that he was speaking to her because Amihan wasn't around, so she gave him an uninterested "Really?"

He didn't seem to notice, staring down at her hand. "Yeah. I met her at a party and thought she was pretty, so I claimed her. Simple as that."

Damn. Curiosity overwhelmed her, but she forced herself to play it cool. "It was like that for me too, I guess."

"What was he like?"

"What was *she* like?"

Tezca shrugged. "I was sixteen and she was fifteen. She was tall and refined. Quiet. My parents loved her."

"Cint's twenty. He works for the Priesthood. I suppose he's handsome. My parents love him too."

"Do you think about him often?"

She snorted and answered, "As much as he's thinking about me."

Tezca looked confused by this answer. "But do you miss him?"

Not at all, Myla thought. She was about to share this when she remembered how Tezca had been acting these past couple days, allowing Amihan to come between them. She could play that game too. "Not particularly . . . but he *was* a great kisser."

Tezca looked up at her, then glanced away, dropping her hand. Myla couldn't begin to discern what he was thinking. She hoped it made him feel jealous, feeling like she had felt whenever Amihan had giggled in the backseat.

He looked her straight in the eyes. His deep voice growled, "Better than I am?"

Myla was taken aback. "How would I kn—"

He was kissing her, bending to ease the height difference between them. His hands, those long fingers, cradled her face, angling it up toward his, and his mouth was warm. Myla shut her eyes. She had imagined it several times, but had never seen it coming.

She could hear Amihan calling "Tez" from below, and Tezca stepped away from her, looking at the edge of the cliff. Then he seemed to look at Myla and realize what he had done.

Myla narrowed her eyes and shoved her bracelet in her bag. "No, please, don't let me keep you."

"No, Myla, it isn't like that. I heard my name, that's all."

"You turn into such a different person with her around. You won't even look at me. It's insulting."

"I'm sorry. I'm sorry. But it's . . . it's Ami."

Myla was trying not to look upset. "Figure out what you want, Tezca." She walked away, and then turned around, remembering her conversation with Tona two nights prior. "I didn't want our first kiss to be like this."

She saw him standing dumbstruck before she turned, ran, and jumped off the cliff into the cold water below.

The rest of the beach day occurred without incident. Myla pretended like it never happened, and Tezca did the same, though he did seem to see Amihan in a new light whenever she giggled so unlike herself. He didn't laugh along, he just stared at her.

That night, as Myla was about to enter her cabin, she heard someone whisper her name from the side. She whispered, "Who's there?" ready to run in case it was another of Amihan's attacks. Tezca stepped forward.

"Myla, I don't want to end things like they were earlier."

"I don't know what you want from me. I hope you realize that Amihan is acting like a twelve-year-old to try to draw you away from me."

"I know, I know. I can't explain it, but she does love me, in a way. And I, her. But she's acting immature now, I know."

"If there's not room for both of us in your life, then please let me know now, before . . ."

"Before what?"

"You know what." Myla was getting tired of the mind games.

"Look, Myla, there's something you should know. I must admit, I've trusted that you're on our side for some time now. I haven't agreed to let you see your brother for another reason, a more selfish one."

Myla was astonished. "What?"

"What if he convinced you to come back? What if you left us, me?"

Myla wasn't sure how she felt about this. She was upset with him for putting himself before her brother, and angry with herself for being the slightest bit thrilled. It was a stupid thing Tezca did and Myla hated herself for being so happy he cared.

"That's unfair of you, Tezca."

"I know. Which is why I'm telling you now. I don't want you to suffer worrying about him, even if it means you need to leave. I was thinking about it and . . . if you want, you can call him tomorrow from the factory. Just for a minute, though."

"Thank you, Tezca. That lifts a huge burden. I won't take too long, I promise." She took his hand. "And *you* should know: I'm not going anywhere."

He smiled with his eyes. "I'm not going to let Amihan get between you and me anymore."

"She's your best friend. I understand. You should do what makes you happy, even if she does hate my guts." At that moment, Myla longed to tell him how Amihan had attacked and threatened her, but then he spoke.

"I can't believe I thought you were the person I thought you were for even a moment. Thank you for forgiving all that."

Myla shrugged. "You ruined my life." She stood on her tiptoes, whispered, "Thank *you*," and kissed him goodnight.

They woke up and ate the next morning. Myla and Mectel were given walkie-talkies that could connect them to the rest of the group. Myla was also handed a gun, a knife that she hid on a leg holster, the green dress she wore the night of her birthday, a fake file, her medic pack, and some luggage that she supposed had been high quality once but looked as if it had been thrown out several times. It would have to do. The dress barely fit her. She must have lost weight at the compound, though her wide hips had remained.

Mectel was going to drive Tezca's group to get ready and then head over to the factory with Myla. When they arrived at the first group's destination, they wished each other good luck. Myla hugged Lisbeth and Tona and nodded at Amihan.

Before they left, Tezca took Myla's hands in his and told her he'd come for her and everything would be okay. She was pleased that he didn't even glance at Amihan as he did so. He meant what he'd said the night before.

There was still a five-minute ride between destinations. Myla took a moment to get into character. She had to be Priesthood Myla, Scared Myla, who cared most about whatever party was happening that night.

"Everything okay?" Mectel asked.

"Yeah. I'm trying to think like this past month or so never happened. I'm a good talker, but straight up lying is more difficult."

"You can yell at me for a while, if you like." Mectel smiled. He never cracked jokes, but Myla appreciated this one.

She smiled. "That won't be necessary, but I'll keep it in mind."

"Good, because we're here."

The van pulled up to the guard booth on the factory's driveway.

Mectel nodded at the guard. He wore false tattoos on his left cheek to show he was a chauffeur.

"Myla, the owner's daughter, here to see the foreman."

"Can I see some ID?"

Myla was warned this would happen. She leaned forward in sight of the guard and rolled her eyes. "Is there a *problem*?"

"I need to see some identification."

"Yeah, well, I forgot it. Look, my dad sent me *three* hours out of the city to deliver this stupid file. Can I *please* see the foreman? Or do I have to call my dad?"

Myla hoped this would work twice. The guard looked on the fence until she told him, "He *hates* being bothered."

The guard sighed and waved them in. They parked and Mectel turned to Myla. "Nice work. Before we go in, you clear on the plan?"

Myla nodded and got out of the car. She made a big show of tapping her foot as Mectel got the luggage from the back. Then she handed him the file as well, flouncing toward the entrance of the factory.

The sliding doors welcomed them into the lobby. It was pretty much as Myla had remembered it, with a security checkpoint that she and Mectel approached. For a second, the words caught in her throat. Myla didn't remember her lines. Then, it clicked.

"I'm Myla, Tlazo's daughter. He's the owner of the factory. I need to see the foreman on my dad's behalf."

The guard glanced at Mectel. Myla jumped in. "He's my Under. I don't like carrying luggage."

"If you'd like we could hold it here for you, miss."

"No. I don't like it to leave my sight. Please take me to the foreman's office."

"I'm going to need some verification on who you are."

"Look, all I know is that my dad woke me up today, like, way too early and gave me this file. I was running late and I forgot my ID. Are we going to have a problem?"

"It's protocol, miss."

"I was here three years ago. Can't you check the security tapes or something? I came in with Tlazo. He *owns* this stupid factory."

"Here comes the foreman now."

Myla turned to see the balding, little man— Molnem, she remembered—hurrying toward them. She huffed, "Finally!"

"Miss Myla! Good to see you again. It's been a while. You're all grown up."

The guard spoke. "All good here?"

"Yes, yes, it's fine. I know her. We'll go to my office now."

He rushed them past the security office and toward the elevators. Once they were inside, he turned to Myla.

"I'm surprised it's just you, Myla. It's somewhat unusual for a daughter to visit on business."

"Yeah, I know. But my little brother is too young and my dad didn't trust a messenger with this file."

"Ah, good. How has the family been?"

Myla inspected her nails, resisting the urge to bite them. "They're fine. My dad sends his regards."

"Please send him mine."

"Will do." The elevator pinged, showing they were on the top floor. They stepped out into a huge office that overlooked the entire factory. Myla remembered the tour she had gotten three years prior. The housing was right in front of the building they were in, with storage and assembly facilities farther away.

"Would you like anything? Some water? Coffee?"

"Yes. Do you have a secretary that can fetch some?"

"No, but I can call someone up from the ground floor."

Perfect, Myla thought. "No, thank you. That won't be necessary. Anyway . . ." She strolled nonchalantly—she hoped—closer to her luggage. "Get the rest of the files out," she told Mectel. Then she turned again to the foreman.

"I'm here on behalf of my father. He has urgent, private business to discuss. If there are any receptionists or guards around in earshot, you would do well to inform me now."

"No, no. This is a private office. I assure you, your father's business is safe here."

Myla paused, glancing out of the corner of her eye at Mectel, who was still rummaging through the bag. She could feel her heartbeat in her fingertips.

"Excellent."

On cue, Mectel whipped out a handgun with a silencer. Myla strode over to the luggage and grabbed one of her own. She turned to face Molnem as Mectel circled around to watch his back.

"Myla! What are you doing?"

This was the important part, Myla reminded herself. She had to channel Tezca the night he and the rebels took her: commanding, stern, and sincere.

"Thank you for the warm welcome, Molnem," she enunciated. "Please raise your hands above your head and step away from the desk." He obeyed as Mectel came forward and laced his hands together behind his back and tied him to his office chair. Myla felt bad. This man was always nice to her; he didn't deserve a scare like this.

She put that thought out of her mind as she approached the desk. Mectel knew what she was about to do, facing Molnem away, and he slapped a pair of silencing headphones over the foreman's ears just in case.

Myla laid her gun on the desk, picked up the phone, and dialed. She was glad she remembered the number off the top of her head. It rang twice as Myla prayed that, as usual, Aktu would be home alone.

Then, someone picked up.

CHAPTER 18

"Hello?" Her little brother's voice flowed out of the phone and brought a new strength to Myla.

"Aktu?"

"Myla?"

"Yeah. It's me."

"Mom and Dad said you were on vacation, but they won't tell me where! I miss you a lot and I want you to come home."

"Yeah, yeah. I know, buddy. Look, I only have a minute. Are you okay? Everything's fine with Mom and Dad?"

"It's okay. I'm by myself in the house a lot because they're out all night sometimes. I got a new tutor, and yesterday I went to Tlacopan. The food was good."

Myla felt she was going to cry out of relief. He sounded absentminded and energetic as usual. He was going to be okay.

"That's great, Aktu. I'm glad you're having fun."

"But where *are* you, Myla?"

"Aktu, you can't tell anyone."

Mectel looked up in alarm. Myla shook her head. She continued. "I'm hiding out in the jungle outside Tenochtitlan. I'm okay, but Mom and Dad do not know where I am. Do not believe anything they say."

"Why are you there?"

"It's hard to explain, Aktu. But I'll come for you, I promise."

Mectel gestured to his watch. They had seconds left.

"I have to go now. But I love you and I miss you. We'll see each other soon, I promise."

"Myla, don't go, please! Tell me where you are and I can come meet you."

"Aktu, listen to me. You sit tight and do nothing until I tell you. Do you understand?"

". . . Yes."

"Okay. I should go now. Stay safe. I'll see you soon."

". . . Bye."

It took all the might in the world to put the phone down and concentrate on the mission. But somehow, Myla did it. She wiped her eyes and turned to Mectel, who looked wary of her.

"Okay. Let's do this."

They removed the foreman's headphones and gag. Myla sat down on a chair opposite from him and laid her gun in her lap next to the pad and paper. He looked at her with a fear that made her feel powerful.

"Okay, Molnem. You have thirty seconds. Tell me where the security office is, how to get there, and any codes I may need to get into your computers."

"Why do you want to go there?" His voice shook.

"We have our reasons. Now, Molnem, you forget what a powerful family I belong to. I know about your family. About your wife and kids. Please remember that later, if you live. If you tell anyone anything, we'll find you."

He was crying. Myla wondered if she looked that way when Tezca, Tona, and Amihan first found her. She hoped not. She felt bad that she had to scare him like this, but it had to be done.

She got up, crossed over to him, and pressed her gun to his forehead, discreetly clicking the safety on. He was sweating and sobbing.

"Tell me what I want to know, Molnem, and no one gets hurt. You have my word." Her gun trailed downward until it was digging into his cheek.

"Okay! Okay. Security office is sixth floor to the right. You need the code 4-9-3-2 to get in and the code 3-2-6-1 to access the computers."

Mectel scribbled down the codes. He nodded at Myla and crossed to the elevator as she fastened on

Molnem's gag and headphones. Once he left, Myla radioed Tezca that phase one was nearly complete.

Two minutes later, Mectel's voice crackled on her walkie-talkie.

"I'm twenty feet outside the security office. Do it now."

Myla kept her gun trained on the foreman as she hurried over to the wall. She paused for a moment, and then pulled the fire alarm.

Two more minutes passed and Mectel resurfaced. He had erased the tapes of him and Myla on the premises as well as disabled every security camera in and around the factory. Myla had already radioed Tezca once more to let him know the alarm was triggered. They could see through the giant glass windows the thousands of workers pouring out of the factory. The guards had left too. Hopefully, she and Mectel were alone.

As far as keeping things anonymous went, it wasn't a bad plan. Myla's face was seen entering the premises, but it had been unavoidable. Later, if she had to after being captured, she could claim to the Priesthood that she had been kidnapped then instead of the night of her party. Only the foreman knew her true intentions, and hopefully she had frightened him into silence.

"Okay, as of now we have eighteen minutes," Mectel informed her. "Let's get downstairs."

They wheeled the foreman into a closet and took off his gag and headphones.

"Thank you for your help, Molnem. We'll be on our way. Remember what I said. You have no idea how many of my agents are in this building."

He nodded, shaking, and Myla closed the door on him. She and Mectel grabbed the luggage and made their way downstairs, hearing the sirens of the approaching fire truck. They had just reached the lobby when the firefighters came running in.

The tallest one came up to Myla. She felt her heart beat faster with apprehension as Tezca lifted his visor, smiled that smile with his eyes, and said, "Hey, Myla."

"Good to see you. The storage facility is this way."

Tona came up to Myla and Mectel and handed them two extra fire suits from his pack. After, the five left the administrative building and snuck over to the assembly facility through a walkway, careful to not be seen.

As they progressed, Myla spoke with the group. "So, no problems with the interception?"

"Nope," Tona answered. "There's this region's fire department tied up on the road two miles from here seminaked and truckless, but we'll get them after."

"And you made the call?"

"Yes, at least some of this region's Priesthood patrols are heading in a different direction. And even if they split up, we still have twenty minutes."

Mectel interceded, "Make that sixteen."

They reached the door to the factory left ajar and hurried in. Inside were rows and rows of gleaming-white assembly lines piled up with electronics. Myla and the crew split up, running in different directions to find the storage facility.

"Over here!" Lisbeth called. They all turned and ran in her direction.

Mectel informed them, "Thirteen minutes!" Amihan blasted the lock off the door with her gun, and they filed in.

Inside the storage room were rows and rows of metals shelves filled with boxes of equipment. As they did before, they split up to cover more area. Myla went left, scanning each shelf of boxes for the microphones. She saw plastic switches, wire sleeves, and . . . there! She called over the group and rummaged through the boxes.

She had just found the microphones when the rest of the group arrived. The factory had two boxes of them, perhaps two dozen microphones in total, but it was enough. They each stuffed some equipment into the oversize pockets of their jackets.

Tezca turned to Lisbeth. "They were supposed to hook up chargers for these here. Will we need to get those too?"

Lisbeth was inspecting one microphone. "No. These are compatible with our systems. Let's grab all we can and get out of here."

"Good. Split up and do one last check for any remaining mics," Tezca ordered them, and Myla set off as she had done before.

She turned a corner, running her hands along the wall of cardboard boxes as she searched them for labels. She stopped at one tall, metal shelf, spotting more equipment at the top. The bottom shelf seemed to be able to hold her weight. Boosting herself up, she started climbing.

Myla was near the top when suddenly, her foot touched air, slipping on the smooth metal shelf. She felt herself falling, grabbing at the shelf for support, and it wobbling.

She felt the concrete floor slap her back, saw the shelf tilting over toward her, and then, darkness.

Myla couldn't tell how long she'd been out when she came to. She was aware of a heavy pressure on her legs, pinning them to a cold floor. She could barely move.

She looked down at what was crushing her. The heavy metal shelf had fallen on her, pinning her to the ground. She tried to move her toes. She still could — that was good.

Were her friends still there? Did they think she had slipped away to rejoin the Priesthood and sell them out? Oh, the Priesthood. They'd find her and take her away to be sacrificed any minute. She had to get out of there. She struggled with all her strength, but couldn't lift the shelf.

"Tezca! Tona! I'm back here!" Myla tried yelling. She couldn't hear anyone else in the room, but didn't stop.

Then, a noise from behind her. She craned her neck and saw Amihan, arms full of equipment, staring at Myla.

"Amihan, help! The shelf fell on me."

But she did not reply. Myla tried again. "Please, please get me out of here. We need to get back to everyone and rejoin the mission."

She didn't like the look Amihan was giving her, thoughtful and cold. "What the hell are you doing, Amihan? We have to go!" Myla argued, panic rising.

But Amihan, eyes still trained on Myla's trapped form, walked backward the way she came, not speaking a single word.

"No, no, come back! Please, Amihan, I'm begging you."

But she turned a corner, casting Myla one final look, and then hurried away.

The door shut behind Amihan and Myla was trapped in the darkness. She propped herself up on her elbows and tried to lift the shelf once more. It creaked and groaned, but stayed put. Her left foot had already gone numb. Had the group left yet? Would they come back for her?

She tried sliding farther under the shelf, allowing her to plant her feet and bend her knees, then lifting with the combined effort of her arms and legs. But it was no good. She gave in, lying flat on her back and struggling. She felt like she was going to die in there. She struggled to keep back tears.

Her lifetime passed before her in seconds, but only everything after her birthday seemed watchable. She felt like she hadn't lived until the night she was taken. What *had* she been doing with all that time?

What had she been doing before Tezca? Granted, he was moody and fickle and impossible sometimes, but Myla still couldn't imagine living without his knock on the infirmary door. If she got out of this, she was going to be up front from now on. Companionship, both romantic and platonic, was so attainable, she found. She closed her eyes and remembered the feel of Tezca's lips on hers, the first happy memory she thought of.

Light blared from the outside of her closed lids. She sat up, apprehensive of who might round the corner.

"Myla?" she heard Tona calling.

"I'm over here!" she hollered as loudly as she could.

Soon the whole group came running up, even Amihan.

"What happened?" Tezca asked.

Myla glanced at Amihan. They had to get out of there. "The shelf fell. Thank you for coming back for me."

They all teamed up to lift the metal off her and Tezca lifted her to her feet. His hazel eyes found hers, a new crease burrowing into his brow.

"Are you okay?"

She touched a hand to his cheek. "I'm fine. Now we need to run."

Tezca smiled and kissed the inside of her palm. "Okay."

Tona had been staring at them, bug eyed. "IS THIS THE TIME?"

They ran.

CHAPTER 19

They should have had two minutes left before the Priesthood patrol arrived, but they were pulling in to meet the factory's guard as Myla's group exited the administrative building. The patrol would have no reason to believe they weren't real firefighters. They had planned for this and strolled over to the fire truck, covering their faces with the helmets' visors. Fifty or so officers entered the administrative building.

One guard stopped Lisbeth on the way out. "All clear in there?"

Myla's blood froze. If Lisbeth spoke, they'd know she was a woman, and they'd all be done for.

Tezca jumped in. "Yeah. Minor electrical issue, but it's all fine now."

The guard grunted and headed inside as the group breathed a collective sigh of relief.

But suddenly, the sighs turned into something more inside Lisbeth's helmet. She was gasping for air.

"I'm having . . . an asthma attack," she wheezed.

"Keep walking," Tezca told her. "We'll gather around you and block you from the patrol so you can use your inhaler."

They all crowded around her and walked as Lisbeth fumbled in her bag for her inhaler. Myla looked back and saw two guards exchanging words. They were still a couple hundred feet from the fire truck and fifty feet from Mectel's van. Lisbeth flipped up her visor and raised the inhaler to her lips.

Myla turned back toward the building and saw Molnem walk out, gesturing to a guard. Then he looked her way.

"It's . . . it's empty," Lisbeth rasped. "The inhaler's empty."

"Hey! You there, stop!" The guard was jogging toward them.

They all looked at Tezca, who uttered one word under his breath: "Run." Then, it all exploded.

Myla and Mectel split from the group, sprinting to the van. The other guards ran in their direction, radioing for backup. She was twenty, ten, five feet from the car. When she jumped in the passenger seat, Mectel already had the engine running.

He turned the van to face where Tezca, Tona, Amihan, and Lisbeth were. Twenty or so guards were closing in on them already, as the rebels had to help Lisbeth move, carrying her and slowing their process. Mectel revved the engine and drove to where they were. Myla loaded her gun.

They made a stand, walking backward to the fire truck. Amihan took down target after target with each shot. Tona assisted her, and Tezca focused on keeping Lisbeth moving. The guards were gaining numbers from inside, and they blocked them from view.

Myla only processed Mectel's intentions as the bones of the guards crunched underneath the van's wheels. He had cut a clear line through the circle of guards approaching Tezca's group. One rolled over the windshield, cracking it. Myla was thankful they hadn't hit one of their own.

Mectel turned around and readied for another pass. Myla rolled down the window and shot at the guards, missing often but occasionally making a hit. She had never shot at humans before, but she took one look at her friends inching toward their truck and her hands stilled.

Suddenly the patrol that had arrived earlier streamed out of the building and toward them. Myla saw a small, new hole appear in her window, and then heard the gunshot that accompanied it. The Priesthood patrol had guns. They needed to move.

The group of guards had reached Tezca's group. They were fighting hand to hand, being overpowered by numbers. Myla saw two guards dragging a limp Lisbeth away from the scuffle. She took aim and wounded one, but Mectel already had the van on the move.

Bullets now were making noises like rain on the van as Mectel moved it to plow down the rest of the guards fighting Tezca, Tona, and Amihan. Those three saw their chance and bolted, sprinting for the fire truck. Mectel pointed his van toward the exit.

"What about Lisbeth?" Myla yelled over the gunfire. Mectel didn't even glance at her. She looked around for signature blond braids, but she had already been taken inside the building. A weight dropped in Myla's stomach. Too late.

Meanwhile, dozens of Priesthood officers were getting closer to the van, taking better aim. The rest of Myla's passenger window was shattered, and she ducked down. The van passed by the now-empty guard booth and lurched onto the road. In her mirror, she saw the fire truck following them. It turned the other way. Before they went back home, they'd have to free the real firefighters.

So Myla and Mectel drove back, attempting to comprehend what had happened. He sat stone faced at the wheel, knuckles white and clenching his teeth.

Finally, he spoke. "They have enough time to get her to the city before sunset."

"What?"

"They'll use her tonight. They won't give us a chance to rescue her like we did Tona. So she's tonight."

And Myla let herself cry.

The grieving for Lisbeth was unspoken. It seemed that no one cared how it had happened, just that it had. Myla had cried as Tezca addressed the camp. Amihan had stalked off to the jungle to be alone. Tona looked like he was lost. And Tezca told the compound the details of Lisbeth's capture. He spoke as if he hadn't been there, like he was reading the information off a piece of paper.

"But, everyone, the mission was successful. We retrieved the microphones . . ." He trailed off, unsure of what to say next. Then he cleared his throat and said, "Tonight's is Lisbeth from Sweden. She was a technician on a rebellion's base. We were her family."

Gasps arose from the crowd when they realized what he meant. People turned to each other for comfort, others pelted Tezca with questions, and even more stood in silence.

"What happened?" most seemed to be asking. It took Myla a moment, but she realized with a start that some were asking her. She could barely find the words to speak.

Tezca held up his hands for quiet, and the crowd calmed down. "I'll draft a mission report and have it circulated soon. Give us"—his voice wavered as he struggled for words—"Give us a moment, please."

Myla followed Tezca into the mission center. He seemed to notice her presence and waved her forward. He took her downstairs to a new room filled with monitors, each showing a different scene of the Temple Mayor. Some depicted the outside of the pyramid, where already Unders crowded for the daily sacrifice. The tunnels of the pyramid where Cint had taken her were also there. And one view of a small cell with two guards posted outside.

A young girl with long, blond hair was curled up inside. It took Myla a moment to recognize Lisbeth. They had unwound her braids and her face was beaten bloody. Myla wondered in that moment whether she should have aimed for Lisbeth instead of the guards carrying her.

"Are you sure you want to watch this?" Tezca asked her, his deep voice shaking.

Myla nodded. Her imagination had been running wild with all the ways it could have turned out differently, ways Myla could have saved the day and Lisbeth.

Amihan opened the door and sat down with them, careful not to meet Myla's eyes. Myla decided that then was not the time to tell Tezca how Amihan had trapped her. If she hadn't done it, they would have gotten out of there quickly and it was possible Lisbeth would have been with them now. Maybe the consequences of her actions would weigh on her enough to leave Myla alone. Either way, it could wait. Their friend was in the pyramid.

The chief speaker had come for Lisbeth. The two guards held her still as he injected her with something that made her go limp. As she had been taken away, the two guards dragged her out of the cell and out of the camera's vision.

Amihan turned to Tezca. "Do you think . . .?"

Tezca didn't even look at her. "No. She wouldn't tell them anything." He paused. "She knew she was dead the second the inhaler reached her lips. She knew . . . that we wouldn't be able to get her out of there."

Lisbeth had appeared on top of the pyramid. It occurred to Myla that Quinel and Cint and her family were there somewhere, toasting over Lisbeth's blood.

It was over quickly. Matutslan made his speech, brought Lisbeth over, and slit her throat. There was a laugh in his voice as he recited the ancient prayers. Myla would have liked to think that Lisbeth fell to the ground gracefully after, but in reality, it was the clumsy flop and jerk of a body losing its blood. The other priests set upon the body with their blades, and Myla struggled to bear the crushing guilt that accompanied this sacrifice more than any other. Well . . . maybe any other.

"Not for nothing," Tezca whispered.

"Not for nothing," repeated Tona, standing in the open doorway, tears running down his face.

Later that night Myla lay awake in her bunk, replaying when it had all gone wrong earlier over and over in her mind. *If* Myla had had an extra inhaler on her for Lisbeth. *If* the patrol had been two minutes later. *If* Tezca had decided to not go back for Myla—everything would have ended differently.

She looked at the woman snoring next to her and swung her feet out of bed. Myla dressed and headed out to the main cabin. Something had changed. The air tasted different on the compound. The grass flattened itself under Myla's feet.

Myla walked through the cabin's main sitting room and into the memorial room. A few candles were lit to honor Lisbeth and her newly chiseled spot on the wall.

Myla advanced on the wall and stared at it. Then someone closed the door behind her. Tezca looked her up and down, unsurprised to see her there.

"Myla, I need to talk to you."

"It's late, Tezca. Maybe I should go." She tried to walk past him. She could tell where this was going.

"No, this is important." He placed his hands on her shoulders, keeping her in place. He continued. "When you went missing earlier today, Amihan claimed you snuck away to rejoin the Priesthood."

"And you knew better. Thank you again for saving my life."

"No, but she was *so sure*. I didn't want to believe it. I was relieved to see you trapped like that. But it seems . . . a little too perfect."

"I told you, it fell on me." That wasn't the whole story. But he was distraught. How would he react to the truth?

"Myla, Lisbeth is dead. If someone did something to endanger the mission and the people in it, I must know. If someone tried to hurt you, *I have to know*."

"Tezca, she's your best friend."

"Not if she hurt you."

Myla's will weakened. Tezca already knew it all. The old feeling in her gut to cover up injustices and lies and emotions and pretend like everything was okay was rearing up.

But she spoke, albeit quietly. "She didn't knock the shelf onto me or anything. But when the shelf fell on me . . . she saw it. She was there and I called out to her. She saw me and . . . and then she left. In fact, ever since I got here she's been threatening me, trying to scare me away. But I never thought she'd leave me for dead like that."

Tezca put his hands at his sides, fingers curling into fists. He stared forward, straight over Myla's head. "She wouldn't do that."

"She would and she *did*. If you hadn't come back for me, I'd be dead."

"She wouldn't do it."

"I told you that you didn't want to hear it. But it's the truth. You should know it, before she feeds you some line about how I'm trying to turn you against her or something."

Tezca's eyes snapped onto hers, like she had struck a nerve. Myla could sense that Amihan already had fed him some line like that.

"You asked for the truth. I told you that she's been harassing me for weeks. Why would I lie about this?"

Tezca seemed to deflate. He put his head in his hands and sank against the wall to the floor. "You're right, I'm sorry. I just can't believe that she would do this."

"She has a lot of hate and mistrust. I think she believes I'm still loyal to the Priesthood."

"I . . . I don't know how to resolve this, Myla. I feel split in two. She endangered the whole mission by not telling us where you were, held us up, and now Lisbeth is dead. But she was the second person to join the cause, my best friend. I have no idea what to do." She was certain he had never admitted something like that to anyone before.

Myla sat next to him, back pressed against the wall, and closed her eyes. Tezca believed her, that's what mattered. She felt a rush of relief that he had made it out that day, that they were there together and he was listening to her. She wished she could do what she swore she would when she was trapped under the shelf, articulate to him how he made her feel, show him how much she cared.

It had been a long day. A game changer. She rested her head on his shoulder for a few moments more, and then stood.

She crossed to the wall of names and ran her hand along it. Her pointed finger landed at a name carved about a foot above her head. Tezca squinted to read it.

"Citla?"

"My sister."

CHAPTER 20

Myla remembered it all, despite her efforts to blur the edges in her mind. It remained. Sometimes she couldn't remember childhood pets' names, what month it was, what she did yesterday, but this one memory lay in the back of her mind, popping up at will.

She was ten and her sister, Citla, had been eighteen. Citla was the one who had taken care of Myla, and later, Aktu, when their parents would often disappear. When it happened Aktu was two—he remembered none of it. The spitting image of Myla now, Citla had been cursed with the same untamable hair, the wide smile, and the wide, brown eyes.

Citla was smart, overwhelmingly so. She had nurturing instincts and could chat with anyone about anything. Everyone spoke of her beautiful singing voice. She used to take Myla to the movies during the day when no one was there so they had the whole theater to themselves. She was Myla's hero. Until that night.

Citla had been claimed a month earlier by a man well into his forties, the head of the patrol, high profile. There was nothing their parents could do about it, so Citla took it all in grace. He was an intimidating man, but by all accounts, polite and chivalrous. He opened doors for Citla, sent her gifts, and more, and Citla seemed happy enough to find a man capable of looking after her.

She stayed out until the early hours of the morning with him often. Myla saw how happy it made her parents that Citla had been claimed and shared their joy. She let them think for her. Yes, she was young and didn't know better, but some of her readiness to celebrate the match must have come out of her own apprehension. One day she would be claimed, and she willed herself to believe that it would make her happy, willed herself to believe Citla was experiencing couples' bliss.

Then one night Myla crept out to their apartment's small balcony to watch the stars disappear. It was a still night, so Myla heard a car pulling up four stories below. The sound of her sister's laughter wafted up to her, so she hung over the side to see what was going on.

A shiny black car was pulled up in front of Myla's building. Citla and the man who had claimed her were standing outside it, chatting. He kissed her. Myla felt like she shouldn't be watching but couldn't look away. He pushed her up against the car, hands traveling, and Myla could see that she resisted, pushing him back and shaking her head. Myla wasn't sure what was happening.

He became angry, yelling at her and shaking her. She tried to walk away but he grabbed her hair and flung her to the ground. He took out a gun. Citla grew quiet, inching backward, hands out in defense. He kneeled over her and pressed the gun to her forehead.

Suddenly, she knocked his hand away. A shot rang out over the street. The gun clattered and landed a few feet away. He grabbed her neck as she reached in vain for the fallen gun. He held her there for ten, twenty seconds until she went limp. He sat back, panting and looking upward. Myla hid, holding her breath, counting to ten.

Then she heard another shot. She peeked out over the railing and saw Citla standing over the man, blood pooling around him. She stared at the gun for a solid minute. Then she cleaned it, threw it on the ground beside the corpse, and walked inside.

Later when a Priesthood patrolman asked Myla if she knew anything about it, she confessed. She told him everything she had seen that night.

Why? Why had she done it? The question drove Myla mad. Was she trying to protect herself? Trying to protect Citla by coming clean and hoping for a lenient punishment? As the years went by, she was less and less sure.

Citla never knew that it was Myla who had blown the whistle.

Myla had turned it over in her head for years. At the time, she had been scared, but with time her guilt had grown. She tried to avoid the thought that had plagued her for years: that she was partially responsible for her sister's death. She clung to how the Priesthood was a force of good and justice to ease her own conscience. Seeing Lisbeth killed had opened her mind up wide. She allowed that guilt to wash over her, allowed herself to miss her sister.

She told all of this to Tezca, her voice shaking, and he listened without interrupting. She finished her tale with "I allowed her to die and attended her execution."

She was afraid Tezca would be disgusted with her. Instead, he seemed shocked.

"Myla . . . I'm so sorry for your loss."

She looked up at him in awe. After Citla was killed, her parents never talked to Myla about it. They grieved in their own way, a way which involved closing themselves off from their other children. They had never been exemplary parents, but since their firstborn was taken from them, and the community had turned against her, they shut down.

Their elite friends wrinkled their noses when they gossiped about her behind their backs. Everyone seemed either glad to be rid of her or insisting she never existed. No one was sorry for Myla's loss.

"You are?"

"Of course. I know what it's like to lose an older sibling."

"I loved her so much. Why couldn't I protect her?"

"You were a child."

"I should have known." A couple small tears splashed down her cheeks.

"Nothing can change what they did to her. All we can do is try to prevent it from happening again."

"I have so many regrets, Tezca."

"It hurts because you loved her so much. Never regret loving anyone. It's the best thing we've got."

It was hard to deny this as he kissed her.

The compound had a small ceremony to honor Lisbeth. Tezca spoke beautifully, praising Lisbeth's selflessness, bravery, and sacrifice. Tona sat near Myla. He seemed to be done with the tears—instead his fists were clenched, knuckles popping out, on the side of his seat.

Myla treated the funeral as if it were Citla's as well. She had never gotten a funeral. Myla didn't even know where her body went, assumed it was cremated like all the other sacrificial bodies. But it helped to say goodbye in an official ceremony. She wondered if, had Citla lived, she would have joined the cause with Myla.

A day went by and the compound still seemed in a fog. They had been "rebels" for two years. They had had a few natural deaths, but nothing could have prepared them for losing one of their own. Even the extremists who would glare and mutter at Myla looked at the ground as she passed.

The next day, Myla found Tona sitting by himself in the amphitheater and jogged over to join him. He was wringing his hands.

"Are you okay?" Myla asked.

"Yeah, yeah, I'm fine." His tone indicated that no, he was not. He seemed angry with Myla.

He took a deep breath. "I had a little chat with Amihan . . . crazy how a shelf fell on you like that." He had figured out what happened.

Myla was shocked. She didn't expect anyone to care about how Amihan had messed with her. She realized that this was a product of years of her being a plaything of the Priesthood and her parents.

"Thank you for coming back for me. I'm sorry it cost Lisbeth her life."

Tona turned to her, eyes wide. "*Amihan* cost Lisbeth her life."

"Tezca knows. He'll make it right."

"How can you be so submissive? Are you going to let Amihan keep going until she kills you?"

She was getting angry. "What else am I supposed to *do*, Tona? If I introduce a 'her or me' ultimatum to the camp, it could go either way. I could be signing my death warrant or my exile by calling her out."

"You don't know that. I don't know why you're letting a hypothetical hold you back."

She paused, looking at the sad boy in front of her, pushed so far. "I'm scared," she responded. "I always have been."

He stared at her, then looked at the horizon, and the two sat in silence. She realized this was one of the longest stretches he had ever gone without making a joke.

Myla resumed her work in the infirmary, though she thought she'd cry every time she passed by the supply of inhalers.

Zuma taught her how to bandage a punctured lung. The two ate lunch together afterward, taking a much-needed rest. They'd do this often, but this time Myla noticed something.

Zuma, before eating, bowed her head, said a few words under her breath, then dug into her food. Myla couldn't help asking about it.

"Were you praying?"

"What? Oh, oh yeah. I know, some people think I'm a little crazy."

"Oh, I don't, I promise. I'm just wondering why. Do you believe in the gods?"

Zuma shrugged. "As of right now, yes. I can't help but feel someone, something gave me a purpose and has a plan for me."

"That's comforting." Until she was enlightened, she had always thought the gods were punishing her for everything, that they existed to exact justice, and if she kept her head down, they'd leave her alone. After her chat with her parents and after studying other religions, however, she found herself convinced they didn't exist. But did that mean there was *nothing* out there?

"I don't feel bad praying to the same gods who the priests sacrifice our friends to every night, in case you were wondering." There was a defensive edge to Zuma's voice. "The priests take advantage of the gods, creating false messages that benefit themselves. I think the gods are good for creating us." She paused. "Do *you* believe in them?"

Myla thought about it. "So much has happened, you know? And it's not like I thought about this thing before I came out here. So, I guess . . . I'm still not sure. And I think that's okay, knowing all we know, to be unsure."

Zuma smiled. "Smart girl. People can get carried away here. Those extremists have talked about killing anyone who believes in such a murderous faith. It's good to be somewhere in the middle, levels people out a bit."

Myla considered that as the two continued to eat their lunch, then got back to work.

She avoided Amihan as much as she could, hoping that another attempt on her life wouldn't be made by the time Tezca figured out what to do. At least Tezca knew. It was good to have someone on her side. Things continued as normally as they could, and Myla counted herself lucky.

Until one afternoon two days after the mission, when Tezca entered the infirmary without knocking, no absurd ailment to grant him admission. Zuma was about to kick him out until she saw the look on his face.

"Myla, you need to come with me right now."

She looked at Zuma, who nodded. Myla handed her the sterile solution she was using to clean out a wound, washed her hands, and left with Tezca.

His long legs left her jogging to keep up across the field. "What's going on? What happened?"

He wouldn't even look at her. "Something happened. It doesn't look good."

Myla worried. What could have happened that would have involved her? Had the Priesthood figured out she had deserted?

He led her to the monitor room in the mission center. Tona was already there, the door closed behind him. He looked grave, a rarity for Tona. Myla bit her nails.

Tezca turned to her. "So Tona and I were down here about ten minutes ago, planning the placement of the microphones. And I noticed something on one of the monitors."

Tona cut in. "We should take care not to lose our heads. Something can be done about it."

Myla prepared for the worst. "Will someone please tell me what happened?"

They glanced at each other. Tezca nodded and Tona opened the door to the monitor room. Myla rushed in and scanned the screens for anything that would pop out. At first, she noticed nothing different, the outside of the pyramid empty, several priests milling about the lobby, and in the cell, two people: an Under and . . . her brother.

Sitting in the cell below the pyramid, the same prison that Lisbeth had been curled up in two days ago, was Aktu. Myla gasped.

"What happened?" she whispered.

"That's what we've been trying to figure out," Tezca admitted. "But when he was brought in, he had a small backpack with him. We think he was trying to run away."

Myla sank into one of the chairs and stared at her little brother on the screen. "That's it. He said on the phone he'd come for me. But . . . I told him not to come!" She felt like she was ten years old again, like she was trapped, powerless.

There was a prolonged silence as she watched the monitor, willing herself through it, and Tezca and Tona were trying to communicate silently behind her. Then, it clicked.

"This . . . is *my* fault. They're going to kill my nine-year-old brother. I can't believe this is happening again."

She had been stupid and careless to think her brother would obey without question. She had been stupid and careless to trust the Priesthood so quickly when the time came to judge her sister. The age-old guilt reared its head and came crashing down around her until she wasn't sure where she was anymore.

Tezca looked worried. "If they choose him tonight for the sacrifice, we have no time to go in for a rescue mission. But if he's tomorrow, we might have a chance."

Tona nodded. They both seemed so ready to help. It would break Myla's heart if anything would happen to them now. But what position was she in to decline their offer? Her brother stretched onscreen.

Had her parents been notified about his imprisonment? Did they even care? And did Aktu know where he was and what was going to happen? No, she wouldn't let it happen. She was going to save her brother and kill Matutslan herself.

That evening, they studied the monitors, jumping in their seats at any movement onscreen. Finally, two guards and Matutslan came to the prison, and he took a moment deciding who to slaughter. He walked over to where Aktu was sitting, and every muscle in Myla's body tensed, gripping the edge of her chair.

"No," she whispered. "No, not him. Not now. Don't. Don't do it." She didn't feel good about wishing that the poor Under stuck in there would be chosen, but Aktu was her little brother. She couldn't watch him die.

Like a switch flipped, Matutslan turned and pointed to the Under. He was drugged and taken away. Myla felt a pang for the poor man but also relief. She thanked the gods out of instinct and promised to give Matutslan a quick death.

Tezca had been watching her the whole time, eyes flitting back and forth between the screen and her. He was holding his breath and let it all out in a sigh when she looked at him.

"Okay then," he broke the silence. "We've got a mission to plan." He locked eyes with Myla. "A full-scale attack."

Twenty minutes later, he was standing in the amphitheater in front of the whole camp. He had taken a moment to prepare for his speech, getting himself into politician mode. He had closed his eyes and taken quick, deep breaths. If she hadn't been so worried about Aktu, she would have found it endearing.

"Friends, I have an announcement," he began. There it was, the pull in his voice that caused the whole crowd to lean forward. "A deserter was caught today and put in custody. He's nine years old. He's also Myla's brother."

Myla could feel hundreds of eyes on her. Tezca continued. "As he was potentially one of us and we have twenty-four hours to save him, we've decided to launch a rescue mission that will culminate in the attack we've been planning since the beginning. Now is the time. All of those capable of fighting would be expected to join us, if the vote goes through." The crowd shifted in their seats as Tezca outlined the details of the plan.

Then, he put it up to vote. Council members cast their votes on tiny slips of paper. Tezca then held them up and read them for everyone. There were two votes of dissent, but the mission group had their go-ahead.

Tezca adjourned the meeting, warning everyone to prepare and get a good night's sleep. They would leave the next afternoon.

After, he came up to Myla and explained, "With rescue missions, it's important to go as soon as possible. But I'm sure you'll agree that with the nature of this attack, it requires a certain threshold of time to be utilized."

He was still in politician speak. Myla decided to knock him out of it by kissing him ever so gently and whispering, "Thank you. I know you made the decision you did in part because of me."

He shrugged. "Myla, I'm this compound's leader. I must be impartial and make the right decision. All I'm doing here is deciding to save an innocent nine-year-old boy. This attack has been a long time coming, too."

Myla hoped so. She looked at him. What if she got him killed? Or Tona? She didn't think she could live with herself. Tezca could see straight through to her thoughts and the familiar furrow appeared.

He cupped her face with his hands. "Don't worry. It's nothing we haven't signed up for. This is all for the cause." When she still didn't believe him, he took her hand and whispered, "I have to help Huelta film something to help with the mission—we're gonna try to pull off something crazy—but I'll meet you back here in a half hour."

That stir-crazy energy she had seeing her brother in a cell had channeled into pure adrenaline. She had a purpose—she would get to the pyramid no matter what and save her brother. It was an insane mission, it was insane she was going to do it, but it was real. It was happening, Tezca had ensured that, it was happening.

She waited for him and together they hiked into the jungle, reaching a small clearing about a half mile from the base. He turned to face her. "Now, Myla, since we couldn't make it to the beach this time . . . I thought we'd come out here and continue our self-defense lesson." And he smiled with his eyes.

CHAPTER 21

Myla's brain buzzed until the next day, hypotheticals flying left and right. But as she prepped her medic kit and watched the troops streaming out onto the main field, she felt a new wave of calm wash over her. Today, things were going to change.

They had about an hour before they had to leave yet, so Myla headed over to the infirmary to see if there was anything she could do to help. Zuma would be staying behind. Myla found it hard to say goodbye.

"You've come a long way," Zuma said. "We'll see each other again."

"Thanks, Zuma. I—" Myla's voice caught in her throat. She took a deep breath. She was getting better at expressing her feelings. "You've been such a wonderful role model and friend. Thank you for all you've done."

Zuma pulled her into a hug and left for the main cabin. Myla continued preparing, when the door banged open. She looked up to see Amihan and two of her extremists framing the doorway. They had guns. Myla's handgun for the mission was back in her cabin waiting for her. She had hoped Lisbeth's death would have quelled Amihan's rage. She was wrong.

"It's your fault Lisbeth is dead," Amihan spat. "If you had never come here, none of this would have happened."

Myla swallowed her fear. "*You're* the one who left me under the shelf, holding up the whole mission."

"We should have never gone back for you. But I underestimated Tezca and his childish fascination with you."

She handed her gun to the man to her left and then pulled out her knife. "You have no idea what it's like to suffer, to be a factory worker, to be an Under. So I'm going to show you."

Her knife was close to Myla's face. The man behind her grunted, "Hurry up."

Amihan smiled that viper smile. "I'm deciding what Myla here is going to be, what I should take. A finger? A nose? An earlobe?"

The door banged open behind her once more. The two men aimed their guns at the figures of Tezca and Tona, who ran in, guns drawn.

Tezca looked nervous for once. "Ami. Please put down the knife." More people, Mectel and Quent, arrived, also holding guns. There was a moment of uncertainty, of indecision. Then, it became clear.

The two extremists bolted toward the back door of the infirmary while Amihan lunged at Myla with the knife. They fell backward, Myla holding Amihan's wrist with the knife right above her face. She felt a sharp pain on the side of her face before Amihan was wrestled off her.

Myla clutched her cheek and removed her hand to see blood. Amihan had made an inch-long vertical slit on Myla's cheekbone. It wasn't that deep, but blood dripped down her face onto her clothes. She was surprised at how calm she felt. Blood had never bothered her, even her own, it appeared.

Myla glanced up to see Tezca holding Amihan, pinning her arms at her sides. She looked so tiny in comparison to him, struggling with all she had. The bloody knife lay a foot away from Myla, who picked it up. Tona, Quent, and Mectel still had guns pointed at the fighting pair.

Myla was picking herself up to her feet when Amihan elbowed Tezca's jaw and wrested his gun from his grip. She leaped back from him, her aim jumping from person to person, unable to cover them all.

Tezca looked up at her, his eyes full of hurt as he clutched his jaw, and gasped, "What the hell, Ami? Who *are* you?"

For a second she appeared to be seeing him in a new light. Her eyes filled with tears as she whispered, "Tez . . ." She opened her mouth to say more, but nothing came out. Then she was backing up, new resolve on her face and her gun trained on Myla, and she was out the door.

Once it slammed shut, Tezca turned to the group and instructed, "Go after them." They complied, and Tezca and Myla were left alone. She grabbed some gauze and a sterile solution to clean their wounds.

Tezca noticed her presence. His eyes softened and he murmured, "Your face, Myla."

"It's nothing I can't fix."

He nodded and stared at the door after Amihan, looking like he was going to cry. Myla didn't know what to say.

She patched him up and then turned her attention to herself using a mirror. The cut would leave a scar, no doubt, but she was lucky to still have her face. It didn't even need stitches.

"She's not who I thought she was," Tezca spoke, still staring at the door. "I thought I could see through everyone, but she was there, right under my nose."

Myla sat by him and put her hand on his unaffected shoulder. "Nobody knew. Don't blame yourself, Tezca. I'm fine. We're going to go save my brother and we're going to be fine."

"I've lost so many people."

Myla didn't like where this was going. She shuffled around to face him and looked him in the eyes. "You've got to keep it together, Tezca. We have a mission."

"She cut you. She got close enough to cut you. Myla, I wanted to do something about her after she left you for dead, you need to know that. But with Lisbeth's death, and your little brother . . . I thought . . . I don't know what I thought. I didn't think she'd jeopardize the peace of the camp at a time like this. I'm so sorry."

The pain on Myla's face had reduced to a slight stinging. "Focus. We don't have the extremists anymore. Does the plan need to be changed?"

Something clicked inside him. "Yes." He stood. "I need to address the camp." Myla sighed in relief.

The cameras showed that the passage they came out of last time had been sealed off. The Priesthood had figured out that was where they had exited. There were plenty of sewer tunnels weaving about underneath the Temple Mayor. The problem was getting up into the actual pyramid.

The plan was this: Huelta, Tona, Tezca, Myla, and Mectel were going to use the submarine to access one of Tenochtitlan's private beaches, where they would appear to be a bunch of kids out on a day-trip while Huelta took the submarine back. Then they'd make their way through the city, reaching a service door leading into the depths of the pyramid tunnels, which Mectel had used in his days as a sewer worker. Once inside, they'd open the door they'd used before, letting in hundreds of rebel fighters when the time was right.

Amihan and her extremists had gotten away, disappearing into the endless jungle around them. It didn't matter much to Myla. She wasn't going to fear a knife carving up her face in the night, because after tonight, she'd either be living in Tenochtitlan or dead.

Myla, when packing her bag, encountered Tona removing his eyebrow ring and fastening a small piece of tan plastic to his ear. With his long hair covering it, he didn't look like an Under at all. Mectel did the same with the gauges in his ears.

"Where did you get the prosthetic earlobe?" Myla asked Tona, curious.

"Oh . . . well, there's a doctor in Texcoco. He helps Unders who want a fresh start. He gave me this."

Myla hadn't realized that maybe they weren't the only rebel force out there. There could be hundreds of small parties out there wishing for the fall of the Priesthood. Maybe they would join Myla's group tonight.

The time came for Huelta's van. Myla had her medic kit, Tezca had the radio, Mectel carried the ammo, and Tona hauled the maps and mission's computers, as Lisbeth used to do. They all held their own guns.

As the van hurtled to Lake Texcoco, Myla felt the thrill buzzing in her head leaking down to mix with the apprehension in her stomach. Last time it had not ended well. Whom would she lose this time?

But she took comfort in Tezca's presence next to her. In the final minutes before the departure, he had been running around, updating people on final changes to the plan and making sure everything was perfect. He regained some of his confident composure then, and now, despite some sad hollowness in his eyes, his brow was smooth. He was ready to lead them to victory.

He reached out and took her hand, squeezing it. He whispered in her ear, "I want to live forever with you. And I'm sorry if that's not how this ends." His deep voice still gave Myla chills.

Myla couldn't think of anything to say to that, so she removed her green bracelet. Rolling down the window, she flashed him a sad smile and threw it out of the van.

Before Myla could count minutes, they were in the submarine and underway on the mission. Tona took on Lisbeth's role as captain and only faltered once or twice when obstacles arose. Myla pondered how far she'd come. It was strange to think that before, she'd sat handcuffed to a cot in the corner, and now she was awaiting orders from one of her captors—when to pull which lever.

The beach they were headed to was the one Myla had gone to with Quinel and Aktu on her birthday. The rocks extending from shore would envelop their submarine. She hoped nothing had happened to change them. Anything could be waiting for them up there.

Tona maneuvered them to what he deemed the perfect spot and took a deep breath. His voice rang out. "Prepare to surface!" Myla ran to her spot by the hatch, removing her black top to reveal a flashy swimsuit Huelta had dug up. She stuffed her shirt in her pack for later.

At the right signal, she twisted open the submarine's hatch. *Show time*, she thought. Something Citla had told her once about giving the world hell popped into her mind. She agreed, swearing to do so, and swung open the door, feeling the warm sun on her face.

CHAPTER 22

It was a perfect landing. The rocks came out from shore to form a hook that Tona had steered right into. If Myla stood straight, she'd be seen by the beachgoers, but the submarine was concealed.

Myla inched her head up for a peek and made a note of her target. She took a deep breath to calm her mind and then stood and strolled onto the rocks. She took breaks to look out over Lake Texcoco, like any tourist would, and settled on the beach, lying down to sun herself. She made a conscious effort not to glance around too much.

The beach was full that day and no one seemed to notice when another teenager, Tezca, popped up on the rocks and strolled over to Myla. He greeted her with a deep kiss. She stared at him as he sat next to her and whispered under her breath, "That was not part of the plan."

"Just you and me, a normal couple enjoying a day at the beach." He was grinning.

"You are such an ass. We need to focus." She could see Tona and Mectel making their way over.

"So you admit I'm a distraction."

Myla opened her mouth to say something witty and devastating, but her mind was blank. She gave in, shrugging and turning toward the lake. Tezca stifled a laugh.

Once Mectel and Tona reached them, Tezca and Myla made a small show of greeting them and packing up their stuff. The swimsuits the boys had to wear were terrible and antiquated—full body, thick, and bright orange—which Myla found hilarious and Tona found unfunny.

The group headed over to the beach's exit, hoping they looked like a small party out for a day-trip. Myla liked the idea that they still would have all been friends under different circumstances, if the resistance never existed and they had met some other way.

Her heart raced as she saw guards standing where the sand met the road. She turned and pretended to chat with Tona as they passed. There, they were on the main road. Myla flagged down a cab as the rest of her group threw regular clothes from their packs over their swimsuits. Myla did the same in the cab next to Tona and Mectel. Tezca sat in the front, instructing the driver to take them to a café they'd picked out near the Temple Mayor's courtyard.

Once they arrived, they pretended to wait outside the café until the cab had departed. The café overlooked the pyramid and its giant, circular courtyard, soon to be full of Unders and, closer to the pyramid, the upper class. They had the cross the concrete sea to reach the pyramid. They'd be out in the open.

Myla whipped out her camera, setting off across the courtyard, pointing to the Temple Mayor and talking to her friends. They too had cameras and were snapping photo after photo of the pyramid.

Finally, they reached the base of the pyramid. Mectel directed them around to the side, where the service door was. Tezca stayed at the corner, pretending to text but watching for guards. Mectel tried the handle—nothing. He pulled with all his might. It still wouldn't give. Then they all noticed a control panel, waiting for a password, to the left of the door.

Tona turned to Mectel. "Is this supposed to be here?"

He looked more serious than usual. "No. It's new."

Tona whipped out his computer while muttering to himself, "Four-digit code, most likely two letters, two numbers. Hm . . . would it be there? No, no, no. They wouldn't have it. The distribution network might."

He looked at Mectel and Myla. "To crack the door's code, I'm going to need about a half hour."

Around the corner, Tezca coughed. That was the signal for approaching guards. They needed to either get in or get the hell out of there.

"Do you need to do it here?" Myla asked.

"No. I need time . . . Lisbeth would have been able to do it quicker."

"There are guards coming. We need a place to hole up," Mectel insisted.

Myla racked her brain. Her apartment was on the other side of town. Then, she had it.

"Pack up the computer. I know a place."

"Myla, where the *hell* have you been?" It was good to hear Quinel's voice.

"Hey, Quin. Sorry I've been out of touch. Are you home alone?" Myla stepped past her friend through the open door, looking for anyone else there.

"No, it's just me. What's going on? You disappear off the face of the earth and your parents won't tell me anything and—"

"Quin. Listen to me. A lot has changed. I need to know I can trust you."

Quinel seemed to notice Myla's appearance for the first time. Her eyes widened in horror at the old-fashioned clothes, lack of makeup, and the state of Myla's hair.

"Yes, of course you can trust me. What's going on?"

Myla walked back out into the hallway, called her friends in, and went back into the apartment.

"The first thing I need to tell you is that the Priesthood has been lying to you your whole life."

"What are you talking about, My? Why are you acting so weird? Who's . . .?" Her voice trailed off. She was staring at Tona, who had just entered the premises. In the same moment, he saw her too.

They both spoke in unison. "Who's your friend?"

Myla sighed. It was still true that nothing could focus Quinel like a boy. The two were grinning now at each other.

"Um . . . Quinel, this is Tona. Tona, Quinel."

Tona had regained his composure. He strode over to Quinel and swooped down to kiss her hand. "Tona, at your pleasure."

She looked up at Myla with a slight grin on her face. "All is forgiven, Myla."

Myla rolled her eyes. "Glad I could be of service. Now Quinel, please listen to me." She wrested Quinel from Tona's grip and sat her down on her plush couch. Tona set up his computer on the coffee table and set to work.

"These are my new friends, Tona, Tezca, and Mectel. We are . . . the rebellion."

"What?"

"You need to give me time to explain. As I said before, the Priesthood is lying to you. They don't know if the gods exist or not."

And so, Myla filled Quinel in on her life for the past several weeks. It took ten minutes, and Quinel listened with rapt attention. When she was done, Quinel was silent, sitting with her hands on her knees.

Finally, she spoke. "So all those people . . . all the wars . . . it's all for nothing."

Myla nodded. "To promote a system that doesn't even work anyway. Most of the population is enslaved and the senate is corrupt and inefficient."

"That . . . is . . . ridiculous!" She stood, pacing around the apartment in her pajamas. "Why haven't my parents told me this? Why haven't they *done* anything?" She was furious. Myla had never seen her this angry. When Myla had been enlightened, she felt sad and confused. Quinel seemed pissed off.

"Your parents weren't allowed to tell you until you came of age," Myla told her.

"Still! Crazy people pull a giant scam like this and no one tells me anything? I feel so stupid!" She walked straight up to Tona. "Okay, I'm in. Sign me up. I want to kill some priests."

Tona smiled, in awe of the force of nature that was Quinel. "Whoa, you processed that quick, didn't you?"

Quinel's smile dimmed the slightest bit. "Well, to be honest with you all, I feel like I always knew deep down that something was up. I'm too much of a skeptic. But I didn't ask any questions, didn't trust my gut enough to say something, and for that I am sorry. I am upset, I promise, I'm just more angry with myself than upset."

"Well, in any case, you can help us now," Myla said, standing. "We need to get into the Temple Mayor first. Quin, they have Aktu. We need to get in to save him. And then we attack."

"I'll come with you. I'll get him out of harm's way."

Myla smiled at her old friend, blown away by her. "Thank you."

The computer kept running, decoding the door's password. "Nothing to do now but wait." Tona shrugged before going to sit next to Quinel.

There was a moment of awkward pause as they decided where to even begin. Tona started, "Hey, Quinel? Are you oxygen? Because I don't think I can live without you."

She smirked and rolled her eyes. "Hey, Tona? Are you dough? Because I knead you."

His body shook with silent laughter. "Are you a magnet? Because I find you attractive."

"Are you a lightning bolt? Because you're a knockout."

"Are you a door? Because I a-door you."

She was laughing out loud now. "That one's terrible."

He shrugged. "You expect me to be able to think around you?"

Quinel blushed and looked at Myla, patting her knee. "This will do nicely, thank you." She turned back to Tona, who filled her in on the history of the rebellion. Myla walked away. Tezca was seated with the radio, communicating to the rest of the group the slight hiccup in the plan. He wrapped it up as soon as he saw Myla.

"Your friend's nice. Tona seems to like her."

"Yeah, she's cool. And they seem to like each other. Too bad I only play matchmaker right before we're all about to die."

Tezca smiled and rubbed the seat next to him. She sat and tucked herself under his arm. "What will you do if you get out of this?"

"Well, the plan has always been to build a new government, a better, impartial one. I suppose I'd try to lead it. You?"

"I don't know. I'd like to continue in the medic profession. Oh . . . would I have to get a *job*?" The thought had never occurred to her.

Tezca chuckled and rested his head on hers. She moved with his chest rising and falling. Myla loved being intertwined with him, feeling his warm body against hers. It felt right.

They stayed there until Tona announced that he had pulled the right code from the Priesthood's servers. "And what *are* the rest of us doing with our lives?" Quinel said.

He beamed at her and said, "That's what *I've* been telling everyone."

Tezca interrupted their ridiculous outpourings. "So we're back on schedule, then. Quinel, we appreciate your hospitality, but this is the real deal. People have died, and will die. If you're in, welcome. But if not, we understand."

Quinel took in their leader, fingers interlaced with her best friend's, and for once was serious. "I feel angry. But I trust Myla, and the idea that I've been lied to my whole life is believable, my parents aren't great at it. Like I said before, I sat back and watched it all happening. And now is my chance to make up for it. So, am I in? Abso-freaking-lutely."

Myla gaped at her—she'd never seen this side of her before. Quinel, after all their years of friendship, was still managing to surprise her.

The two girls walked arm in arm out of Quinel's building, like they had months ago, now trailing a group of rebels.

Myla gushed, "I missed you so much, Quin. It's so good to be back in your presence. I love you so, so much."

"Whoa, whoa, all the feelings! I love you too, sweetie. What, did you not have any girlfriends at the camp or compound or whatever?"

"Well . . . I did, but one died and the other tried to kill me."

Quinel stared at her, not sure if she was joking or not. "That . . . sucks?"

"Yeah . . . Tona's nice, though!"

Quinel laughed. "Of course he is. And I noticed you found a guy out there too . . . the tall one who hates fun."

"He doesn't hate fun. You gotta get to know him."

"I will. But he's hot, good job. Seems smarter than Cint, anyway." Quinel paused, gauging the situation. "I'm sorry about your brother," she ventured. "We'll get him back, I'm sure of it."

"Thank you for listening and being open minded and joining and stuff. You have no idea how long it took me to even get used to the idea of overthrowing the Priesthood."

Quinel glanced at Tona. "It's my pleasure . . . and hey, Myla? I'm happy *for* you, you know? Like, you seem centered and focused. I like it in you."

"You too."

"And one more thing. I'm sorry we never talked about your sister."

They were nearing the door now. Myla and Quinel only had moments more to get it all out in the open.

Quinel kept going. "I allowed it all to happen, I didn't even ask you about it. I'm sorry."

"Please, if anyone was repressing anything, it was me. You're here for me now, which is more than I could ever ask for."

They had reached the door. The two reunited girls hugged for the first time in months.

This time, the door swung open after Tona inputted the code. He nodded at Mectel, who led them down into the base of the pyramid.

The tunnels so far were as Myla had remembered them: long, dank hallways that stretched and zigzagged for miles, but Mectel seemed to know the way.

"It's twenty minutes to sundown. Myla, to the armory . . . with Quinel, I guess. It's that way," Mectel said, gesturing.

Tona jumped in. "Tezca and I know the way to the cell. We'll be waiting for you there."

"All right. I'm going to open up the sewers."

Tezca warned him, "Remember, if the bomb isn't contained, everyone will know we're here."

Then he turned to Myla. "In case this is the last, love." He swept her into a deep kiss that did nothing for her focus on the mission. When he let her go, everyone was looking everywhere but at them.

A short pause, and then Tona broke it. "You know, Quinel, it could be the last for us as well . . . love."

She thought about it, shrugging, and then jumped him. He reciprocated until Mectel cleared his throat.

"Well, if we're done with whatever that was, we should go."

Quinel came up for air. "Yeah, yeah. We're done, spoilsport."

Myla took her hand, pulling her away from Tona. "Everyone ready?" The group took one deep breath, a moment of silence before Myla said, "Give 'em hell," and they broke off. She ran down the hallway, Quinel at her side.

A series of passages and stairwells took Myla and Quinel to the same level that Cint had taken Myla to on that fateful night. Myla looked at the map Mectel had drawn for her of that floor. There were offices for about three hundred more feet until they reached the armory.

She and Quinel stalked past the dark offices, turning left and right, moving as quickly as they could without making much noise. Myla brought the pace up to a jog when she felt Quinel tugging on her sleeve. She pointed ahead to one office with a lit window. Myla's stomach dropped and she took out her gun. They crept forward. The door was ajar.

Myla peeked in, then felt sick to her stomach. Sitting on the desk inside was Cint. Myla flattened herself against the wall, wincing when to her right, there was a dull thud. Quinel had dropped her bag. They froze.

Inside, a girl's voice said, "I think I heard something."

Then, footsteps approaching as Cint said, "Stay here."

Myla turned to run, pushing Quinel, but she wouldn't move. Then behind her, Cint's voice.

"Hey, babe."

CHAPTER 23

Myla hid her gun behind her back, sticking it in her waistband as she turned, hoping Cint hadn't seen it. She could talk her way out of this. But what should she do with Cint?

He gaped at her. "What are you doing down here? Where have you *been* the last two months?"

"I've been away, Cint." Her cool tone seemed to sound alarm bells in his head. His eyes darted to her right wrist.

"Where's your bracelet?"

Myla paused, then decided, what the hell? "Who's your new friend?"

"That's none of your business. Myla, I'm angry with you. You can't leave town and not tell me!"

"Why not?"

He was turning bright red, making a face that couldn't be further from his usual dazzling smile.

He spluttered, "B-because . . . I claimed you."

Myla maintained her composure. "And?" She stared at him, daring him to go further.

"Have you cheated on me, you little hussy? I should remind you that if I were to go to the Priesthood, you'd be executed for that . . . on just my word."

"I haven't been claimed by anyone, Cint." She turned to go and could sense him softening, giving in.

"Babe, please. Why are you doing this to me?" Cint wore a sad, little smile. He took a step closer to her. "You know I need you. Don't leave me again."

"Oh, Cint." She reached out and cradled his face with her palm. "As if you had a say in it." Okay. That felt good.

He became enraged again. Quinel squealed in fright as he lifted one hand to slap Myla. Myla didn't even need to think. She ducked the blow, stepped behind him, and used his own momentum to push him over. For a second she wanted to go further, but remembered her sister. Cint was a bad guy, but he didn't deserve that. She held back, subduing her shock that he'd raise a hand against her. Man, she'd dodged a bullet.

He looked up from the floor, bewildered by his new location. Quinel stared at her in awe. Myla heard the door open and pulled out her gun, stepping back to cover Cint and the girl he was with.

The girl shrieked and Cint gasped at the sight of the gun.

Myla realized she had been wasting time telling Cint off. She needed to deal with these two. "Stand up," she ordered Cint. He was cowering from her, trembling because of the gun. *Very attractive,* she thought.

He pulled himself to his feet. Myla waved them both inside. "Get in and sit in opposite corners of the room. Quin, grab the rope from my bag and tie Cint to that pipe and whoever she is to the desk, tight."

Quinel obeyed as Myla covered the two with her gun. Then she checked their pockets for anything sharp, coming up empty.

"You're going to hang out here for a while, your favorite spot. Is that okay, Cint?"

"Myla, what the hell is going on? Why are you doing this?"

"You'll see soon enough." Myla glanced over her shoulder at the girl who was now crying. Though cute, she was one of those people with ugly crying faces. Myla was glad Cint would be stuck with it for a while. It was something that would bother him. She walked over to the girl.

"Oh, don't worry. Your night's not ruined. He," she gestured with the gun to Cint, "he thinks you're *great.*"

Myla was silent on the last bit of walk to the armory. Quinel had a weird spring in her step. She kept looking forward, grinning, turning to Myla, opening her mouth to say something, and turning back forward.

"If you want to say something, say it, Quin," Myla said exasperatedly.

"That was badass, My." She giggled. "That was so badass. Who *is* this new badass chick I see before me?"

"Cint's a jerk. He had it coming."

"No doubt about that . . . but the way you *handled* it was awesome! No, it's more than that. You would always take so much crap, Myla. But then I lose you for two months and you come back all cool and free, and I think it's so awesome."

Myla grinned. "Well, thank you, Quin. But we can discuss this later. We have to access the armory. It should be around two more corners." Her voice trailed into a whisper, a finger on her lips showing that they should be quiet. She screwed the silencer onto her gun. It was time.

Light and low conversation came from the next hallway over. Myla took out a small mirror and set it at floor level, lying down with it to see around the corner. Two Priesthood guards stood chatting in front of the armory. Myla nodded at Quinel. The two girls straightened up, Myla hid her gun, and they strolled around the corner arm in arm.

Myla giggled at a high pitch while Quinel staggered around, pantomiming her own drunken state at her last party.

"Excuse me," one of the guards said, "you girls can't be down here."

Myla hiccupped and smiled at the guard. "I'm s-sorry. We . . . got lost." She pouted as Quinel hung off her arm. "Could you maybe show us out? Please?" She gave them the best innocent smile she could muster.

It worked. The first guard nodded at the second and started down the hall, intending to lead Myla and Quinel upstairs. He was five feet away when Myla spun around, whipping out her gun, and shot the second guard in the chest. She twisted to the first guard and shot. He was midturn, reaching for his holstered gun, when she got him in the neck. He clasped it, making terrible gurgling noises. Myla forced herself to stay calm. She had never more wished she were a better shot.

The first guard was dragging himself to the wall, reaching for the phone there. Myla kicked him away and shot him a few more times, then made sure they were both dead.

When Myla caught her breath, she noticed Quinel pressed up against the wall, her eyes wide and her hand pressed to her mouth. She walked up to her and took her hand.

"Quin, trust me, I didn't like it. But we discussed it back at the base. They're just more to fight when the time comes."

Quinel blinked and focused on Myla's face. "Yes, I know. Of course. These guys were going to help murder your brother. I've just never seen so much blood up close."

Myla hadn't noticed before, but yes, blood was pooling around their feet. She felt used to it. She had just shot two men in cold blood, but it was only the beginning. She'd have to kill more before the night was over.

"We've got to keep moving, Quin. My brother needs us." Quinel nodded and reached down to the second guard, plucking the keys from his belt. There were a few drops of blood on them. She held them out from her like they smelled bad.

It was a good thing Quinel had joined up, because Myla wasn't sure if she would have been able to get the door open herself. It looked like a bomb shelter from the outside, but the door creaked open to reveal rows and rows of guns and ammo.

Myla ran along the shelves, taking out Mectel's list and looking for the specific items. She hoped there would be room in her pack for all of it. Quinel called to her from the entrance, "Is there anything I can do?"

Myla paused, uncomfortable, before calling back, "Well, if you wouldn't mind doing it alone, we need to move the bodies inside before someone sees them."

Quinel's silence told her what she thought of this mini mission. "It's okay, Quin. I can do it," Myla shouted.

She heard a quiet "no" before Quinel's voice strengthened. "No, I'll do it." She sounded resolved to do so. Myla felt proud of her friend, then reminded herself to get back to work.

She picked up several handguns and two semiautomatic machine guns. That was all they could use—Tona and Mectel were the only ones who knew how to handle them. Myla also filled her pack with all the ammo she could fit.

This all took about four minutes. Myla expected to reach the entrance and see Quinel waiting for her, but there was no one there. She proceeded out of the armory . . . and came face to face with another guard, his arm cutting off Quinel's windpipe, his other hand holding a gun pointed straight at Myla.

"Who are you? What do you want?" The guard had a harsh look in his eyes. He would have no trouble taking her and Quinel out. But he was one guard. They could take him if he didn't sound the alarm. *Don't think.* She did the first thing that came to mind.

Myla walked toward the guard, staring at him in the eyes. "Now let's all calm down and not lose our heads." If she could distract him for a second, she could overpower him. Her voice took on a new nervous tone. "Let's not do anything drastic." She flicked her eyes over to the phone on the wall three feet away.

The second his eyes followed, she spun outside his outstretched arm. He turned to follow her, gun in hand cutting a wide arc, but she circled him as Tona had once done to her. Then, she was behind him, and put a bullet through his head.

A minute later, the three bodies were hidden inside the armory. There was nothing Myla could have done about the blood, but she hoped that it was less noticeable than three bodies lying around.

Myla and Quinel melted the lock into the door with a blowtorch. No one would be able to get inside in a hurry. Granted, this cut off their weapons supply, but it would cripple the Priesthood as well.

They were behind schedule. She and Quinel jogged back to the elevators, following the map they were given to the holding cell. Myla had given Quinel a handgun she found in the armory. She had no idea how to shoot it, but Myla couldn't leave her friend unarmed.

They had four minutes before Matutslan was due in the cell. She and Quinel needed to be there when he arrived. They loped through the twisting tunnels of the pyramid until they came to the door of the cell, propped open. Myla took out her gun and edged into the room.

The cell was covered by a dark curtain guarded by two officers. One looked up when Myla came in. Her anxiety cracked—Tezca's face was above the uniform, sure and steady despite being in the belly of the beast.

"Where did you put the guards?"

"There was a closet three doors down. Did you have any trouble?"

"There was an extra guard. But it's fine. No alarms pulled. Everything good with Mectel?"

Tona chimed in. "He checked in on the radio. He's ready whenever we are. And one more thing, Myla." He nodded behind her and Myla whirled around.

Despite being locked up for two days and scared out of his mind, Aktu smiled when he saw her, running to hug her.

"Myla! I tried to come looking for you!"

"Aktu, I know. That's why I came for you. I missed you so much, buddy."

"You look so tan and messy."

Myla had to laugh at that, but was cut off by a stern Tezca. "Sorry, Myla, but he's going to be here any moment."

Tona removed the guard's uniform to reveal his regular clothes underneath. He handed them to

Quinel, who put them on and tied her hair up under the cap.

"Listen to me, Aktu. Go with Quinel now. She's going to take you somewhere safe."

Tezca put a hand on Myla's shoulder. "It's okay, I talked to him." He turned to Quinel. "The hallway to the left is clear. You should be able to get out that way."

Myla hugged Aktu one last time and then Quinel. "Thank you for taking him."

Quinel looked at her old friend through wary eyes. "Just come back for him. And for me, My. I don't know what I'd do without you." She handed her a cell phone. "Take this, please. I'll grab my spare at home. The number is in there."

Myla nodded and they were out the door. Her throat closed as they left, but she managed to keep her emotions under control, stepping into place behind the door next to Tona. Tezca stood still by the jail cell, his hand on his gun.

A minute passed and they waited. Then another. And another.

"He should be here by now," Myla whispered to Tona.

"He'll be here. Hang in there," he whispered back. Myla tried to take his words in but they fell out of her head, replaced with mounting unease. They were supposed to access Matutslan when he was at his most vulnerable, but what if he had caught on to their plan? They couldn't take anyone else hostage. Matutslan would let them die if threatened. Getting to him was the only way it would work.

Footsteps echoed down the hall, the squeak of expensive, leather shoes, like Myla's father's. Through the crack near the door hinge, she saw a tall figure entering the room. Matutslan. He walked over to Tezca, took out a long syringe, and spoke.

CHAPTER 24

"Open the door for me," he instructed Tezca, not even glancing at him. His voice was deep and menacing, casting chills down Myla's spine. She and Tona crept forward from their hiding spot, guns trained on the chief speaker.

Tezca paused. The gears inside his head turned as he contemplated the point of no return before him. He took a step back, and then drew his gun.

"Unfortunately, Chief Speaker, I can't do that."

Matutslan glanced up in confusion, noticed Tezca's gun, and stood up straight, pensive.

"What is it that you want?" He seemed calm, bored even, like he wished this would be over with because he had more important things to do.

Myla looked at the man who had killed her sister, drank in the creased lines in his worn face, the slick black hair, and those large, dark eyes.

"Let me see your hands. Drop the syringe," Tezca commanded, and Matutslan obeyed. The needle meant for Aktu fell to the tile with a small clink. Myla stepped out from behind the door and pulled rope out of her bag.

"Let her tie you up," Tezca commanded. "You have three guns trained on you right now."

Matutslan gave him a modest bow of the head. "Of course." Myla circled him, pulling his wrists behind his back. She knotted them as quickly as she could.

"You're done, Chief Speaker," Tezca said. "The revolution has begun and this is the last you'll ever see of any power."

Something caught Myla's eye, a glint near Matutslan's wrist. She stood to investigate when it moved. Myla jumped back, but he grabbed her and propped her up before him, the minuscule knife he had been hiding now digging into her neck.

She hated knives.

"Drop her!" Tezca ordered, but panic came off him in waves. He had his gun trained on Matutslan's head.

"This is a two-inch serrated blade," Matutslan said in a borderline-friendly tone. "It will take me half a second to send a message from my brain to the muscles into my arm and to pierce this little girl's carotid artery. Do you think you can kill me before then? She will bleed out instantly."

Tezca was calculating the risk in his head. They wanted him alive. Was Tezca going to let him kill her right then and there?

Matutslan moved to the door, his left arm around Myla's rib cage, carrying her like she weighed nothing. Tezca and Tona didn't shoot. The swaying motions Matutslan made carrying her pressed the small blade into her neck farther and farther. A small trickle of blood traveled down her skin.

Tezca and Tona followed them at a distance, their guns on Matutslan, but Tezca's eyes on Myla. He was several paces away from the elevator now. As he moved, she wiggled, her toes touched the ground, and she shifted to support her weight.

Matutslan was inside the elevator and left her outside, one arm extended, continuing to threaten Myla's neck. She dared a small sigh in relief. He wasn't taking her with him. The elevator doors closed, his arm disappeared, and he was gone. They were running to her.

Tezca put his hand on her neck, applying pressure. "Are you okay?" he asked.

She removed his hand and saw a spot of blood. "I'm fine, I'm fine. What do we do now?"

Up close, she saw the real fear in Tezca's eyes. Until she saw his reaction, she hadn't processed how close she had been to death.

Tona spoke. "Tell Mectel we have to move now. He's setting off the alarms as we speak. We need everyone up here, on top of the pyramid."

Tezca took a moment to plan their next move, clearing his head, ready for anything. He pulled out his radio and jogged down the hall away from the elevators. Myla and Tona followed. Higher up in the pyramid, the walls were decorated with miles of murals of the Aztecan gods and their feats. Myla recognized the one she was running past. It was of the great reconsecration of the Temple Mayor in 1487. The Priesthood had given eighty thousand prisoners of war to the gods over a period of four days.

"Mectel, charges, now! Gather everyone and meet up on the pyramid. They know we're here," Tezca called into the radio.

As Mectel radioed back confirmation, Tezca pulled open a door to a small, dank stairway. He turned to Myla and Tona. "Climb, I'll explain on the way." They headed up the stairs.

"This is no longer an ambush. They know we're here but not how many we are. We still have a chance if we surprise them at the pyramid's peak. Like the original plan, we need to hold out as long as we can."

Myla was worried. The original plan involved little actual combat . . . and now they were waging all-out war on the Priesthood?

Tezca paused, thoughtful. "We have to hope the people below join us."

Then Myla knew she was running toward her death.

Her legs burned from the climb, but she ignored it to keep up with Tezca as he picked up the pace. She believed in the cause and she believed in him.

At last, they reached a heavy, metal door. The buzz of the massive crowds waiting outside, waiting to see her little brother slaughtered, was overpowering. Her fist tightened around the butt of her gun. Everyone was still talking . . . that meant Matutslan hadn't arrived yet.

"What are we waiting for?" Tona breathed to Tezca.

"Mectel needs to be in place before we attack. Otherwise, we'll be killed."

"Okay, but what if they proceed with the ceremony? We have to stop them before they do."

Tezca looked from Tona to Myla. "It has to be with everyone."

There was pain in his eyes as he delivered this, understanding the choice he had to make. She banished any tears of fear and agreed. "We don't stand a chance otherwise."

The crowd outside quieted. The chief speaker had arrived. Myla held her breath. Tezca shook the radio, as if that would make Mectel ready faster.

"I bet he'll choose someone from the crowd," Tona whispered. "He has to, now that he has no sacrifice."

Myla pictured what was happening outside: Matutslan stepping forward in an elegant suit, the scythe he would wield, the crowd looking up in admiration, respect, fear. She had seen it a thousand times. Her mind drifted to how she'd observed the ceremony no differently the time her sister was at the top of the pyramid. She would make up for it now.

He walked forward, his footsteps echoing around the platform on top of the pyramid. Finally, he spoke. "Greetings, people of Azteca. The gods have granted us twenty-four more hours of sunlight. The apocalypse has been pushed back one more day. But we must remember the sacrifices we all must make to keep the sun in the sky every day. The earth we walk on is sprung forth from the gods who sacrificed themselves to give it to us. From them, life. And so from us, life.

"But wicked, destructive forces are among us. We must cleanse ourselves of the demons who try to plunge us all into eternal darkness. So I must turn to you, Azteca, for help with this mission."

"What is he doing?" Myla whispered to Tona and Tezca. The latter had gone white as a ghost.

Matutslan continued. "This night, three devils in human skin conspired to kill me and end the good we do for the world. I scared them away, but they are still here, in the pyramid somewhere. We must use them tonight for our sacrifice to ensure they can never wreak havoc again.

"I spoke with the gods. And they have decided that we must turn to you, Unders. The first Unders to bring me one of the demons hiding here will be granted by the gods the ability to join the upper class."

That did it. The crowd was buzzing now, anxious to get their reward.

"We have reviewed security tapes and found their faces. Here they are. Remember them. They look human, but I assure you . . . they are evil."

They were probably showing on the large screens outside security footage of Myla, Tezca, and Tona. She wondered if they had figured out whether Quinel was with them. If so, she wasn't safe at her house. Someone was bound to recognize her. Myla also realized that her parents were down there somewhere, looking up at her face. She pondered what they were feeling at that precise moment.

"Unders, you now have access to the pyramid through the side doors. We must complete the ceremony before the gods decide to unleash darkness on us all."

Tezca clicked a button on the radio and spoke, "Mectel, did you get all of that? Are you ready to go?"

The radio squawked, "Yes. And we need more time."

"Now," Matutslan was yelling, "go forth and do the gods' bidding!" He took a dramatic pause. "For the sun!" Myla pictured him raising his hands to sky, demanding her head.

The crowd below screamed back, "For the sun! For the sun!"

Then, chaos. The tens of thousands of Unders swept toward the pyramid, howling for blood penance.

Tona looked up at Myla and Tezca. "Well . . . this isn't good."

Myla turned to run away from the impending squabble but was stopped by Tezca. "They think we're still downstairs somewhere. We're safer up here, holding out until Mectel's group is ready. Plus, there are cameras down there. We'll be found in two seconds."

Her hysteria rose. "So we just sit here and wait to be found? They're right outside! Someone's bound to come in this way."

Tezca put his hands on her shoulders. Somehow, even in their darkest hour, a connection between their two bodies relaxed her. He gave her a contact high of whatever allowed him to think.

"Myla, calm down. We're sticking with the ambush plan. They don't know we're all here."

"Who's all here? Four hundred people? There are at least a thousand guards swarming this pyramid and thousands more on the way. And now an army of Unders!"

"They'll join us when the time comes. I know they will. All the people whose doors I've knocked on in the middle of the night will realize who we are and fight."

Tezca sounded like he believed it, but then again, he *was* a politician. Inspiring people to follow him like he had Myla was what he did best.

Myla fell silent and leaned against the wall. Tezca seemed like he wanted to say more, his brow crinkled, but instead he sighed. He tried Mectel again. "Where are we on getting everyone in?"

The bombs underground answered him. The tiny explosives barely shook the gigantic structure, but everyone heard them going off. Mectel had blown the charges. He radioed up, "We need to get everyone upstairs. Be there soon."

Hopefully, no one would be able to pinpoint where the noise had come from. They needed to hold out until everyone was inside the pyramid.

Tezca spoke again to Mectel. "If you encounter anyone on the way up, pretend that you're looking for us. You'll blend in. They don't know you're here yet."

"Good idea. We should be up there in seven minutes or so," Mectel responded.

Tona paced. Myla's eyes jumped back and forth watching him. Outside, they heard the rabble of the crowd. Those who had not already disappeared into the pyramid could be coming their way. It was nerve racking.

"What do we do if someone comes in? Do we shoot them? Run?" Myla asked.

"They're Unders," Tona said. "We can't kill them."

"Yeah, well, they *are* hunting us down to kill us," Myla said, annoyed.

"Because they think we're demons, Myla! They've never heard one word against what the Priesthood has been telling them their entire lives."

Myla looked at Tezca. "What do we do?"

He was sitting on a step, pressing his knuckles to his lips. He had a deep look of concentration on his face, staring at the floor in front of him. Finally, he straightened up, looked up to the low ceiling, and uttered, "I . . . I don't know."

They all waited in silence for a moment. Myla tried again. "What if we try to reason with them? Tell them who we are and our mission?"

Tona snorted. "Yeah, I guess we could try that."

Then, the decision was made for them. A door two or three floors down banged open and the sound of excited voices found their ears. They all froze. Several people were making their way up the stairs to where they were hiding.

Tezca reached out to Myla, grabbed her hand, and pointed upward. Myla whispered to him, "That goes to the main deck!" The look he gave her meant he didn't care that they'd be out in the open.

"Are you crazy? We can't go out there! The upper deck will be swarming with priests," Tona whispered to Tezca, who looked solemn.

"We don't have a choice."

The landing they were on opened to the main upper deck, the gathering place of the Priesthood for the ritual. Two more flights of stairs above them was another deck, a smaller one, for the most elite priests. This higher floor was a track going around the perimeter of the main outside deck. There was another stairwell on the other side . . . if they could get across. They had no idea how many priests would be waiting for them once they got there. They were going to run for it.

The Unders below them were one floor down. Myla gave in and let Tezca lead her up the steps, Tona following. Luckily, their footsteps were covered by the commotion below. The landing above was clear.

Tezca hissed into the radio, "Mectel! Are you ready?" There was no response. Tezca threw Myla a desperate look before placing both hands on the bar of the upper deck's door. Myla heard a voice below scream, "There they are!" and Tezca flung open the door.

They charged across the deck, taking everyone by surprise. Tezca barreled through the people on the platform, Myla and Tona in tow. They were close to the other side, the other stairwell, when the priests realized who they were, screaming and jostling each other.

A foot stuck out in front of Tezca, and it was enough to send him sprawling, Myla and Tona adding to the pileup. Two priests set on them, punching and kicking. One grabbed Myla by the shoulder and she took her stance, planting her side and delivering three quick punches—one, two, one—to his side.

One priest landed a blow on Myla's head. She felt a sudden wave of dizziness, falling to her knees. She didn't see where the priest went.

Everything seemed muted. Tezca was shaking her. Tona was nearby, yelling something, holding his gun out trying to ward off several approaching guards.

Tezca was also saying something. Asking something. She nodded. She was okay. Then it all came into focus. And it got loud.

The priests on the upper deck had circled them, some carrying guns, some wielding nightsticks. Tona twirled around, threatening anyone who had come too close. But Myla looked down and knew it was over. There were over a hundred guards, dozens of guns pointed straight at them. She looked around from the pyramid's upper deck. She saw all of Tenochtitlan from there. They had been foolish to think they'd make it all the way to the other side so exposed.

Tezca had stood, arms raised, and was now talking to Tona, who lowered his gun. Myla pulled herself to her feet. There was a group of Unders crowding the entrance to the stairs, all screaming and taking credit for the rebels' capture. She saw Matutslan on the main platform below, smiling the smallest of smiles, gloating, his plan to smoke out the "demons" a success.

The ringing in her ears faded as several priests came up behind Myla, Tezca, and Tona, pressing guns to their temples. "Drop your guns! Drop them now!" And they complied.

They were pushed and prodded down the stairs to where Matutslan was standing. They were forced to their knees.

At this point, the disappointed mobs of Unders were beginning to file out of the pyramid to watch the ceremony, but no doubt some were still down there, searching for a shot at survival. A priest apprentice was sharpening the scythe's long blade nearby. Myla and Tona craned their necks around, desperate for help. Tezca stared right above him, into Matutslan's eyes, carrying as much hate as a look had ever borne. Matutslan himself scanned the crowd, absorbing the power of the city's focus.

Matutslan was talking, addressing the city in triumph. Myla didn't care to listen. Little flecks of spit came out of his mouth when he talked, and she noticed he was wearing a lollipop microphone, like an auctioneer. She had never seen it before.

Myla had always resembled her sister. She wondered if one compared the footage of her sister's death and hers, would they be identical? Was Myla in the same spot Citla had kneeled in seven years ago? If Myla looked out to the upper-class pavilion, left of the pulque bar, would she see her ten-year-old self staring back up at her?

"Tezca . . ." she managed.

He turned his head toward her. "I'm so sorry, Myla."

"What?"

"I never should have taken you away from here." His voice was so low, barely a whisper.

Myla paused, swallowing back hot tears. "You took me, but I *chose* to stay."

They shifted on their knees until their sides were touching, looking deep into each other's eyes. Myla shut out the grand scale of the scene behind her.

"Great," Tona noted. "I get to die as I lived, third-wheeling."

The apprentice priest handed Matutslan the scythe, who raised it high above his head. Myla hoped she'd somehow end up in her infirmary,

Zuma teaching her something new, Tezca faking some stupid new illness, Myla complete.

And then, all hell broke loose.

CHAPTER 25

Mectel's group burst out of the stairwells as Tezca tackled Myla to the ground. She heard the swish of the scythe missing her head. Matutslan raised it again for a second strike but Tezca, Tona, and Myla rolled and ducked until they were out of reach. He growled and went toward them, then realized he had brought a scythe to a gunfight. He ducked and headed toward the other stairwell.

Myla, Tezca, and Tona felt bullets fired by both rebels and guards whiz past as they ran to Mectel, who was taking cover behind an altar. The rest of the rebels too had found spots to conceal themselves on the two decks of the pyramid's peak.

People screamed like no one was hearing them. The Unders on the pyramid ran down to safety when Mectel and his group had burst forth, but some still were caught in the crossfire. Most were watching the fight with shock on their faces, unsure what to do.

"Glad you could find your way here," Tona yelled, ducking in beside Mectel.

Mectel was carrying a ridiculous number of guns and ammo in straps all over his arms and chest. He handed Tona a semiautomatic machine gun and Myla and Tezca handguns.

"Let's establish some nests on the upper deck," he said to Tona. "Myla and Tezca, you know what to do."

They nodded.

Tona took a deep breath. "One . . . two . . . three!" He and Mectel jumped out from behind the staircase and, dodging bullets, sprinted up the stairs to the upper deck.

Myla and Tezca waited, but no shouts came, no sudden pain. Their friends must have made it all the way up.

Myla caught glimpses of what their group was doing. Izel and a small platoon took the west stairs, hopefully preventing any guards from infiltrating the rebels' line from underneath. Other groups had moved altars in front of the main, giant staircase that led all the way down. A horde of guards had gathered at the bottom, trying to find a way up.

It all worked out as they had planned it. They were holding the top of the pyramid. All they needed to do was clear the small corner of the main deck that fifty or so Priesthood officers still held. But that wasn't Myla's job.

As if on cue, a rebel on the east staircase dropped from a bullet, letting loose a yell that kicked Myla's brain into high gear. She looked at Tezca. "Ready?"

He held up his gun. "I've got you. One . . . two . . . three!"

They darted out from below the staircase, Myla firing everywhere, Tezca taking calculated shots as he ran. Bullets greeted them in return, but they were fast and made it to the east stairs unscathed.

Twenty or so rebels were taking turns popping over the railing to fire on a squadron of guards below while one rebel lay away from the rest. A female rebel kneeled over him and stood back when Myla came running up.

Tezca switched on a flashlight he had brought with him. The sun had disappeared and they couldn't see much in the cool night. Well, his job *was* to assist and cover Myla, more making sure she didn't die. But this counted too.

Myla dropped to her knees. The man was bleeding in growing spurts from his upper collarbone. She applied pressure with both hands, feeling the blood soak up between her fingertips, and told Tezca to get a bulky, gauze dressing from her bag. He fumbled for a minute and then produced what she'd asked for.

The man's bleeding slowed, but his skin had already gone pale, cool, and sweaty. Myla wished she had a blanket with her to treat for shock, but had to be content with just the dressing for this patient. At last, the bleeding stopped under the dressing and her pressure, and the man's eyes fluttered.

"You're going to be okay. Don't move or you'll tear the arterial bleed," Myla told him. He blinked once. Myla stood, nodded at Tezca, and ran off under his cover to her next patient.

Through the inky night, she managed to catch where Matutslan had ended up. He had a gun now and was taking control at the base of the pyramid, sending guards charging up to be battered back by the rebels' fire.

Finally, the rebels claimed the entire deck, pushing some Priesthood down the great staircase in the process. Myla didn't know how she felt watching them fall. It seemed like justice, but she tried to focus on what she needed for the next shooting victim.

She was doing a good job, and as the hours sped by, most of her patients had been able to get up and keep fighting. Some were past her help, and if they were still conscious, she'd hold their hands until they died. But Tezca was next to her the whole time, and it made the fear seem like excitement, the bullets like mere air, the impossible futility that was the battlefield medic's job like something hopeful.

They ducked around from nest to nest without suffering too much fire. Priesthood snipers had been set up in buildings around the pyramid's courtyard, and they were taking more rebels down than the massive crowd of guards and Priesthood patrol at the base of the pyramid. The crowds of people, both upper class and Under, had retreated to the outer courtyard but were still watching, impartial.

Myla sighed when she had a moment. "They're not joining us."

Tezca shrugged. "We don't know that. When Quent's group clears the east stairs so Huelta's set can get to the control room, we can play the video."

The video had been Lisbeth's idea, over six months ago, they had told Myla. When they took the pyramid, her plan was to hijack the giant screens and use them to broadcast a message, to explain why they were there. Huelta had made the video the night before, using Tezca as her speaker. It was three minutes long and spoke of the Priesthood's injustices and Tezca's cause. Myla hoped it would work.

Thirty minutes passed, then an hour, and Tezca checked his watch. He radioed Quent. "Clear? Just to three floors down?"

"Yes, all clear. Huelta's group just went through. Four people. She thought it better for getting around with guards down there."

"What? I thought we agreed it was better for her to have cover!"

"Sorry, she was out of here before I could do anything."

Tezca cursed and changed the settings. "Huelta, can you hear me? Are you in place?"

"Yes, Tezca, we're closing in on the main—" She cut out.

"Huelta? Huelta?" Tezca's eyes were wide and unblinking. He tried her one more time, and then the arm holding the radio dropped to his side. He said, his voice quiet, "We can't rely on the broadcast message anymore."

A yelp from above drew Myla's attention. Tona and Mectel were still up there, holding off any priest who got too close on the ground.

"We have to get up there," she told Tona.

He locked eyes with her, counted down, and they darted inside the east stairwell. Bullets rang out from below, and they emerged on the upper deck unscathed.

"There are snipers all around us," Tezca told Myla. "We need to be quick."

Myla's legs ached, but she suppressed it as she and Tezca dashed across the upper deck and to the makeshift fort Tona and Mectel had been using as cover. It had been a huge marble statue of Mictlantecuhtli, an Aztecan god, until they shoved it over. Now the face was disfigured, the statue nameless. Tona was slumped against the inside of the wall, and for a moment the world stopped around Myla, but then he moved. Myla and Tezca crouched next to him.

He said, "One of the snipers got me." He nodded toward his left shoulder, which was oozing thick, shiny blood.

There was no exit wound. The bullet was still inside his shoulder somewhere. She sat with him and tested his ability. He could still move his fingers, and his wrist's pulse was strong, but he was in a lot of pain. It was hard to concentrate under fire from the snipers and guards as well as next to Mectel's operating machine gun.

Myla was running out of gauze. She improvised with a square of the stuff and part of Tona's shirt, first cleaning the wound. Then she applied pressure until she was content that the bleeding had stopped.

Mectel joined them. "They have a helicopter coming. We need to break out what I brought."

Tona flexed his arm. He winced but seemed capable of using it. He opened a long, black box and set up a tripod on the floor in front of him.

Myla heard the chopper getting closer above the occasional sniper shot right above her. The helicopter had guns, and all of their cover would be useless from that vantage point if they got too close. They had to maintain the high ground.

But Tona and Mectel didn't seem worried. They operated as a fluid team, pulling a long tube out of the case and setting it on the tripod.

"You got aim?" Mectel asked Tona.

"Affirmative. Ready when you are," he responded. The helicopter was two hundred yards away.

Myla gasped, "Is that a—"

Tona cut her off with a sly smile. "Yes, it is." Then, he flicked a red switch and pushed a button.

A rocket burst out of the tube with wicked speed and sailed through the air. It struck the helicopter from the bottom and engulfed it in a fantastic explosion. Small chunks of debris rained down from the sky on the courtyard until the burned husk of the chopper crashed at the feet of the pyramid's main stairs. Myla felt a wave of heat pass over her like a gust of wind.

She and Tezca took advantage of this distraction to charge across the upper deck. There were more and more patients springing up all over. The snipers' accuracy was improving.

Myla found herself at the front line, kneeling in front of the thick, stone altars peppered with gunfire from below. This girl had a hole in one of her lungs, a spontaneous pneumothorax, as Zuma would call it. These were tricky. She couldn't breathe and would soon pass out. The blood seeping from her chest had little bubbles in it.

Myla had run out of occlusive dressings. She grabbed a plastic wrapping that the gauze had come in and pressed it over the wound, taping down three sides. Then she waited. The way occlusive dressings worked was to preserve the pressure inside the lungs to allow them to inflate. The girl sucked air in, and the plastic flattened against the hole. She could breathe, and then so could Myla. The cool night air chilled her forehead, damp with sweat.

Tezca checked his watch. Myla knew he wasn't as confident as he had been, much as he tried to hide it. Most of the rebel force had been holding the front line on the main staircase, but their numbers had been cut in half by the endless gunfire from below and from the snipers.

Tezca had wanted to send out another party with Myla's blowtorch to open the armory downstairs and replenish their supply. But after Huelta had gone down into the pyramid and hadn't come back up, it didn't seem wise. They just had to hold out as long as they could. The dead were everywhere: people Myla barely knew and people she saw every day.

While Myla cleaned the girl's wound, Tezca radioed the platoon leaders, checking in on their numbers and position. He was talking to himself. "Losing people too fast . . . need to buy time . . . what if we . . . how many left . . ."

Myla knew better than to disturb him when he was in this state, but she had an idea. "Tezca?" He didn't look up. "What if I call Quinel and ask her to come here, start spreading around word that we are the rebellion among the Unders?"

"We lost the video with Huelta. There's no other way to enlighten them quick enough."

"She could try."

He furrowed his brow, thinking hard, and then nodded. "Call her."

Myla dialed Quinel's spare phone with shaky hands. She picked up on the first ring. "Myla? What's going on over there? The rest of the city is deserted." Even in what could be Myla's last night, it felt good to hear Quinel's voice.

"Yeah, everyone's here watching the fight." She had to yell over the sound of ricocheting bullets on the altars. "Quin, we need you to do something. The people in the courtyard still think we're demons, what the Priesthood announced to them. We need you to tell them they're wrong."

"How do I do that?"

"I don't know, find groups of Unders and try to make them listen. We're going to lose if they don't join us. If there's anyone—*anyone*—on the fence about it, you need to convince them."

"Okay. I'll see what I can do. Be careful, Myla."

She closed the phone. There was other work to do. Some officers were making their way up the stairs. The force to hold them off on the front line had been decimated to about two dozen people. Tezca was running along the line, informing whoever was left to fall back.

One by one, the remaining shooters fled to the back of the main deck, taking cover behind staircases and pillars. The Priesthood didn't seem to realize that only Myla and Tezca were left, firing the occasional warning shot down.

"Ready?" he asked her. The marble was cold against her hands as she planted them to kiss him once. They counted down together and dashed from the line of altars to where they'd started.

An hour passed, and then another, before the Priesthood braved sending officers up past the line of altars. By that time, the rebels had refortified their line farther back. The Priesthood hadn't sent any more helicopters—they didn't know how many rockets the rebels had stockpiled. So the rebels had retained the high ground. The Priesthood didn't know how their numbers had shrunken yet.

Myla's side had been reduced to a third of the original raiding party. They were cornered on all sides with no escape and dwindling ammo. The first of the officers used the front-line altars as cover and shot over them. The rebels fired back. The bullets whizzed past and dug themselves into the staircase where Myla and Tezca were hiding for what seemed like an eternity.

Then, a yellow flag arose from behind the altars, a sign of peace. The bullets stopped and Myla heard the squawk of a megaphone. Matutslan's deep voice settled on the rebels hidden in the nooks and crannies of the decks.

"Demonic creatures, stop this violence! You have no hope of winning, you are outnumbered, and we will kill you all if this goes on longer. If you surrender now, we can guarantee a fair trial for each and every one of you. If not, we will be forced to keep pushing your lines back."

Tona's voice came out of Tezca's radio. "We're not listening to this guy, right?"

Tezca flicked a switch that allowed all the leaders' radios to hear him. "If we give in now, it will all have been for nothing."

Then Myla heard Tona shouting back, "Come and get us, toots!"

They fought on into the night, losing more ground to the Priesthood. Myla hastened from base to base, treating an endless line of wounded and dead. All through it, the gigantic crowd of Tenochtitlan citizens stood nearby, unmoving, curious.

Myla thought about how others would take her death. In Aztecan belief, the highest heaven was reserved for dead infants. Then those who had sacrificed themselves: soldiers who died in combat, mothers who died in childbirth, and, of course, those who went up willingly on the pyramid and came back down piece by piece. Myla knew the honor-by-death-in-combat one didn't apply to her as a woman. The best she could have ever hoped for was to die during childbirth. It was then that Myla once more wished for change.

Then they lost the east staircase. The Priesthood forces had blown back Quent's people holding it and the survivors came to join the center of the main deck. Then they lost the west one. Maybe fifty or so people fought the Priesthood's oppressive gunfire, and there wasn't enough of Myla to go around. The Priesthood's warfare was meant to injure, not kill, to obtain as many prisoners of war and potential sacrifices as possible.

The rebels felt claustrophobic. There were too many of them. Guns clicked, chambers empty, and the paths from cover to cover were barraged with bullets, unsafe to cross.

The shooting slowed, then stopped. They were cornered on all three sides. And even so, by the time the Priesthood got close enough to threaten the rebels point blank, Myla and her friends had run out of bullets. One by one, each rebel surrendered, unable to do anything else when cut off on all sides by guns.

Soon, they reached Myla and Tezca. The rebels from both flanks were herded in to meet them, all standing together powerless and with nowhere to hide. People were dragged out from behind pillars, statues, and staircases and thrown into the small throng of survivors.

Myla saw Matutslan's head peeking out over the main staircase. When he saw Tona and Mectel thrown out from their cover, their machine guns empty, he emerged, victorious. He strutted among the fallen, even stepping on some as he passed. Myla winced as she heard Izel's glasses crunching under his leather shoes, their owner fallen a foot away.

Matutslan stood in the center of the main deck, and then raised his arms.

It was over.

CHAPTER 26

The Priesthood took the rebels' guns and herded them to the front of the pyramid. Myla felt naked in front of the Priesthood's guns and all Tenochtitlan. The sky lightened, and Myla saw the entire crowd below her.

Matutslan addressed the crowd, thanking the gods for delivering them the demons among them, wearing his microphone. The group of rebels shifted to allow Tezca to move to the front. They did it slowly, so no one would notice the tall boy, brow furrowed, making his way closer and closer to Matutslan.

"We need more time," Tezca whispered to Myla. "Spread the word. When he's done with his speech, we need to execute Plan D."

Myla slipped around the rebels, grateful for her short stature, letting everyone know the plan. "Stall," she whispered. "Plan D. Do whatever you can." When she reached Tona, she grasped his hand. "We can still pull this off."

He smirked, nodding his head toward Matutslan, still speaking. "We're lucky he's such a long-winded ass."

Matutslan seemed eager to revel in his victory. He prattled on for minutes about his mission for the gods, Azteca's past victories, even the most recent accomplishments of the senate. He raised the scythe and concluded with "It would seem the gods deserve some blood about now."

All the rebels held their breath and Myla thought, *Now.* Now.

Tona stepped forward. "My holiness, please wait. I have something to say." Matutslan's microphone picked up his voice and carried it through the speakers.

Several officers and priests raised their guns at him, but Matutslan held up a hand. "What is it that you want?"

"I'd like to pledge my undying loyalty and volunteer to be the first one sacrificed."

"Tona, what the hell?" Tezca broke out of the herd and marched right up to Tona.

"I don't work for you. I never have. I infiltrated your ranks all in the service of the gods." He looked past Tezca to Matutslan. "I want everyone to know that I'm not one of these demons here. I am human and I serve you, Chief Speaker."

Myla's turn. She pushed her way past the people in front of her, strode toward the confrontation, and slapped Tona in the face. "You monster! How could you do this to me?" Tezca was holding her back. She yelled at the top of her lungs, "I hate you! You're an animal! You deserve to die." The population of Tenochtitlan was inching their way closer and closer, curiosity overwhelming the fear of becoming collateral.

Tona yelled back, "Well, I never expected you, Myla! I'm sorry! How I feel about you doesn't change. I just . . . need to do my duty to the Priesthood."

Myla scrunched up her face like she was crying, but still spoke loudly as she said, "But I love you. I've always loved you."

The priests glanced at each other, looks ranging from discomfort to shock. No one had anticipated such a raw display of emotion in that moment.

The rebels stirred, hurling curses and slurs at Tona. They surged forward, engulfing him. They all fought, roiling and screaming as they went. Then they turned on each other. Myla and Tezca joined in, screaming and thrashing with the mob. The officers on the outside didn't seem to know what to do.

Matutslan fired a single shot into the air. That quieted the rebels and gave him the power once again. He seemed confused, unsure of what to do in such a unique situation. Eventually, he said, "All right. Bring me this 'Tona' and we shall begin. Come, the gods must make the sun rise."

Tona stumbled forward toward the chief speaker. He kneeled at his feet. Myla hoped the last trick they had was enough. Matutslan proclaimed his usual "For the sun!" and swung the great scythe high above his head. When it reached the peak of its arc, Tona's head popped up with his usual smile.

"There's just one thing," he said. He stood, threw one hand out to the east, and yelled into the microphone, "What a *beautiful* sunrise!"

CHAPTER 27

That little glowing slice of red on the horizon had changed everything.

It had been a week since the battle of the pyramid's peak. The entire city was shell-shocked by what had happened up there. Myla would never forget it.

She'd never forget the standstill, the collective gasp at the mass enlightenment. The anger hadn't even kicked in yet. She'd never forget the way Matutslan had improvised, telling the crowd that the sunrise was an illusion made by the demons. And how no one had even heard him.

"We made it," an awestruck Tezca said to her. She couldn't even summon the words to respond.

The upper class had been the first to run. They tried to peel off, speed-walking to get anywhere but there. That snapped the Unders into focus. Shouts rang out from the crowd, unspeakable rage at hundreds of years of loss. They wanted someone to blame, and he was standing right above them, trying to reason them back into submission.

They surged forward, the Unders with children staying behind, but screaming for blood all the same, clutching their kids to their sides as they did so. Thousands came running up the Temple Mayor's great staircase. Matutslan faltered, his voice shaking as he pleaded with the mob.

That was when the priests and officers saw the way things were going. One by one, they abandoned Matutslan and ran down into the pyramid, hoping to disappear forever.

Matutslan seemed to understand as well. He threw off his microphone and grabbed a rebel from the group, holding the scythe to his neck. "Back off, all of you!" He backed up toward the east staircase.

Tezca and Tona searched for dropped guns, but by the time they came up with one, he was gone, his hostage pushed aside. They nodded at each other and Tona ran off after him with Mectel.

Tezca put up his hands and tried to quiet the crowd. Someone retrieved the fallen microphone and handed it to him. He took a deep breath. He hadn't wanted to show anyone the speech, in case they never made it that far.

"Hello, everyone, people of Tenochtitlan. My name is Tezca, and we are the rebellion and the future."

Many stared at him in confusion, wondering what tyranny this new leader offered. But at least the horde had stopped in their tracks on the stairs.

"First, I must assure you, my best men are going after Matutslan. He will be brought to justice. Next, if you will allow me to do so, I wish to tell you all about our cause.

"You have all been lied to your entire lives. The gods do not need you and your family's blood to make the sun rise. The earth turns as it always has and always will. Nobody knows for certain if the gods exist, but all of the Priesthood and most of the upper class know that the sacrifices exist to oppress you and make examples of those who disobey.

"At the age of seventeen, the upper class is enlightened and told of this conspiracy. When I was enlightened two years ago in Tlacopan, I decided to take action. I convinced my family to run away with me, but they were killed as we left. It was then that I founded the rebellion with . . ." He faltered, then corrected himself. "With . . . the people you see behind me. We are from all classes, from all over the world, and we banded together to end the longest-running injustice in the world: the Priesthood."

The deep glow of the sunrise illuminated his whole body. He did not squint, but rather gazed over the crowd, his deep voice emanating warmth and protection.

"As you can see, we are not demons, just as you are not lesser beings because you were born 'Unders.' The Priesthood took their power from you. They stood on your backs to make this empire what it is.

"And as you have seen this morning, it was all built on lies. Matutslan is fled and the empire belongs . . . to you. You decide what happens now. The people who died tonight died to give that power back to you. I can only hope you honor their sacrifice." He placed special inflection on that last word. "As we say, 'Not for nothing.'"

Myla and the others repeated it back to him, gazing over the fallen.

"Together we can create a nation worthy of its success. I ran the council at the rebellion's base, and I have some ideas as to how to get started. Of course, the decision is in your hands. Azteca can be a democracy, a government built on its people, but not as they hunch over in suffering—as they stand tall, proud, and bearing the load together."

He paused and Myla worried for a moment that he had made his move too soon, too immediate in the wake of the mass enlightenment. But his words seemed to have struck home for some.

"We must move on from our former lives under the Priesthood. It is history now. I know it may seem unfair to let the upper class get away with perpetuating the system, but they are citizens like you and me. I know that you want to revolt against them, cut them down like they allowed the Priesthood to do to you for years. But we will not build our new society on violence. We are not the Priesthood. We must move onward and forward."

The crowd listened to him, their anger deflating as he replaced it with hope. Tezca opened his arms and continued. "Those behind me as well as those dead tonight gave up their lives in Tenochtitlan for the cause. I hope all of you will join us as well.

"I will be forming a new council with council members elected by all of you. Each neighborhood of Tenochtitlan should meet and choose a representative to sit on the council today. It's only a test, but it worked well for our compound. I will explain more tomorrow. For now, please elect representatives among yourselves, someone intelligent with your interests in mind. We will bury our dead and hold services for them today."

He had ended his speech with a dismissal, expecting the mob to clear away and deal with personal business. But none had left. They all stayed to help the rebels move and bury those who had died in the battle. It seemed to be a good sign, a sign of gratitude and respect.

In the days that followed, semireluctant representatives had emerged from Tenochtitlan's housing projects, even one from the upper-class part of town. They must have heard about Tezca's plan somehow. Tezca had been worried about opposition, that the people of Tenochtitlan would be unwilling to adopt his system on his word alone, but there was no one to contest him. There didn't appear to be any resistance from the people of Tenochtitlan at all. Anyone would have been an improvement over the Priesthood.

Tezca hosted meetings at the former Temple Mayor, open and fitted with microphones so that anyone could be a spectator. His anonymous system was implemented first, then a rapid assignment of jobs to the upper class. Some had fled, but others had nowhere to go. They joined the people who used to work for them in food production, transport, and other jobs that made the city run. Just like back on the compound, they could apply for a transfer after a week of work.

Tezca also adapted his own systems to work for a larger population. He adopted Tenochtitlan's currency and interwove it with his own policies, paying those with unpleasant jobs like sewage work more than the standard. It was all met well. People seemed ready to make this new nation work.

All the Priesthood who had been captured were put in the holding cells once intended for sacrifices. This was less of a statement and more of a precaution, as Tezca made ever clear. The one hundred or so rebels who had stayed behind came to join the city. They banded together with the battle's survivors to form a temporary police force. Tezca had confided to Myla that he hoped to propose a method to recruit new police through an application process. He was going to suggest it anonymously tomorrow morning. All of it would take time, he had told her, but he was confident through and through.

Myla's parents had been among those who ran. Myla decided that she would be the one to take care of Aktu from then on. It wasn't like this was the first time their parents had deserted the two of them. They would get on, as they always had.

Tezca and Myla met in her old apartment. It now sat above a small market area some former Unders had set up, full of homemade goods, cheap and swarmed by new customers. Tezca hoped that a watchful, yet loose standpoint on governmental regulation of economy would help close the wealth gap and form a middle class.

Myla was looking over his initiatives for the next day, proofreading them and sharing her thoughts. He watched her as she did so, but it didn't annoy her anymore.

"All of this looks solid, Tezca. I've got to go to work now." Myla and Zuma had taken over the Tenochtitlan hospital, helping to run things in the former upper-class owners' absence. Myla would barely call herself qualified for it, but she had a whole new group of trainees to induct that day.

She stood to leave, but he grabbed her wrist and pulled her back down onto his lap. "You're not getting away that easy." He smirked.

"Come on, Tezca, I have to go." She stood up, and he pouted.

"Oh, don't leave, Myla. I'm stressed. This one rep from Sector Six is giving everyone a hard time."

She smiled sadly. "You know I wish I could stay . . ." She added from over her shoulder on the way out, "You know I wish I could stay with you forever," and brushed out of the door.

Myla hurried to the hospital. Even with the city in a peaceful state, Amihan and Matutslan were still out there. It wasn't like Myla was just another one of the rebels either. Her face and name had been posted up before all of Tenochtitlan. People recognized her in the streets, and the exposure meant she wasn't safe.

But she reached the hospital in one piece. It made her happy how excited the hospital made Zuma. It was a beautiful facility in tip-top shape and Zuma couldn't get enough of it. Myla washed her hands when she arrived and collected the trainees lingering about. She led thirty or so of them up and down the hallways of the great building, giving a tour while adding facts about patient care, both in emergency and nonemergency situations.

She passed Zuma, who was practically skipping down the hallway, clutching a stack of paper half her height. "Hell*oo*." She beamed at Myla, who giggled and gave her a short wave, then returned to her lecture on the importance of sterile surfaces.

During the Priesthood reign, officers would take over looking after the emergency patients so that the medics could attend the mandatory sacrifices. In the small chaos that followed the battle, several patients who had needed constant surveillance were left unattended. It had been Myla first on the scene, stabilizing anyone she could. The plan was that Mectel would join her, but he had been off looking for Matutslan under the pyramid. Luckily, out of the one thousand or so patients left alone in the hospital, only twelve had been in dire condition, and Myla had saved all but three of them.

The trainees continued to follow her as she provided medic work. Most of the Unders who had been employed as low-level medics had returned to the hospital looking to help as well. They were bustling around now too under Zuma's instruction.

The day turned to night and Myla gave up her shift to someone else. She stopped by the space Zuma was now calling her office to let her know she was leaving. Zuma pulled her inside the little storage closet, grinning and gesturing to a file. In the week since the battle, there had been fifty girls born in Tenochtitlan. According to Zuma, about a third of them had been named "Myla."

The next day she had a break, and so she walked to the pyramid, hoping to see Tezca in action. When she arrived, she stood up on the upper deck. The agenda contained more voting on job delegation. Sector Eleven was going to take over mail delivery while Sector Two handled street sanitation.

Suddenly, one of the people on the council stood up, protesting. Tezca quieted him with a raised hand. "Sector Six, please sit down. We have sorted through all the protests given anonymously. Please do not disrupt the system."

But he rose again. He was around forty and a former Under, small and mean looking. He walked around the table, addressing the spectators now. "People, can we allow this 'reassignment' to continue?" He gestured at Tezca. "These upper class are just allowed to get away with what they did to us? To our families? I say we *do* something about it!"

The crowd murmured, some in approval.

Tezca seemed calm, and his deep voice rang out once. "Enough!" All went quiet. "All of you trusted me a week ago, when you approved of the representative system. I want to *help* you. I want success and peace for all of us. But we need a clean slate. All of us must be equal. It's the only way we can move forward."

He was shaken, repackaging his old speech, hoping it would work again. There was a pause as the crowd turned over what he had said.

But one voice called out from the side of the deck. "I care to disagree," Amihan declared, strolling forward, flicking her knife back and forth.

CHAPTER 28

Tezca pulled out his gun that he carried on him now, moving to block Myla from Amihan's view. "Everyone, that girl attempted murder," he called out, voice shaking. Nothing could get to him like Amihan. "She's vicious and as bloodthirsty as the Priesthood."

The crowd was silent as she strolled around the deck. "The people of Sector Six don't think that. They like my ideas." She nodded toward the Sector Six representative. "I sent him in to speak for me, but they elected me . . . once they heard the truth."

Amihan was projecting; she had practiced this. Tezca was having none of it. "Enough of this. I don't care how you got here, but you tried to kill one of us. You don't deserve to walk around freely." He nodded at two of his own men holding guard. "Take her to the holding cells. She will have a trial."

The two men hesitated. They had been on the compound and had most likely known Amihan. She looked at them unfazed on one side, daring them to make a move, while Tezca, on the other, nodded them forward, jaw clenched and brow furrowed.

"You call me extremist, Tez. But I am not extreme. I am justice, pure justice. And the unjust living in your city have had me coming for some time now."

He shook his head. "You persecute based on your prejudices. You are not justice. You are murderous vengeance. And it will poison what all of us here have worked to build. I won't let you kill anyone I love."

That did it for the guards. They approached her, guns drawn, and she dropped her knife. She shrugged as they clasped her arms and steered her down into the pyramid. "We'll see, Tez. We'll see!" she called over her shoulder as they took her down.

There was a moment where everyone at the scene stared at Tezca, waiting for his next move. But he seemed absorbed in the events that had passed, unable to gather his thoughts and move on. Finally, he shook his head and cleared his throat. He paused one moment more and then turned back to face the representative from Sector Six.

"As for you, you have committed no offense, and if the people of Sector Six voted you onto this panel, then you are here to represent them. Everyone is entitled to an opinion, but we as a society should not tolerate bullies and violence. We have had *enough* of that."

The representative looked sheepish and sat. Myla breathed a sigh of relief when she saw the reproachful looks the other representatives gave him. She didn't think her nerves could have handled anonymity of opinion at that point.

The rest of the meeting wrapped up without incident. After most everyone had cleared, Tezca stayed behind with Mectel, the new head of police, to discuss tactics on smoking out and capturing Matutslan. No attempts were to be made to go after those in the upper class who had absconded, as the council decreed. The citizens of Tenochtitlan, all citizens, should have freedom to come and go as they please.

Myla waited for them to finish their talk and wandered over to where Amihan had been standing not a half hour before. Myla didn't know whether her knife-throwing skills were good or not, but she didn't like how close she'd been to her. Amihan's knife lay on the ground, untouched. Myla picked it up, ran a finger along the blade, and put it in her pocket, folded, wondering what Amihan could be planning.

That night, when Tezca came over, he was edgy and distracted. Myla didn't pretend that she didn't know what he was tense about. She sat next to him on the couch, chin resting on his shoulder and rubbing his back with one hand.

"I'm upset with the way things turned out," he managed.

Myla frowned. "Oh."

"No, no. Not in that way. But I always pictured this victory with her at my side. I never thought anything would drive us apart."

Myla didn't like what he was implying. "I'm sorry I ruined the friendship of a lifetime," she said sarcastically.

He rolled his eyes. "You know that's not what I meant . . . I just . . . see now that the reason she didn't like you was not just because you were upper class. She was used to having all this power over me, and you came along and . . . disrupted that hold."

"You make it sound so romantic."

He smiled with his eyes and ran his thumb along her jawline. "It was more than that, Myla. You ignited me. You sizzled through my body and fried my circuits. You burned me through."

Myla had no idea what to say then. All she could get out through her flustered stuttering was "It's . . . the same for me, Tezca. I hope you know that."

Someone giggled who was neither of them. Myla did a mental check. Aktu was at a friend's house, giving her and Tezca some privacy. Her heart raced as she thought of Amihan's wicked smile coming from somewhere in the house.

Tezca put a finger to his lips and rose, drawing his gun. He held it out in front of him and a voice from Myla's hallway closet called out, "Don't shoot!" followed by gales of laughter. Myla relaxed.

Tona and Quinel tumbled out of the closet, laughing their heads off.

"Quin? What are you doing here?" Myla asked, standing.

"Look, we needed a place to hang out and your apartment was right there!" Quinel protested. Tona beamed. Even Tezca laughed.

But Myla was confused. "I left my door locked!"

Quinel nudged Tona with her elbow. "Well, it's a good thing I was with someone who knows how to pick locks."

"And you didn't think to let us know you were here?"

Tona shrugged. "You seemed busy."

"So . . . you hid . . . in the closet." Myla couldn't believe them. She was starting to think she had created two monsters.

Quinel winked at Myla. "It was fine in there."

Tona jumped in. "Yeah. It's a nice closet, Myla. My compliments."

Tezca smirked. "You heard all the stuff we said?"

Quinel nodded. "Yeah! And we *would* have heard *more*, if *someone* could have kept his hands to himself." She punctuated each inflection by jabbing Tona in the ribs with her pointer finger.

"I didn't know you were ticklish!" he objected.

She gave him a skeptical look. "Oh yes, you did," she said, to which he shrugged.

"I hate to do this," Tezca started, "but Tona, shouldn't you be helping Mectel with the new mission preparations?"

"I promise I was. I just wanted to discuss it with our newest mission partner!" He threw out his arms, presenting Quinel like she was a new car.

Tezca chuckled. "We'll see."

Quinel whined, "Oh, please let me join, Tezca! I'm terrible at everything else, I promise!"

He laughed and the four friends collapsed in a heap on Myla's rug, unloading the events of their days on each other. But all were glad to share the burden.

A few more weeks passed, and Myla enjoyed watching Tenochtitlan grow. Messengers were sent to Tlacopan and Texcoco to incorporate them into the new government, and most of the Priesthood occupying those cities had fled by the time Tezca got there.

He took on too much. He created a meticulous system of taxation. He helped the city's necessary utilities get back on their feet. After a careful application process, he sent some new managers to the factories in Tlaxcala and Tarasca with large checks and instructions to improve the living conditions of the workers there. That one he did in the name of Amihan and others like her, though still she sat under the pyramid, waiting for her trial.

Myla wondered once whether he had gone to visit her, and found the courage to ask him. They had been through too much to endure secrets.

She approached him at the Temple Mayor, waiting for the council to adjourn. Once it did, she took his hand and led him to sit on the grand staircase. There was a light breeze blowing Myla's hair all around her in a mess. He laughed and helped her smooth it down.

"I have to ask you something."

"What's up?"

"Amihan's still in her cell?" she probed. He stiffened, anxious to hear where this was going.

"Yes, why?"

"Have you gone to visit her?"

He frowned, nostrils flaring. He snapped, "I did, okay? What does it matter?"

"Whoa. You don't have to be so defensive about it." Myla struggled to keep her tone understanding and even.

"Why do you even care?"

"That's a stupid question. We have history, the three of us."

"You'll just . . . you . . . the war brought out something bad in her, and it's horrible that you'll never know her as I did."

"That doesn't matter now."

Myla paused, debating whether to ask the big question. *Screw it,* she thought, *we're already there.*

She cleared her throat. "Did you ever love her?"

Tezca looked up at her, expression muddled. "Nothing ever happened between us."

"That's not what I asked."

"I . . . I don't know, Myla. I cared about her. And I'm hurting a lot now. And I'm . . . I'm stressed." He put his head in his hands.

Myla felt for him. All the responsibility of running the new Tenochtitlan was weighing on him.

He took a deep breath. "I'm sorry I snapped earlier. I'm sorry I'm so sore about her. I think I'm just anxious about everything that's going on."

And Myla forgave him, threading her fingers through his. "I understand."

The day after the battle, Myla had checked the room where she had left Cint, but he and the girl were gone, from what was left of the ropes on the floor. The thing was, Myla didn't wonder where he had gone. She didn't think about where her parents were at that moment. She didn't care anymore. It was freeing.

One day she had come home from an eight-hour shift in the emergency ward and flopped down on the bed. She felt like she had closed her eyes for a moment before she heard someone banging on the front door.

She pulled out her gun, just in case, and approached the door. Standing there in the hallway was Mectel, an intent look on his face.

"Mectel! What's up?"

"Myla, we need you. We think we have a lead on where Matutslan went. We think he's trying to raise allies, build an army. We're sending a mission squad after him and we want you to come with us. It would be me, a couple of the new police officers, and Tona."

Myla felt like she was still dreaming. There was a two-second delay between when she heard the information to when she processed it. "Why do you need me?"

"You are the most experienced field medic since Izel is gone. It's you or Zuma, and she's running the hospital."

For a fleeting moment, all the decisions Myla had made leading up to that moment resurfaced. She felt like laughing. What a strange series of occurrences to end up back at her apartment, a new friend and partner telling her how valuable she was to a life-and-death mission.

For a minute Mectel was not standing there in the doorway, but Myla in a green party dress. That Myla gawked at new Myla, still in her hospital uniform, unrecognizing. But Myla knew this girl.

The girl in the party dress was out of control, spinning uselessly through her life. She had brushed up against true meaning a couple times, but never pursued it. She was unthinking and, most of all, scared. She was afraid because Citla had hid behind every thought in her head. Because she wouldn't let this Myla out. Because she bottled everything up and felt alone. These two girls couldn't be more different.

Above all, what Myla felt for her old self was pity.

Mectel swam back into focus. Myla nodded and told him she'd have an answer for him by the end of the night. Then, she packed a bag.

Aktu's room was next to hers, and she entered it. He was reading one of the books they had imported from America, one that had been banned in the times of the Priesthood. It was written by a man called Copernicus and Aktu was engrossed in it.

Myla asked his permission to leave. He hadn't had a say when she had disappeared, and she wanted him to know that if he needed her to stay, she would. A part of her hoped he would.

But she hadn't expected him to be so grown up. He hugged her and told her goodbye, but that he'd see her again soon. She assured him that she'd have a phone this time and they'd talk every day.

Next, she went to the hospital and told Zuma what had happened. "I don't know how long I'll be gone, but, as usual with these missions, I don't know that I'll be coming back . . . Can you handle it here by yourself?"

Zuma had a rare serious look on her face. "I can, Myla. I don't want to do it without you, but I can." She chuckled, a cute little giggle that was entertaining coming from such a tough woman. She continued. "I'm going to miss you running around here, so enthusiastic all the time. It's funny . . . people were calling you Mini Zuma the other day."

Myla grinned. "That is . . . the *biggest compliment I have ever received!*" It brought on a new wave of giggles from Zuma as Myla continued gushing. "You have *no idea*! I have been *waiting* for that for ages! I'm so, so happy right now!"

And she was. Zuma put such life in her work, and Myla loved her for it.

They hugged before Myla departed, wishing there could be some other way to stay in Tenochtitlan. Her brain ran wild with stupid plans of rapid-training one of her protégées. It was impossible. This was something she needed to do. She left the hospital, brushing away a few tears as she did. She called Quinel's phone several times, but got no answer. She would find her before she left.

Then, in some ways, the hardest one. Tezca was at his usual spot during sunset, the pyramid. He had implemented his old practice of reading a name every sunset to commemorate those who had been taken by the Priesthood—except now he was working his way backward through the list, retracing history.

Myla caught ahold of him after as he descended the great staircase. The wind whipped her hair around, frizzy and impossible as ever. He chuckled when he saw her having trouble with it.

"Behold: the great Myla! She enabled the revolution but can't handle her hair!" he said, smiling that irresistible smile with his eyes. "What's the plan for tonight? I need to relax." But something in Myla's face tipped him off. "What's wrong?"

"Tezca, Mectel came to me earlier. They think they found Matutslan."

Tezca nodded. "Yeah, he showed me. It's good news."

"No, that's not all . . . he wants me to come with him."

For once Tezca's brow stayed smooth, but his gaze dropped. "Oh. What are you going to do?"

"I think I have to go, Tezca. I have to find Matutslan and end this."

"And what about *this*?" He held her hands in his. He was tearing a hole in her heart, but then again, she had known this was going to be hard.

"I'm sorry." It wasn't enough, and she knew it.

"Myla, I don't know if I can run this without you."

She smiled sadly. "Of course you can. Don't be stupid. All of this is you. *All of it* is because of you."

He shook his head. "You have no idea how wrong you are."

"It won't be for that long. Your best men are on the job. We'll get him and I'll come back to you, I promise." She took out a piece of green thread from her pocket. It was the best she could do on short notice. She handed it to him. "I'm always yours," she said, offering her wrist.

He stared at the thread in his hand for a moment, and then met her eyes and he tied it around her wrist. He chuckled. "How old fashioned of you."

"Well, I'm yours. There's nothing I can, or want, to do about it now."

"Still . . . so archaic."

She held up another piece of thread. "That's why I got one for you too."

As she laced it around his wrist, he said, "You know you changed everything, right?" She finished tying it, but he wouldn't let her move her hands. "I'm going to worry so much about you," he said.

"Me too. And . . . thank you for respecting my decision."

He did a little shrug. "We are the makers of history. We have duties to fulfill. Our personal lives can't get in the way of the people we have to help. Even though we're finally safe and together." He looked out over the pyramid. "Wow, we're idiots."

On the way back to her apartment, she couldn't help thinking of Lisbeth, who had at one point said goodbye to her family, leaving for a brand-new world. Had she had any idea what she was getting into? Had she wished she could have said something she didn't at that goodbye? Before she left for her last mission?

Nothing was certain. And everything was wild and unpredictable in retrospect.

Tezca saw her back to her apartment, where she said a more extensive goodbye to Aktu. Tezca had promised to take care of him while she was gone, and she trusted him with her little brother.

The group Mectel had promised soon showed up to Myla's apartment, a few officers she didn't know, Tona, Mectel, and . . . Quinel, who it turned out assumed she'd be coming along. Typical. Myla was glad.

When Mectel confronted her, Quinel raised her eyebrows and said, "Oh, I'm coming along. Sorry."

Tona smiled. Tezca looked jealous.

Later as they set out, he took her into his arms and whispered, "I wish I could go with you. I wish I could drop everything and go with you. It's selfish, but I wish I could make you stay."

She cupped his face with her hands and said, "I wish I could stay. But like you said, we're idiots."

He looked everywhere but at her and then straight into her eyes. "Idiots in love?"

Her answer and more was unlocked by a kiss.

They used a car and one of the major highways to leave town. It felt strange—Myla was used to sneaking around in the sewers. But it also felt right, sitting shotgun next to Mectel at the wheel, Tona and Quinel all over each other in the back, the car loaded with guns and supplies and who knew what else as they set out to climb their next mountain. Myla hoped that Tezca would be waiting for her at the peak.

The pyramid gleamed red in the rearview mirror. Myla lingered on it for a moment, knowing she'd see it again soon.

As it had been hours before, she saw earlier versions of herself, now standing on the side of the highway and disappearing as the car sped past. There she was as a child, unknowing and naïve, which didn't change as the years went by. One bump when they passed ten-year-old Myla, eyes widened in horror. Then her at eleven, texting and wearing glitter lip gloss. Soon, the girl in the green party dress reappeared, and dirty, frizzy-haired Myla, her own reflection, smiling back.

ABOUT THE AUTHOR

Val Bodurtha has won over two dozen writing awards, mostly in humor. She is a classics major at the University of Chicago, where she practices her improv, sketch, and stand-up comedy. This is her first novel.